Ladykiller

Ladykiller

A Novel

Lawrence Light
and
Meredith Anthony

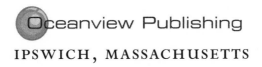

Oceanview Publishing

IPSWICH, MASSACHUSETTS

ISBN-13: 978-1-933515-05-2
ISBN-10: 1-933515-05-8

Published in the United States by Oceanview Publishing,
Ipswich, Massachusetts
www.oceanviewpub.com

Distributed by Midpoint Trade Books

2 4 6 8 10 9 7 5 3 1

PRINTED IN THE UNITED STATES OF AMERICA

For our families — Nancy, Cindy, Martha, and Troy.

ACKNOWLEDGMENTS

Thanks to Bob and Pat Gussin, Susan Greger, and the entire fantastic team at Oceanview; to the world's best agent Cynthia Manson; and to Gwen Arner, Donna Ahlstrand, Nancy Schreiber, Melissa Leo, and everyone who helped make the short film "Ladykiller" that grew up to become this novel.

Ladykiller

ONE

"Of course, I know what that is," snapped the whore. "I went to college." She kept walking, irked at having to turn down a trick, but she had an appointment to keep. She left the forlorn john by the stairs with his fat wallet in his fat hand. Every time she was too tired or too sick or — like now — too busy, it was money lost. Money that she needed. She moved through the disinfectant stink of the lobby of the cheap SRO she called home. In fact, single room occupancy hotels were almost exclusively the address of choice for the working girl. She strode into the jiving maelstrom of 42nd Street. The Deuce. 1991. The beginning of a hopeful new decade. Yeah. Right.

She passed a pizza place and realized how hungry she was. Maybe on the way back, she would buy a slice. That was all she could afford since her cash position was on the short side. At the corner was a bank machine in a claustrophobic enclosure behind a door with a busted lock. New York had millions of them. This one was full of garbage and bums. No respectable soul, not even the poor horny bastard she had just turned down, would venture in there to do any banking. Her bank, of course, was a shoe box safely hidden in a locker at the bus station. Direct deposit. That's what she called her job, too. No withholding, no taxes, no FICA, whatever that was. FICA sounded like what she did every night. But not now, darling.

The whore wrapped the coat tighter around her against the cool vapor of the early spring evening. She had borrowed the coat from a much taller hooker, off duty tonight with a hangover. The coat was so long it rode down around her shins. The whore figured that guys wouldn't bother her if she were covered up. Nevertheless, men she passed gave her those hard-dick looks anyway. She wondered how they knew, with her wrapped up like that. Maybe it was the shoes, high heels of Lucite that looked fragile but were actually as tough as bulletproof glass. The shoes, which had come in the box that was her bank, were called fuck-me's. A tall black dude waggled his tongue at her. Not now, darling. The whore had an appointment. And she wouldn't earn any money from it either.

She smiled fleetingly at the dude and turned her head back to the direction she was going. And gave a sudden start. A massive moving presence loomed in front of her. She momentarily wobbled on the heels, then stepped smartly out of the way. It was a heaping shopping cart with extra bundles tied to the sides, wide as a truck.

"Hey, girlfriend," the whore called, delighted. "Hey, Stinky."

The bag lady ignored the greeting and kept pushing her cart forward on the rutted sidewalk to nowhere. She wore a stained, ripped overcoat from some Dumpster and Salvation Army-provided running shoes that had holes in the toes.

The whore playfully jostled one of the bags and heard a muttered curse.

"What you got in there, girl? Ann Kleins? Ralph Laurens? Naaah. I figure you for the Bill Blass type. Clothes make the woman, girlfriend."

The bag lady stopped and faced the whore. "A few more years, you'll be me," she said, her voice an ominous snarl, her mouth full of snaggled, discolored teeth. "If you live that long."

"Hey, now. Jackie Why takes care of his girls," the whore shot back, stung. "Ain't nothing going to hurt his girls." Actually, if Jackie saw her parading around the Deuce covered up like a nun, he would probably do some major hurting himself. Maybe her appointment wasn't such a good idea. She wasn't keeping up her cash flow.

The whore resumed her brisk walk, leaving the bag lady, still muttering, behind. She stepped gingerly around a raw hole in the pavement, badly protected by broken sawhorses. She glanced at the yellow and orange clay in the hole and marveled. In the middle of man-made Manhattan, there was actual dirt so close beneath the surface. The thin veneer of civilization. The phrase popped into her mind. She chuckled. You can never be too rich or have too thin a veneer.

No, she should call off the meeting and go earn some money. She reached the corner of 42nd and Tenth, and spotted a pay phone half a block up Tenth. And what do you know: It still worked. She stuck in a quarter and punched out a number.

The line was ringing when the homeboys lounging outside a nearby bar started up. The usual from that kind of crowd in their stolen leather jackets and boosted Reeboks. Repetitive cries of *"puta."* Kissing sounds. Assorted gestures.

"You don't have to call me, baby," the biggest one called. "I'm right here." They all laughed and grabbed their crotches but made no moves. She flipped them a weary bird.

A message machine came on. The whore hung up. Shit. She'd have to go.

The homeboys had vanished, probably into the bar. She walked up Tenth. Only a block from the Deuce this time of night, Tenth Avenue was empty and silent as a graveyard. Funny how people thought the Deuce was dangerous. The whore knew that the teeming crowds meant safety. Filled with pimps, punks, winos, homeboys, homeless, and assorted other street vermin though it may be, the Deuce was a damn sight safer that the chilly, lurking emptiness that stretched before her. A parking lot off Tenth Avenue. Great.

The killer strode through the New York night, its brisk, crystal air vibrating with electric bloodlust. The killer had a purpose — a purpose that the police and the news media could not begin to fathom. As the killer glided past a newsstand, a tabloid headline whined: LADYKILLER STUMPS POLICE. ASK PUBLIC FOR CLUES. Ladykiller? Beyond stupid.

On impulse, the killer bought a copy of the paper and stood reading it under the fierce buzz of a streetlight. An academic expert with indifferent credentials was quoted on the nature of serial killers: How they often suffered head injuries as children, came from broken homes, lacked social skills, were addicted to killing. Some expert. He probably smoked a pipe and wore a tweed jacket with suede elbow patches. He probably seduced his most impressionable female student each year. "This killer is filled with incredible rage," the expert said. "In everyday life, he may appear sane. But no one who shoots his victims in the head with a .45 caliber pistol at close range is sane."

A strange expression wormed its way across the killer's face. No, professor, this was not a matter of sanity. It was a matter of purpose. A purpose you can't fathom. The shining .45 rode in the killer's pocket like the hard stone of salvation.

Tonight, in the shadowy angles of the concrete night, a woman would die. And another headline about the Ladykiller would tantalize the fearful hearts of the cretins who read the tabloids. And the professor would pull on his pipe. Oh, yes.

The killer folded the paper neatly and dropped it into a trash receptacle. And strode on to mete out another killing. A killing with a purpose.

The pretty young blonde left her large, rundown, pre-war apartment building at a brisk trot. Her long legs fairly loped along the bustling Broadway sidewalk, on fire to get to her job, the night shift that most of her colleagues dreaded. Get there and watch and listen. And maybe, if she was lucky, say or do something to impress the one whose approval she craved. The night held such radiant possibilities.

She glanced at her reflection in a long store window and made a face. She was dissatisfied with her looks although any observer would, did, look twice. She felt barely put together after a two-minute regimen of eye liner to emphasize her blue eyes, mascara to darken her pale lashes, and a swipe of rose lipstick. The person she cared about most liked people who made an effort. "Otherwise, you don't make a difference." She hurried on.

The pavement, flashing beneath her determined stride, sparkled like a thousand diamonds. The sparkle came from quartz in the concrete that caught the city lights, but she had a secret fantasy that the city had actually imbedded diamonds for her to walk upon on Broadway.

She waved a spirited hello to the counterman at the all-night doughnut shop that she frequented. It was a virtual home to a potpourri of interesting humanity. Tonight's group included a jet-fighter pilot, a jazz musician, and a U.S. congressman. They turned to look at her bouncing past with her thick, shiny, reddish-blonde hair. Even though she didn't like her looks, she knew that men liked her. Several of the customers in the doughnut shop had made overtures, but she wasn't interested. Her life right now revolved around one person and she rushed through the night to get there.

The elegant woman's sensible, low-heeled shoes moved briskly over the piss-stained pavement. They skirted a used condom, lying there like a dead snake. At least they had used one, she thought philosophically.

She walked past a bearded man with a pot belly and a paper bag-covered beer can standing in front of a deli. He had the expected impulses throbbing in what was left of his brain.

"Looking good, pretty momma," he said thickly.

She was not one to cringe from some boob's advances. She scowled, letting him know she could not be cowed. That usually worked. Not now, unfortunately.

He fell into step beside her, the beer held in front of him like a communion chalice. "Some brew, pretty lady?"

"No, thank you," she replied with a degree of coldness calculated to freeze the testicles off a saber-tooth tiger.

The oaf persisted. "It'd warm you up."

She said nothing.

"Don't you like beer?"

She stopped and faced him. "Get lost."

Her resistance inspired him. "You seem like a lady who would benefit from male companionship." She assessed him. He was large and possibly dangerous.

"I'm not interested," she said levelly, without the slightest trace of fear. She glanced behind him. The nearest other person was a half-block away. He stepped closer, menacingly.

"Before you say that, check this out." He unzipped his fly.

"Why, that looks remarkably like a male penis," the elegant woman said with a laugh. "Only smaller."

The old joke worked. He snarled but backed up and slunk away with his beer can dribbling.

She resumed her purposeful stride. She briefly considered suggesting that the man seek counseling. But the man had lurched off across the street.

Her smile died abruptly. Footsteps. Behind her, nearly matching her own. Careful not to change her pace, she frowned in concentration. She tightened her grip on her bag and kept walking purposefully into the dark night.

The whore turned into the deserted parking lot. The expanse of asphalt was empty and unlit. A chain stretched across the entrance. No one was on duty at the shack, which sat in the middle of the lot. The dark cold seemed more intense here.

She paused, getting used to the darkness, shivering in the coat that now seemed too lightweight. Then she struck out across the lonely lot. Her heels clattered on the paving. The abandoned guard shack had trash heaped up against one side. There was one discarded Christmas tree, dripping tinsel. She caught a movement around the plastic garbage bags and thought, *rats*. She hated this.

The pretty blonde's gaze searched the shadows. What was that sound? A scuttling rat? She looked over her shoulder. No one was behind her. A brief wind off the Hudson sent a shower of grit against her face. Crumpled paper swirled down the street, an unholy, whirling white phantom.

She turned a corner. No one else on this block either. Her heart fluttered like a trapped bird and she walked a little faster. Her destination wasn't far. A hand shot out of the ground and swiped at her ankle.

Dodging awkwardly with an ineffective squeal, she stumbled and almost fell. Then she began to run. When she looked back, panting, she saw the dirt-caked face of a wino, who crouched in a stairway down to a basement entrance. He laughed maliciously but made no move toward her. Too wasted on bad wine.

The footsteps were close. Right behind her. The hair bristled on the back of the elegant woman's neck. Alarm sparked up and down her spine. She tensed for the hand on her shoulder, the knife at her throat, the junk-soaked breath hot on her cheek. If she turned around now…?

She rounded the corner. Up ahead shone the beacon of a neon beer sign on a deli. It was open, a sanctuary in the forbidding expanse of limestone facades and gated shop fronts. The footsteps seemed to fall back.

She slipped into the deli. The beer cooler exuded a rank smell of unwashed refrigeration. As the front door closed, she turned. There was no one behind her. Without opening the door, she leaned close to the dirty glass and checked out the street in either direction. Nothing. Where had her pursuer gone? Had she imagined it? Was she paranoid? Was she insane?

"What'll it be?"

The guttural growl made her start.

The stooped, bent gnome behind the counter was leering at her with dark malice. "What'll it be, honey?"

"Excuse me?" Another dysfunctional member of society.

"What do you want?"

"Nothing."

"Well, get the hell out of my store then."

"I'll go when I'm ready," she snapped. Could her pursuer be hiding outside, waiting for her to emerge? She hated not being in control.

"What are you afraid of?" the gnome asked, laughing unpleasantly. "The Ladykiller?"

"Nothing."

"The Ladykiller," he nodded wisely. "He blow your head clean off." The gnome chuckled with obvious relish at the thought.

"Let him try," she said shortly, with more conviction than she felt.

*   *   *

Turning tricks, you were almost never really alone. Even when some john was heaving into her, back in her room, she wasn't alone. Her SRO hotel had tissue-thin walls she could scream through if a guy went nuts. In an instant, Jackie Why or one of the other girls or somebody would be there with a knife. Even the time when she was blowing a guy on a walkway of the Queensborough Bridge, she had more company than now. Lots of people around, that was real life insurance.

She leaned against the small shack, uncomfortably close to the garbage. This was where she was supposed to wait. Just as well. If some creep passed by on the street, he wouldn't see her as easily. It was cold and she was irritable. She didn't need this. What she did need was a cigarette. She fumbled out a Virginia Slim and flicked her disposable lighter. And saw something.

She didn't scream, but made a high-pitched, involuntary, animal sound. The face hovered nearby, illuminated by the sashaying flame. Even after she registered the face as familiar, she still croaked a little as she lit her cigarette. The flame trembled.

"Shit." The whore pocketed the lighter and dragged deeply on the cigarette to steady her nerves. "Thank God, it's you. I thought I was going to have to wait." Thinking it was funny that she hadn't heard a sound, she exhaled, a little jittery, but better, and glanced up. "Did we really have to meet here? It's creepy."

No answer.

"Nice gloves," the whore said, trying to make conversation. What was this all about, she yearned to ask. "They leather? Expensive?"

A glint from a far-off streetlight caught the chrome .45 pistol as it emerged from the shadows. Held in the leather-gloved hands.

"What's that for?" the whore asked. Jackie sometimes carried a piece for protection. She wasn't truly alarmed until she saw the gun was pointed at her head.

The familiar face had become twisted into an ugly Kabuki mask. This wasn't like the person the whore knew and trusted. What was going on?

The whore's hysteria built with every word: "Hey, it's me. What the hell are you doing? Quit kidding around. This isn't funny."

The .45 fired, a brief thunderclap that rolled across the parking lot. Its bullet smashed through her right eye, brutalizing the softest, most vulnerable membrane. The bullet tore through her brain and burst out the back of her skull in a spray of bone and blood and tissue. Her soul, startled, fled. Her body, already cooling, slowly slipped, dropped away, and fell back into the welcoming trash.

The killer remained holding the .45 in a two-handed combat grip, held it where its fire had reached out and kissed the whore's eye. The killer's leather-gloved hands relaxed finally; the silver pistol lowered and pointed toward the ground.

The bag lady continued her slow, painful progress up Tenth, pawing through each trash heap, adding the occasional bottle or can to her burgeoning shopping cart. Each one brought a nickel at the one deli where they put up with her. Not much around, though, this time of night on this well-picked-over block. Go through the motions, she told herself. You'll be okay. Spring was almost here and she could sleep outside tonight, which was much better than in those hellish shelters where they stole everything.

Wait. What was that over there? She pushed the creaky old cart wearily across the dark parking lot to a promising heap beside the deserted guard shack. Stinky ignored the customary twinge in her back as she bent to rummage through the trash pile, avoiding the brittle spikes of a discarded Christmas tree.

"Lord God must've made garbage about the same as He made men," she muttered to herself. "It dirty, it smell bad, it stubborn." She tugged at an auspicious piece of cloth. Despite the darkness, her instinct told her the fabric was good quality. Probably the hem of a coat. "It like to break your heart, the things people throw away."

She tugged and met unusual resistance. She set her jaw and hunkered down to pull harder while trying not to tear the fabric. A stiletto stab pierced her back. She grunted with the effort and gave one more desperate, angry tug.

The entire heap shifted suddenly. The old lady, caught off balance, fell awkwardly beneath the weight of something far heavier than a coat. She blinked and pushed up her stocking cap, which had descended over her eyes, and with her other hand pushed at the weight that held her down.

Swearing, spitting lint and God knows what, her nose running like a gutter in the rain, Stinky took a full fifteen seconds to grasp what lay in front of her. She found herself gazing into the cold, timeless face of the dead whore, inches from her own, with its parade of slow, sad, red tears leaking from the terrible crater that had been its right eye.

She let out a demon screech of terror.

TWO

Detective Dave Dillon listened to the informant talk. You listened first, then you asked questions. And tonight, amid the crackling, otherworldly neon light of Times Square, Dave was listening very closely.

"I know this is the dude, man," Finesse said. "Scary motherfucker. Cold." Finesse pumped his head up and down, in agreement with himself, and the three rings in his nose tinkled against each other.

Dave said nothing. He watched Finesse with a blank Irish cop's stare and let him talk.

"I seen him before. He smacked some brothers around once. Stay clear of that motherfucker, no shit. He big. Big white guy. Like you. Bigger. He said he done them women. I was in the bar and I heard it myself. Motherfucker's drunk off his ass. Say he shot them bitches in the head."

Dave's eyes narrowed a millimeter. He needed more detail.

"He had a .45. Stuck in his pants. Stuck in like, it went off, it'd blow off the family jewels."

Dave watched impassively. Anyone who read the papers knew the victims were shot in the head with a .45.

"Said he shot them in the eye."

Dave's reaction didn't show on his face. "In the eye?"

"Said he didn't like the way they looked at him. Said they could give him the fish-eye in hell. I mean, this is one scary motherfucker. I ain't lying."

"This was last night?"

"Yeah, last night. Like I told you," Finesse said nervously, check-ing up and down the sidewalk to make sure no one was watching. "At the Foxy Lady. I didn't want my ass near this mean motherfucker. I was with this dude, Ace. Ace the kind of dude likes to be close to the action. Fucker's going to get himself killed nosing around that kind of shit. Anyways, Ace is buying this hard-ass drinks — actually, I'm paying — and the mother starts up about killing them bitches, shoot-ing them in the eye. I figured he was jiving. Trying to impress us. But he hauls up his windbreaker and shows us his .45 in his pants, pointed at his goddamn dick. I mean, I like to've shit my pants."

"What color windbreaker?"

"Blue. Maybe green. It's dark in there, you know. They keep the lights down so's you can't tell how old and ugly a lot of them dancers getting." Finesse drew a breath.

"What else did he say?"

"Damned if I know. I got out of there so damn fast, you'd've thought my ass was on fire."

"He have a name?"

"Shit, all I wanted to know about him was how many miles be-tween him and me."

Dave pulled a photo out of his leather jacket. It was a criminal booking shot, taken by the Miami Police Department, cropped to omit the biographical information on the board that the prisoner held beneath his chin. "This him?"

Finesse's nose rings clinked. "That's him. Mean looking, ain't he?"

Dave got up and grabbed Finesse's hand high in a brother's grip. The crisp bills clasped in Dave's palm were easily transferred to Finesse's. "Stay in touch."

Without examining the money, Finesse slipped it in his pocket. His palms had eyes. "You generous tonight, Dillon."

"In honor of spring." He turned to go.

"You nail this dude, it make up for the bad mark on your record, huh?" Finesse gave Dave a small, superior smile.

Dave was back in his face so fast that Finesse jumped a little. Dave grabbed a handful of collar. "What did you say?"

Finesse's cool expression slipped a little. "Sorry. People talk, is all."

Dave leaned toward him until his teeth were close enough to Finesse to tear the rings off his nose. "You tell me what goes down on the street, not your opinions on my career," he muttered with barely caged ferocity.

"No problem," Finesse blubbered.

After a few seconds, Dillon relaxed and stepped back. "Now, you just get back to living the life."

Finesse edged away, crab-like, into the swirling honky-tonk night of 42nd Street's eternal carnival. Dave watched the Deuce swallow him up. He felt a twinge of guilt for leaning on the brother, but certain references to his past triggered a knee-jerk reaction. He should have more control.

Dave sighed as he stepped into the doorway of the shuttered electronics store and pulled out his radio.

Lt. Blake was at the other end. "Positive ID?"

"Pretty good. Sufficient for questioning. Last night, suspect was in a blue or green windbreaker. Carries his piece in his waistband. Last seen in Foxy Lady. I'm close. I'm going there now."

"I'll send out an APB. Wait for backup." Dave clicked off the radio.

Blake had personally requested Dave for this task force. If not for him, Dave would be back in a uniform, with the coldhearted brass waiting for him to slip up one more time so they could bounce him out. Blake was an old friend of his father and one sodden evening at McSorley's, Blake had told him: "I couldn't help your dad because I didn't have the rank back then. I do now and you're his boy. Don't let me down, though, Dave."

Not a chance, lieutenant. Dave trekked toward the Foxy Lady. This case would save his life. This case *was* his life.

He took out the booking picture. New York had its share of homegrown bad guys; it didn't need to import them from Miami. Billy Ray Battle had killed a man with a pipe in a fight over a woman outside some redneck bar. Next, he had kidnapped the poor pecker-wood's girlfriend, raped her repeatedly, and ripped up her face. He told the cops he'd done it for love. Billy Ray did five years hard time in the Florida penal system before convincing the local yahoos that he was a reformed man. After that, he was chief suspect in a series of rapes. One had resulted in a woman's death: from a .45 to the head. Unfortunately, the Florida cops were too busy sucking on oranges or skinning gators or whatever they did. They could pin nothing on him. And now, Billy Ray Battle had shifted his horizons.

Dave saw two uniforms walking ahead, a man and a woman. They were giving each face they passed a hard look.

One of them, a pale kid with the nametag "Blitzer," nodded to Dillon. "Green or blue windbreaker, right?" he asked.

"You got it," Dave said. The all-points bulletin had gone out quickly.

"I hear he's dangerous," Blitzer said. "Carries a .45."

"Yeah. Be careful." Dave glanced at his nametag again, then at his face. "You're Zoltan Blitzer's younger brother. Vic, isn't it? I heard you were out of the Academy. Welcome to hell."

Blitzer grinned sheepishly. Veteran cops usually weren't friendly to rookies. "Sir."

"How's Zoltan? I haven't been to see him in a month or two."

"He's okay. Working on weights in the basement a lot, y'know. Builds up his upper-body strength."

"Tell him I said hello," Dave said. "And give my best to Cathy and the kids."

"He talks about you all the time," Vic Blitzer said.

Dave interrupted him by clapping him on the shoulder. "Let's get back to work." He nodded at the kid's partner, a tough female cop who sported an admirable arrest record and a reputation for street smarts. "Keep an eye on this guy, Martino."

The Foxy Lady was exactly what high-minded city planners meant by cleaning up the Deuce. They talked of bringing in Disney, But if Donald Duck set one webbed foot in the Foxy Lady, he'd end up rolled and sodomized. Actually, 42nd Street had no more hope of being cleaned up than a plutonium dump site.

The Foxy Lady was so sleazy that Dave, after a visit, felt like taking a shower. Major slimeballs hung out here. Billy Ray Battle would naturally gravitate to it.

You couldn't avoid knowing about the place. On each street corner for blocks around, skeevy types passed out handbills promising: "Hot girls and more at the Foxy Lady." The street-corner touts snapped the handbills like a lash, catching attention. The "more" that they promised had provided numerous arrests when Dave was working the street. Still did.

The Foxy Lady had a life-sized neon sign, the red silhouette of a woman that flashed back and forth as if she were dancing. Loud 1970s rock tunes blared out the door. As usual, Tony Topnut, the owner, stood guard at the front door, repeating, "Check it out, check it out, check it out," into the auto exhaust of the traffic heading for the Lincoln Tunnel.

"You back?" Tony Topnut exclaimed. "They let you back?"

"They do a lot of things without consulting you," Dave said dryly. "Busy tonight?"

"Not bad." Despite the cool temperature, Topnut wore a garish short-sleeved Hawaiian shirt that covered his ample gut. The hula girls on the shirt were lifting their grass skirts to expose themselves. His short goatee failed to give the desired Satanic effect due to his bulging triple chin.

"Seen a big white guy in a blue or green windbreaker? Southern accent."

"You know my memory's shitty, Dillon."

"Sort of like your taste in clothing. I'll just have a look inside."

Dave shouldered his way into the bar. A dancer, clad in a G-string and tiny bra, undulated on the small stage. Her body was nice for the Foxy Lady: a tight, snaky torso moving with the music. But her downcast face would have been more at home at a funeral. The major stripping action was a while off. This act was just to keep the clientele's blood moving.

Every physically and mentally misshapen boulevardier of the Deuce seemed to have found his way into the Foxy Lady tonight.

Horny, pimply college boys. Horny, alcoholic businessmen. Horny, chain-wearing street hustlers. Horny, ugly — well, maybe they were extra-terrestrials on shore leave. They sipped their watery drinks and waited patiently for more skin.

The bartender nodded at Dave, squirted club soda into a glass, and passed it to him without being asked.

Dave took the glass and walked along the bar, peering at the hunched-over horny toads as they ogled or pretended not to ogle the bored looking woman on the stage. He heard Billy Ray Battle before he saw him.

"Where's the tits?" he bellowed. You could tell he had enough mule muscle packed in his arms and shoulders to disconnect a man's life with a punch. Never mind the .45 in his waistband. Dave could see the L-shape outline of the weapon through the fabric of the windbreaker.

"Where's the pussy?" Billy Ray foghorned across the bar. The smaller men seated on the stools near him stared straight ahead as if he were not there. No sense riling the boy up.

Keeping Billy Ray Battle firmly in view, Dave dialed Blake on the pay phone. Using his radio wasn't an option.

"We're on the way," Blake said. "Five minutes. Tops."

As Dave hung up, Tony Topnut popped up next to Billy Ray, who was busy drinking shooters. Billy Ray gave a displeased roar at being interrupted. Then he listened. Tony jerked his head in the direction of the red exit sign. Billy Ray made for it. Fast.

"Shit," Dave said. He ran after the man, dodging through the tables, and caught up with him as he was pushing the crash bar into the alley. "Halt, police." Dave had his .38 out now. Just in case.

Billy Ray hesitated for only a moment. Long enough to glance back at Dave with such hatred it was like opening the door to a furnace. Then he slammed the crash bar down and vaulted into the alley.

Dave followed, spinning outside low and quick, in case Billy Ray had the doorway sighted with his .45. He hadn't. Billy Ray's long legs had sped him down the alley and out onto the Deuce. He wore large, heavy work boots of stone-hard leather.

"Halt. Police," Dave called again. He pounded out to the street. If that enormous cracker thought he could run, he was about to learn something. From a cop who wore Air Jordans. The balls of Dave's feet bounced along the crowded sidewalk, darting among the walkers. Stark faces that didn't want to know too much swiveled at him, saw the gun, then looked away. Bright storefronts reeled by on his right. Dave's leather jacket billowed behind him. His breath huffed, locomotive-like, relentless, gathering steampower.

Billy Ray's broad, satin-clad back — the windbreaker *was* blue — heaved ahead, elbows working like pistons, down the sidewalk. He was a strong runner, but the constricting leather of his dead-weight boots sucked the flight out of each stride. And his running tactics made him a bad sidewalk fugitive. Good sidewalk fugitives weaved among the pedestrians. Billy Ray bumped into them, sent them sprawling along the cruel concrete. That slowed him down still more.

"Halt. Police," Dave was almost on him now. Almost within grabbing range. His father had taught him never to let anyone get away with running on you. When you caught him, smack the shit out of him.

Hearing Dave right behind him, sensing the menace in the cop's command, Billy Ray made a sudden, broken-field dodge into a T-shirt store, knocking over a carousel of postcards.

Dave overshot the store and skidded to a stop. He warily inched to the side of the door, .38 ready, crouched low.

Billy Ray had a sobbing Korean salesclerk by the neck in an armlock. His arm was like an oversized blue noose. He held the dull gray .45 against her skull. Sweat cascaded down Billy Ray's mottled red face. His jaw hung open so he could suck in air.

"It don't matter to me," Billy Ray shouted over the screams of the passersby as they fled.

"Let her go, you stupid fuck." Dave sighted his pistol at Billy Ray's head, which was in clear view. But he had to take the bastard alive. Besides, hitting a target in the head, even from twenty feet like now, was never easy except on TV. The best place to aim was the chest. Billy Ray at least knew that. He held the hysterical salesclerk in front of him.

"It don't matter to me." He twisted the gun barrel back and forth against his hostage's head. And showed Dave an opening.

Dave sheathed his .38 in the holster at his hip. He stepped into full sight. "Okay, Billy Ray. Here I am." He held his arms wide.

Billy Ray jerked his head to get the salty, stinging sweat out of his eyes. A sprinkle of it shot from his face. The movement tightened his armlock on the salesclerk, who squeaked in pain.

Dave advanced a few feet toward Billy Ray. "I'm coming to get you, fuck." He looked fierce, his teeth bared in an animal rictus, eyes full of fire, flesh molded to the bone. Scare them, his father had said. Scare them.

Billy Ray arced the gun around to point at Dave. Right where he should aim, at the chest. The center of mass. The cage of his fragile, pulsing heart. As he shifted the weapon, his grip inadvertently loosened on the salesclerk. She wiggled free and scrambled past Dave. Billy Ray, his gun on the cop, didn't seem to notice her departure.

"Coming to get you..." Dave paused and took another step. "Coming to get you, you fuck."

Dave stood inches from the .45's black hole of eternity. Close enough for what he wanted. He could smell Billy Ray's breath, part booze, part landfill. Billy Ray was considerably bigger than Dave — a full three inches. If Billy Ray connected a fist to Dave's head, it would snap his spinal cord like uncooked spaghetti. That's why Dave was glad Billy Ray's hitting hand had wrapped around the handle of a .45.

The first second, not much happened. Dave growled as his muscles knit all his power into his fist. Billy Ray pulled the trigger.

The next second, Dave's fist collided with Billy Ray's right eye. Drove a knuckle deep into the firm jelly of his cornea.

The third second, not much happened. Dave's fist withdrew at rapidly as it had struck. Billy Ray's eye closed up like reverse time-lapse photography of a flower blossoming. His lips pulled apart to howl. His gun-free hand moved upward to clasp his blood-gorged eyeball. The gun fell, skidding away on the dirty linoleum.

The fourth second, not much happened either. Dave brought up his knee so he could kick heel first. Wearing Air Jordans, you didn't kick with your toe.

The fifth second, Dave kicked Billy Ray so hard in the crotch that the boy's genes jangled back for twenty generations of Battles.

The sixth second, Dave watched as Billy Ray did an imitation of a shotgun breaking open, as he bent over from the hips in hellish torment.

The seventh second, Dave clasped his hands together prayerfully and drew his arms over his head.

The eighth second, as Billy Ray bent over in pain-wracked penitence, Dave's clasped hands connected with the four-inch-square patch of nerves where Billy Ray's thick neck met his thick head.

The ninth second, Dave hopped back to permit Billy Ray's face to slam unimpeded against the filthy floor.

Martino briskly handcuffed Billy Ray, who was curled up fetally and moaning. Since the suspect was conscious, she told Blitzer to read him his Miranda rights.

"I don't know that he's gonna say shit," Blitzer whispered

"Don't be too sure," Dave said.

Martino squatted by Billy Ray, reading him his rights. From time to time, she prodded him and he moaned a response. Safir and Wise were the first detectives on the scene. They wore the same brown Florsheims, kept the same dour expression on their gray, wattled faces, stayed tuned to the same telepathic band.

"You got him," Wise said.

"You got him good," said Safir.

"You brought down the Ladykiller," Blitzer breathed.

Knees against chin, eye oozing blood, Billy Ray lay on his side with his cheek against the dirt-caked floor and drew unsteady gusts of breath.

Martino stood up and nodded. Dave kneeled next to Billy Ray. "Testing, one, two."

"Was that incredible?" Blitzer asked no one in particular, staring at Dave.

"When he twisted the .45 around, I could see it was unloaded. He showed me the empty handle. He had no clip," Dave said over his shoulder. "And I was pretty sure that model .45 can't release the one in the chamber if there's no clip." Pretty sure.

He leaned close to Billy Ray and said quietly. "You're not a very smart serial killer, are you, Billy Ray? Testing, one, two."

Billy Ray lowed like a felled bull.

"Nice eye you got, Billy Ray," Dave continued. "Or should I call you Ladykiller, huh?"

Billy Ray managed a nod.

"When you shoot them in the eye, which eye is that?"

"Don't matter." Billy Ray wheezed in pain. "Shoot the bitches in any damn eye I want to."

Blitzer was scribbling furiously in his notepad. "I got that," he crowed. "A confession."

Dave straightened up and walked out of the store. Safir and Wise followed. The crowd parted for them. Safir and Wise had parked their unmarked car at a right angle to the curb. A portable strobe pulsed red from its perch on the dashboard. The two older detectives got in the front. Dave slumped in the backseat.

Safir called in the bad news to Blake on the task force's restricted band — restricted because they didn't want the freaks who monitor police radios to hear. Wise drove off fast, down the mad, flashing, neon-drenched street. No one said a word. They let the cool promise of spring air play over them.

"He was carrying the weapon for show," Dave finally said wearily, giving voice to their frustration, as if that would exorcise it. "He didn't know how to use his own gun. And he didn't know which eye the Ladykiller shoots his victims in."

"You hit him in the right eye on purpose," Wise said.

"You had your reasons," said Safir.

"Doesn't matter now," Dave muttered.

Then Blake came back over the radio, instructing them to head up to a parking lot off Tenth. From his tone, they could tell a woman's right eye was involved.

⇒ THREE ⇐

A crime scene, by night, has a festive and eerie majesty. At this one, police car roof lights flashed with the abandon of a crazed Mardi Gras celebration. Already, the uniforms had cordoned off the parking lot, keeping at bay the ragtag crowd that murder always attracts. The moonscape of the parking lot was empty except for the cluster of cops that circled around its one small building like guests at a macabre cocktail party.

Dave bobbed under the yellow crime-scene tape and jogged up to the site. Safir and Wise ambled behind in their thick-soled Florsheims, confident that the body would still be there when they arrived.

Detective Jamie Loud saw them coming. She stepped away from the corpse to watch Dave's determined advance. Jamie looked young and fresh and cool, her close-cropped hair accentuating the elegant shape of her skull, her off-the-rack pleated pants and unconstructed jacket hanging on her lithe frame with the slouchy grace of the Armani originals they were copied from. Since Dave Dillon had joined the Ladykiller task force, Jamie dressed especially well for work — even when summoned from her apartment for a late-night homicide. Her face, with its high, polished-ebony cheekbones, betrayed only a slight tightening as she turned back to the corpse.

Lt. Blake mistook Jamie's turning away as a reaction to the dead woman. He gave Jamie a penetrating stare, as if searching for a special, sisterly angst. Jamie returned his stare impassively, the way she always did. Some day, she would tell him this murder series wasn't a chick thing. Dead was dead, and all gender problems were over for this poor bitch in the garbage heap.

In fairness, Blake was extremely nice to her for an old-school cop on a force where women still weren't wholeheartedly welcome. A study in gray-templed avuncularity, he never made snide comments insinuating that her race or sex had landed her this plum assignment. He seemed to genuinely appreciate her skills, especially with the computer. She loved this job. Unfortunately, she also loved Dave Dillon. Both involved mysteries.

Dave strode up to the corpse, oblivious to Jamie, as usual. "Nobody's touched her?"

"Not yet," Blake said.

The guys from the Crime Scene Unit hovered nearby and waited for Dave to complete his examination. These forensic technicians, picked by Blake for the Ladykiller case, knew that the lieutenant wanted Dave to give the body the once-over before they so much as touched it. Blake felt that they needed the continuity of one cop — one good, intuitive cop — making the initial exam in each instance of the series of killings. Dave himself was convinced that the smallest act — even scraping under her fingernails for samples — would disturb not only the evidence, but the psychic rhythms of the murder scene. It was his father's influence again, although the old man would never have put it like that.

Dave squatted beside the dead woman. Already, the flies were congregating, as thick as sports fans despite the cold. It didn't help that she had fallen in a pile of trash. He waved the insects away and, with the help of a tiny flashlight, peered into her cratered right eye. He shined the light slowly around her face. Next, he slipped on a pair of surgical gloves and turned her head to the side. The exit wound, several inches behind her ear, was larger still: a volcano mouth from which blood and brain had erupted. He felt under the body's armpit. Some warmth remained.

He got to his feet and, as he slowly peeled off the gloves, nodded to Blake. "All right, Loo," he said, using the cop nickname for lieutenant.

"What do you make of this one?"

Dave turned to the corpse. "Nothing new. Like the others, she died where we found her. Her blood lividity shows she hasn't been moved. Judging by her body heat, she hasn't been gone long. Maybe an hour or two. The M.E. will know better. The killer's .45 was fired from the usual close range: There's the stippling effect of gunpowder burns on the skin. And once we find it, I'll bet he used his usual copper-jacketed slug. As usual, it tore out the entire right hemisphere of her brain."

Safir and Wise stooped to check out the corpse, a task they performed with their typical ghoulish relish. In life, the victim had been an attractive woman. And although death made the most comely into ugly nightmares, they enjoyed delving into a female victim's most private matters. Wise checked her pockets. Safir opened her purse.

"No ID, no drugs, no apparent needle marks." Wise reeled off the tired litany as if reciting a catechism. "No visible bruises on her arms or anywhere else."

"She's a hooker," Dave said.

To anyone else, Jamie would have been openly indignant. "Oh, you can't assume that," she chided gently. "That long coat covers her legs. She'd be strutting her stuff."

"The shoes," Dave said.

"A lot of women wear shoes like that," Jamie insisted.

"She's got condoms in her purse," Safir said.

"Big deal. I have condoms in my purse and that doesn't make — How many?"

"About two hundred."

"Three different types."

"Oh." Jamie raised her eyebrows a fraction and opened her notebook. Blake suppressed a very small, tired smile.

"Who found the body?" Dave asked.

"It was a 911 call," Blake said. "From the sound of the tape, the caller was an elderly black woman. Barely coherent. She gave the address and hung up." He signaled for the crime-scene crew to move in and start scraping and bagging.

"The crime scene is always the same," Dave mused. "An out-of-the-way place. Nobody around. No signs of a struggle, of the victim being taken to the site against her will. You have to assume the victim knew the perp and trusted him enough to go with him to the site or meet him there. The victim is shot precisely in the right eye at close range, every time. That means she trusted the perp to get that near. Trusted him enough to hold still, maybe in shock, when he brought out his piece. If she were moving, dodging, or whatever, the bullet would have hit somewhere else in the head. If she had tried to run, he'd have to shoot her in the back first."

"Very, very nice theory," Safir said.

"But only a theory," Wise said.

"An interesting one, though," said Blake, who aside from allegiance to Dave's father, had brought Dave to the task force for his drive and analytical powers. He had picked Safir and Wise because they were methodical, old-time detectives, content to do the plodding grunt work of gathering evidence and — if any existed — witnesses.

Wise resumed his litany. "Well, we've got dick. Four homicides with the same MO. All done in Manhattan, but not in the same neighborhood. No witnesses. No suspects. No pattern to the victims. Zip."

Jamie, her voice now the same professional monotone of her colleagues, ticked off points on her fingers. "A housewife. A cheerleader. A stockbroker. And now a probable hooker. No discernable connection. Families of the first three say they can't imagine any link."

Safir took up the recitation. "Probable perp: a white male in his late twenties or early thirties. A loner. Possible sexual problems. Comes from a broken home. No obvious signs of psychosis."

Jamie gave a throaty chuckle. "Sounds like half the guys on the force."

"So that's it," Safir concluded. "As I'm sure our wonderful chief of detectives, Big Dick Mancuso, would love to hear, we have nothing. No pattern. Nada."

Dave suddenly banged his fist against the corrugated metal of the lot attendant's shack, making a noise loud enough to startle his colleagues and the crime-scene techies, as well. "No, goddamn it. It isn't that way. It isn't random. There is a pattern."

Safir and Wise exchanged a knowing glance. Jamie looked worriedly from Dave to Blake, who regarded his detective with a deep frown.

"The logic exists," Dave went on. "It has something to do with the victim knowing and trusting the shooter. We just haven't found the pattern yet." He stalked off, his shoulders hunched.

"Touchy," Wise said.

"Like his dad," said Safir.

Jamie watched Dave stomp toward the street. She suppressed an impulse to run after him. What would the others say if she did?

"He's a fine detective," Blake said. "His father was, too." That put an end to all further discussion of the Dillon family.

"Too bad the redneck wasn't our man," Wise said.

"Too bad," Safir echoed.

Blake snapped his fingers. "Get on this. I want her IDed, and I want everything on her entered into the computer. And I want it yesterday. I've got to talk about Victim No. 4 to Mancuso. It will be big news." And once again, he would have to defend Dave, whom Mancuso referred to as "that hotheaded maniac."

The detectives murmured tiredly and started to disperse. Wise touched Jamie's arm, and she turned to him. "Just one thing, detective."

"Yeah, Wise. What is it?"

"About those condoms in your purse?"

"Not for you, pal."

Jamie smiled to take the edge off her retort. Underneath, however, she resented the banter. Old-school cops for you. On the other hand, at least they noticed her as a woman. That was more than she could say for Dave.

"How about me, doll?" Safir could always be counted on to extend Wise's jokes. Jamie smiled tiredly but didn't bother to answer.

She did carry condoms in her purse, a recent purchase. She had been watching Dave from the day he had joined the task force. At first because he was handsome. Then because he was smart. Then it was his intensity, how the work consumed him. Catching this serial killer was like a holy quest for him. Personal.

Unfortunately, Jamie's few tentative overtures went by him un-acknowledged. As far as she knew, nothing stood in the way. No wife. No girlfriend. No black-white problems; her radar on race was very sharp. They got along okay professionally. Outside of work, however, he remained oblivious.

At the edge of the crime scene, the uniforms at the tape barrier still had a throng of late-night rovers to keep back. Dave shouldered past a bear-like man with an enormous, veined nose, who craned his neck to check out the action deep within the parking lot. Reuben Silver took a lively interest in crime.

Nearby, a young vagrant slithered along the nether reaches of the crowd. He almost stepped into Dave's path and gave a small yip. Dave scowled briefly and considered pulling him in to question about Billy Ray. But he was tired and Billy Ray didn't matter any more. Dave kept going.

Ace was jacked up, wired, mumbling to himself. Searching for something. Anything. "You think I'm nobody, don't you?" he muttered after the detective had passed out of earshot. "Wrong, Dillon. Big-time wrong, Dillon. Wrong, wrong, wrong, wrong, wrong."

He licked his lips nervously and whispered to the long-clawed demon that burned bright behind his eyes, "Wrong."

By the time Nita got to work, Megan was sitting at her desk, coat hung up, breathing back to normal. When Nita entered the dingy room, Megan jumped up impulsively, then sat back down, controlling the urge to rush over and help Nita out of her coat, hover around her, fuss. Nita hated fuss.

She was drinking in Nita's careless, heart-seizing, elegant beauty when she read the tension in the brow, the tightness in the lips.

She got up slowly. Nita was slipping her coat onto a hanger. "Are you okay? You look awful."

"Why thank you," Nita laughed. "I'm fine. Really."

Amid the depressing squalor of the West Side Crisis Center, Nita's smile bouyed Megan's spirits disproportionately. Megan found herself telling Nita about her own misadventure with the wino.

"Never show fear," Nita admonished her. "I don't care if you're in a cage of tigers. You're the boss." She was only half kidding.

Megan agreed enthusiastically and followed Nita to her desk, trying not to hover. Nita sat down, shoved the overflowing in-box to one side, and turned on her desk lamp. The big room was poorly lit by high, dirty fluorescent fixtures, but each desk had a lamp. The ones on the only two desks occupied tonight cast yellow pools of light as comforting as beacons in the wilderness. Outside the cozy ambits of their desk lamps, the lone outposts of civilization were the coffee maker and Nita's aquarium, almost identical to the tank she maintained in her own home.

"I sent Tim home and changed the log," Megan told her.

"Thanks," Nita answered absently, starting to sort through the in-box.

Depressing even in daylight, this room spoke of human suffering. Wall posters addressed an entire spectrum of disaster, from AIDS to drugs to child abuse to rape. On one bulletin board, an ancient AT&T ad advised the world to "reach out and touch someone." Beneath it was a handwritten amendment: "And then be sure to wash your hands."

"Do you think, if we get a minute, you could help me pick out courses for next semester?" Megan asked.

Nita looked up from her paperwork. "Sure."

The hotline phone buzzed. Nita picked up the receiver. "Crisis center. Can I help you?" But the phone went dead. They got a lot of hang-up calls. From the suffering urban damned who got an attack of reluctance at the last minute.

Megan sank into her chair and looked at Nita dreamily. Nita was a true warrior against the scaly monsters of human degradation. Alienation, despair, apathy, anger. Nita had rescued so many. She had reshaped wrecked lives and sent them back into the urban jungle stronger. Megan wished she could do the same. Wished she weren't weakened by doubts, fears, inchoate desires. Wished she could trade her frail timid heart for Nita's relentless dynamo.

Shrugging, Nita hung up the phone. "They'll call back. They

always do." She shot Megan a look of mock disapproval. "Hey, let's sharpen up. Magic hour's coming."

Megan sat forward in her chair. Social workers who man hotlines in the small hours, like cops and ambulance workers and reporters, know that between one and five A.M. is the time of the wolf, the time when society's translucent fabric shreds. That's when most people die. From heart attacks and aneurysms. And also from violence. That's when they climb onto ledges, stab their wives, shoot too much junk into their veins, drive their cars into bridge abutments. That's when they call the hotline.

The phone sounded again. Megan listened to a hysterical woman whose drunken husband had just caved in her front teeth and staggered into the bedroom to pass out.

"What do I do?" the woman wailed. "If I call the cops, he'll lose his job. How can we take care of the kids then?"

When Megan hung up, having urged the woman to call the battered wife service in the morning, Nita commented dryly, "They're too dependent on the brutes. Testosterone overloads. Mandatory castration isn't a bad idea."

"They aren't all bad," Megan protested, laughing.

Nita laughed, too. "That's not what I hear."

Before Megan could reply, Nita answered another call.

Megan poured them both coffee and went back to her desk. She was about to grab the call sheet to start the evening's paperwork, when she heard the muffled thud of the building's heavy front door slamming shut.

Alarmed, she looked at Nita, who was still on the phone and didn't appear to have heard. No one else was supposed to be here tonight. Tensed, Megan eyed the door to the room, very aware, suddenly, of their own vulnerability. Two isolated women in the middle of a large, shabby room with help far away.

Footsteps, heavy and slow, came from the hall beyond the door. Megan reached slowly for her phone.

Nita asked her caller to hold for a moment. A phone line buzzed unnoticed.

"Hey, hey, hey. Nothing like Chinese to take the bite out of a cool night, huh?" Reuben Silver emerged from the dark hallway toting a large paper bag.

Megan and Nita traded long-suffering looks.

"What are you doing here?" Megan asked. "Didn't we relieve you? This isn't your shift."

Reuben smiled sheepishly at Megan as he unpacked the white, waxy cardboard containers of fragrant Chinese food. "I figured you girls were going to need some help around here."

Nita, still on the phone, glared at him.

Reuben managed an apologetic grimace. "Women. Whatever. There's another murder. Only a few blocks from here, this time," he mentioned as if in explanation. He unwrapped three packages of wooden chopsticks and jabbed them into three of the steaming containers. "I thought as soon as the jungle drums spread the word, our phones would start ringing off the hook with I-did-its, I-know-who-did-its, and I'm-next-to-dies. You know the drill. Most of them have already called the cops and got shot down. But they know we'll always talk to them, the lousy losers."

He gestured for them to join him at the impromptu buffet of the Chinese food he had arranged on an empty desk.

"Dig in, folks," Reuben said with forced gusto. "I brought enough for everybody."

When the two women didn't move, he tried again. "Hey, don't you ever wonder whether the Ladykiller is one of our own people? One of the real loonies we just try to keep the lid on?"

"Really, Reuben," Nita said, disapprovingly.

Reuben launched into one of his patented comedy routines. "We could start counseling murderers. Sort of like Killers Anonymous. 'Hi, I'm Sam and I'm a serial murderer. But with the love and support of my peer group—a great bunch of guys—I haven't killed in two months.' 'We're here for you, Sammy.' 'Hold me, Ted.'"

Nita simply stared at him. Megan gave a small chuckle. He grinned and shrugged boyishly. As if on cue, two phone lines lit up. Their buzzing filled the room.

With Nita and Megan both on the phone, Reuben stood eating out of a carton, his chopsticks dripping evil-looking dark bits and brown goo. His smile faded as he chewed the congealing Chinese food. And his eyes never left the women.

A half hour later, the calls were coming nonstop. As Reuben had predicted, word of the latest Ladykiller slaying had ignited traumas inside every shaky psyche in Manhattan. Nita felt privately thankful that Reuben had shown up. He manned one of the phones, giving advice through mouthfuls of Szechuan cuisine.

Nita picked up the receiver to field the next call. "Crisis center. Can I help you?"

"It's me," the familiar reedy voice said, investing each word with slow, poisonous menace.

"How can I help you?" Nita decided not to favor him with immediate recognition tonight. Coldness was the best response.

"You know who this is, don't you?"

"Yes, Ace," she said tiredly. "What do you want?"

"I want you. I need you. I need you tonight."

"I'm busy," she said, preparing to hang up.

"I did something terrible tonight," he said quickly.

"And what was that, Ace?"

"I killed a woman tonight."

Nita was no more perturbed than if he were announcing the train schedule. She knew which of her regular clients were capable of violence. Ace was not. "You don't say? Who was the lucky woman?"

"A whore. Like you. You're all whores."

"And you're a pillar of the community." Nita knew when compassion's usefulness had ended. "Listen, I'm busy. We'll discuss this at our session. And not before. Real people with real problems are calling in tonight."

"I'm the Ladykiller, you bitch," Ace yelled. "I killed every one of them. And I'll fucking do it again. Do you hear me?"

But Nita had hung up the phone.

FOUR

"These killings are something else. People are really shaken up,"

Dave glanced over at his oldest friend from Queens, now a well-known crime reporter, running beside him. "The press conference about the latest shooting is at ten this morning," Jimmy went on, panting slightly. "You were there last night, right?"

"I can't help you on this, Jimmy," said Dave, who wished he could. Big Dick Mancuso would trace any leak to him.

"Christ, this is a big story."

"Sells newspapers, right?" Dave said in jest, knowing this would get to Jimmy. It did.

"Get lost. We make money from advertising, not newsstand sales, for God's sake." Conlon's irreverence toward every national institution stopped short when it came to his own, which he viewed as a sacred shrine.

"You're right that people are shaken up," Dave said. "Hey, I'm shaken up."

They were running in Central Park along with battalions of yuppies getting early morning exercise before dressing for success and going to work. The park this early had a promising March snap to it, its grass already succulent with rain-fed green, its tree branches laden with fat spring buds, its blue-domed sky streaked with angelic contrails. Its women beginning to show their skin.

"Jesus, I'm in love," Jimmy said as they passed a sleek-thighed goddess, her breasts bouncing gently.

Dave hadn't noticed. "We're under a lot of pressure. We have to find this hump before he does it again."

"You think you're frustrated?" Jimmy said, chugging along beside his friend, who was almost a full head taller. "My editor's going nuts. He believes that a kid from Queens who grew up with a million cops should be coming up with exclusives."

"We honestly don't know anything, Jimmy."

"It's so stupid." Jimmy loved newspaper reporting but he loathed his boss. "Bunch of snotty, Ivy League assholes who spend their time sucking up to each other on the squash court. This dickbrain asked me, 'Have the cops ruled out organized crime?' "

Dave snorted. "What'd you tell him?"

"I answered, 'Yes, Chip. They've ruled out organized crime, beings from outer space, sharp-hooved giraffes, and you.' "

Dave chuckled. "For all I can tell, a being from outer space is behind this."

They ran in companionable silence for a minute. "Seriously, Jimmy, if we break the case, and I have anything to do with it, you'll be the first to hear."

They ran past a massive shoulder of majestic rock that looked as if retreating glaciers had shoved it into the light of a prehistoric sun.

"Break it," Jimmy said, "and I'll make you a hero. Like you ought to be. Again."

At 8 A.M., Dave Dillon slouched into the operations room that housed the Ladykiller task force. The detectives clustered around a battle-scarred table strewn with manila folders leaking papers, Styrofoam cups leaking coffee, ashtrays leaking butts. Dave pulled up a chair and muscled in between Wise and Jamie Loud.

Jamie, not for the first time, gave thanks that her black skin covered her blushing. Jamie touched Dave's arm, giving herself a tiny frisson as her fingers touched his muscled, honey-colored skin, bare below rolled-up sleeves. When he turned to her, she passed him a sheet of briefing paper. The hooker now had a name.

As Dave read the information on the girl, her short rap sheet, last known address, and preliminary medical findings, Jamie studied him. She had a sudden, hot, vivid image of the two of them in her bed together. Not how it would feel. How it would look. An aerial view of them beneath the slow blades of the ceiling fan, the crisp white sheets crumpled after hard-pumping sex, the large fern beside the bed brushing his golden skin where his arm hung over the edge, his muscular blond nakedness a perfect match for her supple black curves. She shuddered and sighed aloud.

Jamie jerked her attention back to the operations room in time to catch Lt. Blake's entrance. One corner of his mouth was twisted upward.

"Chief of Detectives Mancuso is not pleased," Blake said. "We've got to start moving, people."

"Big Dick Mancuso," Wise said.

"This is no joking matter, Wise," Blake said sternly.

"Sorry, Loo. Too much coffee, too early."

"Or maybe too little," Safir added.

"Thanks to Detective Loud's late-night session with the computer, we have some stuff on our victim," Blake said.

Jamie resisted the temptation to smile at his praise.

"Lydia Daniels," Blake continued. "Age 22, born in Minnesota, came to New York three years ago. Arrested three times for prostitution, twice for possession. Lived in an SRO on the Deuce, the Dixie. Pimp that ran her is a minor player named Jacob Weinstein, street name Jackie Why. Dave, you know him?"

Jamie looked up, startled. She could swear she felt Dave bristle beside her at the question. But his voice was calm when he replied.

"Jackie? Sure. Two or three convictions for girls and possession. Went to Attica on a felony dealing beef, but was back on the streets in a short time. I think he turned over his dealer, which makes it a little more surprising he's still around. He's always had a string of girls and a little dealing action. Kind of a complete entertainment center for traveling businessmen. Not too high class. Not the worst, either. When trade gets slow, though, his girls work the street. He likes production."

"Like Big Dick Mancuso," Wise said in an undertone that everyone could pick up.

Blake ignored him. "Great. You talk to this character, then. The beat guys brought him in an hour ago. Says he doesn't know where Lydia is or where she spent the night. He says she was supposed to be working, but he hasn't seen her."

After Blake issued some marching orders to the twenty detectives on the Ladykiller task force, the meeting adjourned with a tortured scrape of chairs. Dave slouched over to the wall where the hooker's bloody crime-scene photo had been added to those of the other victims. Beneath each glossy picture was a summary of the murder. Dave stood before them, scanning every one, back and forth.

The first murder, six weeks ago, was Evelyn Hernandez, 29, a housewife and mother of four who lived in Spanish Harlem. Her husband worked the desk at a big Midtown hotel. She had been shot on the desolate street behind the SPCA building just off the FDR Drive, the yelps of the dogs no doubt drowning out the gunshot.

The second murder, a week later, established the pattern. It captured the attention of the media, the politicians, and Dick Mancuso. Lucy Cristides, 16, a cheerleader from Queens whose parents owned a Manhattan coffee shop, was found in the Meatpacking District. Nobody ventured there after dark.

The third came three weeks hence: Kimberly Worth, 35, a money-eyed stockbroker who lived on the Upper East Side. She met her killer in Carl Schurz Park, several blocks from her elegant apartment building. This park, bordering the East River, was populated with yuppies by day and by no one at night.

And now, Lydia Daniels.

Blake said to Jamie, "Loud, you go with Dillon when he interrogates the pimp."

"Yes, sir."

"And keep him out of trouble."

"What kind of trouble?"

"Any kind," Blake said as he left.

There was something about Dave that no one was telling her. Jamie joined him as he examined the victims' photos.

He didn't look at her, but acknowledged her presence by saying, "There's a pattern in there somehow. It only appears to be random. Normally, a serial killer will go for one type: prostitutes or coeds or redheads or some other easily identifiable trait. They also rarely kill outside their ethnic group. Here, we have three whites and an Hispanic. One teenager, two in their twenties, one in her thirties. And the spectrum of social classes: a wealthy stockbroker, a middle-class borough kid, a working-class wife, and a streetwalker. Two worked for a living: the stockbroker and the hooker. Two didn't: the Spanish Harlem mother and the high school girl. There's nothing to link them. They apparently didn't know one another."

Jamie nodded encouragingly.

"But there's some thread. Some thread binds them together."

Jamie gazed at Dave while he perused the victims, as intense as if he were determined to penetrate the secret smile of the *Mona Lisa.* "I'm sure you'll find it," she said.

Jackie Why sat in the interrogation room. He sat insolently backward in his chair, his legs splayed to either side. His hair was greased and combed flat back, ending in a ponytail so oily he could lube an engine with it. Jackie Why chainsmoked unfiltered cigarettes. Several burnt-out ends lay crushed on the floor around his cowboy boots.

Dave held the door to the room to allow Jamie to enter first. Then he stepped in and closed it softly behind him.

Jackie Why, his lips pressed around a cigarette, shook his head and smiled. "You got taste for a change, Dillon." He winked at Jamie. "Y'know what they say: Once you go black, you never go back." He sucked hard on the butt and its ember glowed.

Jamie seemed to be taking the insult stoically. Dave stood in front of the pimp and said, "Haven't you heard the new rules, Jackie? No smoking."

"Ain't no rules in a cop shop, Dillon. Anything goes, pal."

Dave grabbed the cigarette out of Jackie Why's mouth and threw it hard at him. The burning end sizzled briefly against his forehead, and he swatted at it and grimaced in pain.

"Hey, watch it, Dillon. Don't go around assaulting citizens, okay?"

Dave bounced a hard finger off the pimp's chest. "Don't worry about it, creep."

Jackie Why was not cowed. "Dillon, I've been sitting here for an hour like a good little boy. No one has charged me with shit. No one has served me with any papers. So unless you get on with your bull-shit, I'm booking out of here."

Dave glanced at Jamie. He knew Blake had sent her along to make sure he behaved. And he was determined to keep his temper in check.

"So tell me, Jackie," Dave began, "who were Lydia's friends?"

"Only me. I was her friend."

"What about other hookers?" They went around and around for a spell. Dave showed Jackie the pictures of the other three murdered women and recited their names. Jackie was aware of them solely from media reports of their deaths; he was sure Lydia didn't know them. Shown the long coat she had died in, he opined that it didn't belong to her, although he volunteered no notion of its true owner's identity. He knew little else about her other than her performance as an employee.

"She was a world-class suction pump." Jackie Why leered at Jamie. "Know what that is, baby? She had the — what they call — labial control. Sit on top of you and blow your mind. Shit, take her to an oilfield and strap her on top of a rig, this country's energy problems would be history."

"She had a batch of condoms in her purse," Jamie said. "But they were in unopened packages. Not one was used. Did she practice safe sex?"

"Fucked if I know. She did with me. I ain't letting none of them scuzzy bitches get around my nice pork without something between us." He winked at Jamie. "I use French ticklers."

Dave persisted. "Did Lydia's customers like to do it without con-doms?"

"Maybe some did. Feels better when you can do it raw." He smirked at Jamie. "Right, honey?"

Jamie said nothing. She kept her eyes fixed on his.

Dave rapped Jackie Why's temple with his knuckles. "Knock, knock, asshole. Anybody home? We don't go around making stupid remarks to police officers. Otherwise, bad, bad things can happen."

Jackie Why sneered. "Hey, I got a lawyer, Dillon. After the heat you took for Mr. Slice and Dice, you don't need another brutality problem. Good break for you that fucking redneck last night was too dense to file charges."

Jamie could feel Dave's tension as he shrugged and got up to leave. She followed and they were at the door when Jackie took one last shot. "Oh, by the way, I had a phone call from a friend of yours. A *special* friend." He sniggered unpleasantly.

Dave's face became a mask, as he held back his urge to go back and bounce Jackie Why's oily head off the wall. Instead, he opened the door and spoke evenly. "You can go, Jackie."

The pimp got to his feet and swaggered to the door, giving Jamie an up and down appraisal as he moved past her. "Nice legs you got, for a cop."

"Beat it, scumbag," Jamie said quietly, "Or I'll kick your butt so hard, you'll be wearing it as a necklace."

Jackie Why left without another word.

Dave looked at Jamie in surprise, as if he were seeing her for the first time.

She smiled. "I'm not partial to pimps."

"Me neither. You can tell Blake I didn't smack him around."

Jamie's smile evaporated. "I'm not here to spy on you."

"Good," Dave said tersely.

"And if you had smacked him around, I might have helped."

Dave allowed himself a glimmer of a smile. "You're okay, Loud."

"Call me Jamie," she said.

Dave decided to like her. She was smart, strong, and steady. Exactly the sort of woman the Dillon men needed but never got.

For the hundredth time that morning, Dave thought of the

woman Jackie Why had called his special friend. She was lost to him forever. His heart ached.

Despite having pulled the graveyard shift, Megan was expected at the West Side Crisis Center's weekly staff meeting the next morning. She had slept only a couple of hours and wore the same clothes as the night before.

She entered the center's main lobby, a dirty cavern where motes of dust jigged in the light from the soot-caked windows. The clientele wandered about the lobby, as purposeless as the dust. A woman strutted by with boxes under her sweater, giving her large, square breasts. A man, his entire head wrapped with mummy-like bandages, sat nodding in a corner. One old woman was taking small steps in a circle, around and around. A hubbub of conversation filled the lobby, although it was mostly from clients talking to themselves.

The staff had crammed into the staff lounge, a tiny room with lockers, a coffee maker, and old furniture that bled stuffing. Reuben sat laughing inanely on a sofa with Tim, a young, gay man with a buzz cut. Nita sat in a chair off in the corner, in a fresh change of clothes; she was absorbed in a file and there was no place near her to sit. Megan ended up on the sofa with Reuben and Tim. She said hello to Rose, the sweet motherly lady who sat on a rickety chair next to her.

"One word about counseling cocaine addicts," Tim said.

Reuben looked at him with great expectation.

Tim giggled. "It's not what it's cracked up to be." He fell apart laughing, rocking back and forth.

Reuben, after a moment, joined him with a huge belly laugh. Rose looked bewildered.

Tim said to Rose, "It's not what it's *cracked* up to be."

Rose finally got it.

Dr. Solomon, the tired and aging head of the center, came in and stopped. He looked vaguely about, ever the academic surprised by the real world. Tim got up to pour a cup of coffee. Reuben assumed a blank expression. Rose was now laughing alone.

"Rose?" Dr. Solomon said. "Are you all right?"

Flustered, Rose took a moment to recover. She glanced at Reuben, who faced ostentatiously away. "Reuben," she said, "you crazy old coot." Reuben relented and chuckled at her.

"Megan," Nita called, "let me show you something."

Happy to be rescued and pleased that Nita wanted to see her, Megan rose from the sofa and crossed the room to kneel at Nita's side as she pointed to a line in the file.

"Look, it's Gloria Steinem and Susan Faludi," Tim said. He and Reuben howled some more.

Nita murmured to Megan, "To think I've got the overnight shift tonight with Tim."

"I can come in to keep you company," Megan offered.

"No, thanks. You have schoolwork to do." She shook her head. "God, Reuben last night and Tim tonight. I don't know which is worse professionally. A burn-out like Reuben or a dilettante like Tim."

"Nita, my dear," Rose called across the room, "I do need to have another little talk with you, if I may. My homeless ladies are all upset about this serial killer. I don't know what to tell them."

"Fine, Rose," Nita said. "Any time."

Megan said softly to Nita, "Do you always solve everyone's problems?"

Nita said to her, equally softly, "It's my curse."

As the staff members settled down for the meeting to start, Megan stayed kneeling next to Nita. Dr. Solomon smiled distractedly and poured a cup of coffee. As Megan looked around the room, she saw Reuben. He was staring fixedly at Nita.

Weeks ago, Reuben had taken snapshots of the two women at work, much to their annoyance.

He had the Polaroids stuck on the dresser mirror of his shadow-haunted apartment. Nita and Megan.

Now that his wife was dead and his two daughters had escaped to the suburbs with their husbands, Nita and Megan were the only women in his life.

FIVE

Nita's small studio apartment bespoke the scholarly life. Bookshelves laden with weighty tomes filled most of the wall space, drinking in the scant light from the two windows. Her desk, from its spot in the exact center of the floor, dominated the apartment. Her computer dominated the desk. Books and papers were neatly piled next to it.

A narrow bed, meant for one, occupied a corner of the room. Beside it, a small clock radio played moody, nocturnal jazz.

"We'll be back with more soothing sounds for all you city folk in need of soothing," the announcer said in a mellifluous baritone that echoed Miles Davis' saxophone. "But first the news."

Nita stood next to the room's only bright spot, a large aquarium. She stared at its colorful, darting denizens, their eyes blank, their beautiful tails idly swishing through the glowing water. Carefully, Nita sprinkled fish food upon the smooth skin of water. Never too much or too little. Her fish were robust, happy, at peace. And so pretty.

"The death toll mounted to more than one thousand in the Peruvian earthquake . . ."

The fish tank was a perfect society. Regulated. Idyllic. There were no surprises.

"A presidential commission declared that a cure for cancer lies many decades away, if ever . . ."

Once, one of the fish at the crisis center's similar tank had taken ill and started attacking the other fish. With ruthless dispatch, Nita had destroyed them all and started anew. She watched in delight as her fish swallowed their crumbs, grateful.

"The latest in a series of brutal slayings in Manhattan has stepped up the pressure on the police department for action. The police admit they have no clues in the seemingly random series of killings. The latest victim of the .45-caliber killer was found early this morning—"

Nita turned abruptly and snapped off the radio. She grabbed her coat and purse, and marched off to work, into the unforgiving night.

Ace strutted along the deserted overpass beside Grand Central Station. Below on Park Avenue, bright-eyed stampedes of cars swished, moving to the rhythms of the city, rhythms that trilled inside Ace's head. He shouted.

"Evelyn Hernandez."

He knew every one of their names. He knew everything about them. He could see their faces. The dumb friendliness of Evelyn, a tentative smile that slid very easily into fear.

Ace climbed onto the balustrade, spread his arms like a tightrope walker, and took a step. The air from the speeding cars below whooshed past him.

"Lucy Cristides," he shouted. Lucy, sweet, pathetic, entirely out of control. She might have even liked him.

Another step. Hard to maintain his balance. He swayed in the air currents pushing up from Park Avenue.

"Kimberly Worth." What a snotty bitch. She had looked at Ace as if he were dog shit smeared on the sidewalk. Of them all, she deserved to die the most.

Two more steps. Getting the hang of this now. He smirked in triumph. You only win by taking chances. The taillights of the speeding cars shone like cinders.

"Lydia Daniels." Ace actually had liked the hooker. Until he scraped together the fifty bucks she charged for street trade, a brief session in her room. He remembered how she had laughed as she pushed him off her, laughed at his forlorn look, laughed at his mumbled apology. "I wish they were all like you. I'd have a lot more time, wouldn't I, darling?" she said as she got into her clothes and left to meet Jackie Why. He should have done something to her then.

Women. They felt great, smelled great, moved great. And yet they always ended up making him feel miserable.

And then came the ultimate woman. The ultimate ballbreaker, the icicle queen, the number one dispenser of disapproval. He shouted her name loud enough to shake his lungs, leaning his head back and bellowing at the silver-pulsing sky.

"Nita."

The sky shook. Ace realized he was teetering over the edge of the balustrade, tilting dangerously above the relentless whiz of traffic below. He spun his arms like propellers. And then . . . and then . . . righted himself.

He hopped jerkily down from the balustrade, onto the firm concrete safety of the overpass sidewalk. And he laughed maniacally, as though hearing every obscene joke in the world for the first time.

Tonight, he knew, was Nita's night. The next time he uttered her name would be in person. Tonight.

The night outside Megan's apartment had come to noisy life at this late hour. She idly thumbed through the course catalog, circling possible classes to take, sitting on her large bed in her bikini underpants and an "I Love New York" T-shirt, drinking a Diet Coke, her menagerie of stuffed animals around her. A car alarm on the street was whooping like Curly in an old Three Stooges movie. No one, to be sure, was stealing the rusty jalopy that contained the alarm. The pavement-shaking vibration of a passing truck had set it off. But for ten minutes, the Stooge-mobile would torment the neighborhood. The wail of a police siren sounded out on the avenue, completing the symphony.

In the ideal society, alarms and sirens would be unnecessary. Megan, weary of the polysyllabic course descriptions in the catalog, closed her eyes. Megan could see Nita describing the best way to reorder urban society, watch the white-hot dedication transform her lovely face as she talked. Nita's words had an intense ring to them: "People wring their hands and say, 'Nothing can be done.' Nonsense. It can be done. You're doing it. I'm doing it, right here, right now."

The couple in the apartment above began to make love. Megan

opened her eyes and looked at the ceiling. Their bed, directly over her own, bumped and creaked like a ship in a hurricane. Megan had gone to a party once in their apartment and had wandered into their bedroom, placing her coat on their noisy bed.

Megan sighed and tried to get back into the course catalog. She turned the page. There was his name — Robin Tolner — attached to the course on clinical methodology. A course she should take, and soon. She would wait until the following semester when someone else taught it. Why was Robin listed as teaching it now? He was supposed to be taking his sabbatical this year, going to Peru to study the culture of Third World crime and poverty. Maybe he had postponed it until fall.

His wisdom and learning had nourished her for six delirious months, introduced her to starry vistas beyond anything she had imagined. His passion for the mental gymnastics of academe had bedazzled her. Robin Tolner had been everywhere and knew everything: the best Thai restaurant in London, the best wine from Australia, the best chamber ensemble in Vienna. He could ski like a champion. He played Debussey on the piano with a master's touch. And he had told her that he loved her.

The plan had been for Megan to accompany him to Peru. She would even have gotten credit as his research assistant. His wife and two kids, certainly, would not go along. The dungheaps of South America were no place for a family. But a wonderful place for Megan and Robin. "Everything's cheap," he had told Megan. "We'll have servants. They'll bring us meals in bed." She had laughed in naked delight.

Then, a few weeks later, Professor Robin Tolner told Megan that seeing each other anymore wasn't a good idea. After all, he was a married man. Robin had spoken and acted so coldly, as if he were a loan officer come to foreclose on her home.

Several weeks later, Megan heard that he had taken up with another student, a long-legged blonde named Lisa. Maybe Lisa would be going to Peru.

Megan had cried for a long time. She couldn't expel Robin from her mind. The loss of him was visceral.

The rhythm of the bed upstairs changed, got faster, more urgent. Megan often wondered whether her neighbors had heard her and Robin. Not that Robin ever made any noise. She remembered how clinically composed he looked, in the middle of the wildest love-making, how he watched her appraisingly as she came.

Closing the course catalog and pressing it to her chest, Megan lay back and listened. She could almost feel Robin, deep inside her.

"No." Megan tossed the memories out of her head. She reached for the phone and quickly stabbed out the number she knew as well as her own name.

Nita's voice answered, low and controlled, but it was only her machine. Megan listened to the message but hung up without a word. She had forgotten that Nita was working tonight. If she left a message, Nita would think she was scatterbrained. And of course, she wouldn't disturb Nita at work.

Once, after two glasses of wine, Megan had made the mistake of confiding in Nita her affair with her married professor. Nita slashed Megan's psyche with two searingly accurate comments: "He probably wears leather patches on his elbows." He did. And: "If it were me, I'd have killed him." She wished she had.

The bed upstairs bucked so much it threatened to crash through Megan's ceiling. A siren went screaming past her window. Who knows? Maybe another Ladykiller murder? Megan held the catalog tightly against her and brought her knees up. At least her neighbors had each other to hold against the terrors of the night. Megan worried about Nita, out in it alone.

Reuben was there already when Nita arrived at work. With the desk lamp shining across his face, he looked like a gargoyle, his enormous nose casting a misshapen shadow on the wall.

"What are you doing here, Reuben?" Nita asked as she hung up her coat.

"Tim needed to switch," Reuben rumbled. He hadn't taken his gaze from her from the second she had entered the cavernous room.

"How nice of you." Nita sprinkled fish food into the tank and studied the creatures' movements.

Reuben pulled himself to his feet and lumbered toward her.

She left the tank before he got there and sat at her desk. She busied herself with the in-box.

After a moment, Reuben turned to her, "Can I ask you a personal question?"

Her answer came before he finished his final syllable: "No."

Reuben nodded dumbly and his fleshy face drooped. He shuffled back to his desk, where he sat mulling what to say next. "I'm really glad you're here. Good thing they put two people on duty. These phone calls." He shook his head and chuckled. "Some nights, you need somebody sane to talk to."

"Just some nights?"

Reuben roared with laughter, as if this were the world's best punchline.

"You know," Reuben said, still chortling, "sometimes I wonder if I'm on the wrong end of the phone. I guess it takes one to help one, huh?"

"Whatever," Nita said absently.

But Reuben, convinced he was getting through to her, warmed up his best material. "Hey, do you know the difference between an oral and an anal thermometer?"

She turned a page in a diagnostic report.

"The taste," Reuben brayed. His guffawing echoed throughout the large room. His merriment subsided when he realized she was ignoring him. Chastened again, he tried another tack: "Say, how's the thesis coming?"

"It's coming." She still was absorbed in the paperwork.

"Good, good. I was figuring that some night when you weren't working and you didn't have to write the thesis, you and I . . . uh, well. Do you like movies?"

She finally met his eyes. "I used to. Bergman, mostly. But I don't have time any more."

"Well, uh, maybe when you did . . ."

"I never have time," she said.

"Sure, sure. We wouldn't have to go to a movie. Maybe a cup of ——"

"I don't have time for much of anything lately, Reuben. Excuse me, but I want to finish this report."

"Oh." His face hung in folds of misery.

The phone rang and he snatched it quickly, eager for a distraction. "Crisis center. Can I help you?" As he talked, he furtively watched Nita. "Okay . . . Yes, those could be some of the early symptoms. Are you still using intravenous drugs?"

Another phone sounded. Nita sighed, straightened some papers, and gracefully picked up the receiver. "Crisis center. Can I help you?" She knew the caller's identity even before he spoke, knew from his breathing.

"I've been waiting to talk to you," Ace said softly. "You know who this is, don't you?"

Nita tensed. "Of course I do. What can I do for you tonight?"

"I want to talk to you."

"Couldn't it wait until morning? Aren't you scheduled for a counseling session?"

"I don't need counseling," Ace said angrily. "I need you. I need you to talk to me."

"Well, you understand we're *all* professionals here to help you. Any one of us could ——"

"Bullshit," Ace shouted. "I need you. I love you. You know I do." He slid into anguish. "If it wasn't for you, I'd ... I don't know . . . Explode or something."

"Look, I could get you in to see a therapist right now. Someone at the free clinic who is open at this hour. You ——"

"No. I don't need to see anyone else. I *need* you. Can't you understand that?"

Nita gripped the phone hard. "I'm *trying* to help. I just don't seem to be doing you any good."

"Why can't we be friends?" Ace exclaimed with growing excitement. "That's what I want. That's what I need. That's all. Just friends."

"Certainly. I am your friend. Don't I talk to you like a friend?"

Reuben, muttering into his own phone, watched Nita.

"I know, I know," Ace said. "But I want to see you. That's all. Just to be with you for a minute. Right now."

"You can't." Nita's voice was hard. "That's not possible. I'm sorry, but you can't. There are rules that —"

Ace interrupted her, intense, almost whispering, maniacal: "I can, too. I can get in there. I'm *close* to you. Very close."

There was a pause. Nita replied slowly, with authority: "Listen. You get hold of yourself. The center's closed except for the hotline. I'm not going to talk to you if you say things like that. You know the rules."

"Okay, okay," Ace said softly, suddenly contrite. "I'm sorry."

Nita licked her lips, the tension within her contained. "That's better."

"I'll do whatever you say," Ace said, miserable. "I'm sorry."

"Now, why don't you get some sleep. Come by for the session to-morrow and —"

But Ace hung up on her, smashing the receiver violently into its cradle.

Nita winced at the noise. Carefully, her mind a jumble of thoughts, she hung up. Then she stood and grabbed her purse. As she turned, she almost bumped into Reuben, who held out a cup of coffee for her. She was startled.

"God, the nuts in this city," Reuben said. "Why didn't you give him to me? I'd get rid of him for you."

"He hangs up on everyone else but me."

Nita took the coffee, but her hands were shaking. Some of the coffee slopped onto the floor. She started past Reuben.

"Hey, are you all right?" Reuben, concerned, followed her as she walked.

"Listen, I'm a bit shaken up. I'm going home. I've never done this before, but I suspect this will be a quiet night. I'll spell you for another shift, whenever you want."

"Fine. No problem." He frowned. "Hey, you shouldn't be walking home alone. I'll walk you." Reuben was surprised — and secretly pleased — at Nita's sudden vulnerability.

"No, thanks, Reuben. I'm going now. It's just a few blocks. I walk it all the time."

"Seriously. I'll go with you. I'll turn on the answering machine and call them back later. These wackos can wait a few minutes."

The phone rang before she could reply. He looked at it, then at Nita.

"Damn it, Reuben," Nita said angrily. "You can't leave. People out there need you."

She disappeared down the hall. Her footsteps receded hollowly. Reuben looked anxiously after her as he reluctantly picked up the phone.

"Crisis center. Can I help you?"

In the half-light of the sepulcher-silent side street, Nita opened the heavy metal door. She closed the door behind her with a clank and pulled on it to make sure it was locked. She turned around.

Then she saw Ace. Standing two feet from her. An odd, hard smile stretched across his face. Nita jumped and gasped.

"I'll walk you home," Ace said quietly.

"Oh," Nita said, struggling for control. "You startled me." She glanced up and down the deserted street. She edged away from him in the opposite direction from her usual path home.

"There's a coffee shop a couple of blocks away," she said. "It's on my way. Maybe we could talk there for a—"

Ace grabbed her arm violently and yanked her in the other direction. "No. You live this way."

Nita pulled away. Her purse fell off her arm, spilling its contents on the sidewalk. They both stopped and stared at it. The danger in the air evaporated. Nita simmered with anger. Ace seemed about to cry.

"I'm sorry," Ace said. "I didn't mean to. I just wanted to see you. That's all."

Nita glared at him and stooped to pick up her things. He squatted, too, and awkwardly handed her a few items.

"I'm going home now," Nita said, coldly furious. "We'll forget this ever happened. Now goodbye."

She rose, shouldered her bag, and walked off briskly.

"I'm sorry," Ace called after her, helplessly, rooted to the spot. "I didn't mean to." Defeated, he shifted his weight and heard a sound. He looked down at his feet. He slowly moved his right boot. Nita's key ring lay on the pavement.

Nita could sense the boots following her. She could feel the leather-soled roll of his feet on the pavement. Her own shoes snapped briskly over the sidewalk, past the dark, brick buildings like so many tombstones. She frowned at a sound behind her, and pulled the coat tighter around herself. Her purposeful walk picked up speed. Not running. Not willing to show panic.

Ace loved her bobbing gait, the utterly female click of her low heels on the sidewalk. Loved how her legs were moving faster. He longed to see those legs, longed to rub his hands up them. Starting at the ankle, over the fleshy promise of the calf, past the dimpled intrigue of the knee, and — fingertips only now — skating up the sleekness of her thigh, drawn into —

Nita reached the front door of an apartment building. Above the entrance, a weak yellow lamp gave barely enough light to make out the outline of the lock. No other human soul was about; the world lay curled up under its blankets, sleeping through the time of the wolf. Nita unzipped her handbag and rummaged frantically in it for her keys. Ace was enraptured. How he had gotten to her.

Nita darted her hands into her coat pockets, then foraged madly through the depths of her bag again.

Ace spoke from close behind her. His grin was demonic. He raised his right hand in the air.

"I have something for you," he said. He jingled the key ring up above his head. The lamp's sickly illumination caught the metal.

Nita whirled to face him. Ace was surprised by the set of her face. It wasn't quite fear she showed. Was it —?

A large hand clamped onto Ace's shoulder from behind and

pulled him backward. The jingle of the keys in Ace's hand sounded in the night. Before he could recover his balance, Reuben stepped around him and smashed his face. As Reuben's knuckles connected with his cheek, Ace let out a wail of pain. He crumpled to the ground and lay still. The keys fell from his grasp.

Nita cowered in the doorway, holding her purse against her with both arms.

Reuben stooped and picked up the keys. Shaking his aching hand, he clumped over to her and leaned against the wall, panting. "Are you okay?" Reuben gasped. "Did he hurt you?"

Pale and shaken, Nita took the keys from him carefully. "I'm okay. How did you —"

"I was worried about you. I turned the machine on and left. Lucky thing I caught up with you. I thought you lived about ten blocks away from here and—"

Reuben was suddenly pushed from behind and knocked off balance against Nita. "What the hell?"

Ace ran away, screaming incoherently, a dark banshee in full flight. Reuben held Nita's shoulders to keep her from falling. Reuben and Nita watched Ace run. Reuben still held her shoulders.

She squirmed out of his hold. "Let him go. It's all right."

"Yeah. Right." Reuben nodded sagely. "The important thing is that you're okay. Let's get you inside."

Nita didn't reply. She shrunk back against the wall. There was an uncomfortable pause.

"Come on," Reuben coaxed. "You'll be okay." In the weak light, she could tell he was warming to the role of protector. His half-smile had a concerned, paternalistic cast.

"I'm okay. I'm fine," Nita said. "Listen, you ought to go back."

"Go back?" He laughed incredulously. "Those crazies can wait." He laughed again, then stopped abruptly. "Hey, you know, we ought to call the cops. This guy is dangerous." He gestured that they should go inside together.

Nita didn't budge. "I will. I'll call them in just a minute. I want to catch my breath. You head back. Listen, thanks, Reuben. Thanks a lot."

"I'll wait. I don't mind. I want to help you. I want to make sure you get inside okay. Hey, your hands are shaking. Let me have those."

He snatched the keys from her quickly. She made an effort to grab them back, but was too late. He turned toward the door, easing his bulk past her. Reuben started trying the keys in the lock and looked back at her over his shoulder. He smiled with pleasure.

"I'll make sure you get in and get settled," Reuben said. "Maybe mix you a drink. Your nerves are probably shot."

He had tried all the keys in the door. Then he turned slowly, inspecting the dangling keys in the penumbral light, puzzled.

"Hey," he said thickly, "none of these keys fit."

Nita had slipped on her gloves. She reached into her bag and produced the .45. She spread her legs and brought the gun up, two-handed, to his head. Combat shooter style.

Reuben's jaw hung open. A small gagging noise came from his throat.

Nita's face was terrifying, a Kabuki mask of rage. Her unearthly snarl was the last sound he heard.

The bullet tore perfectly through Reuben's right eye, blowing out half his skull.

SIX

Nita quickly returned to the crisis center. No messages on the machine. Good. She stood peering into the quiet utopia of the fish tank, as if for inspiration, while her bright-scaled subjects darted randomly about. Nita's breathing fogged the glass.

With effort, her swirl of thoughts coalesced. This was the first time things hadn't gone according to plan. Had she been right to kill Reuben? She had acted on instinct, but had it been a good one? The man had learned that she didn't live at that building. Even someone with his sea urchin's intellect could figure out something strange was afoot.

From a broader perspective, however, Nita was better off rid of Reuben. He seemed to have a fixation on her and was bent on being a pest. From an even broader perspective, he wasn't doing the clients much good at the crisis center.

"It was for the best," she murmured to the fish, finally.

She was actually pleased with how well she had improvised. Her plan had been to take care of Ace on the way to the coffee shop, as they passed through a deserted playground. After he surprised her by spilling her purse onto the sidewalk — thankfully, the .45 was safe in its zippered compartment — it was the inspiration of a moment to leave the key ring. It was a challenge, and she had proved up to it. Unfortunately, Ace remained to be dealt with.

The phone rang.

"Crisis center. Can I help you?"

The crazed laughter on the other end was very familiar. The line went dead.

"She's hot for you, Dillon," Wise said.

"Very hot," Safir agreed.

They were bellied up to the bar at McSorley's, long after midnight. A lot of four-to-twelve uniforms were there, not ready to return to the wives and kids. Deep-throated male laughter punctuated the whiskey-sweet air.

Dave smiled and shook his head. "Let's leave her alone tonight, guys. Besides, you're imagining things."

"A man gets a feel for this," Wise said.

"A sixth sense," Safir said.

"You two got no sense," Dave said amiably and finished his draft. "Listen, I got to get back to my cat. There's a lot of work to do tomorrow."

"I hope we get luckier than we got today," Wise said.

"Hookers ain't such good witnesses," Safir said. "What do they got against cops, Dillon?"

"I wouldn't know," Dave said evenly.

Safir realized he had strayed into forbidden territory. He held up his hands. "Hey, I didn't mean nothing by that. Honest."

The bartender told Dave he had a phone call.

"Excuse me, gentlemen," Dave told the older detectives.

It was Blake. "Looks like the Ladykiller again," the lieutenant said. "Only this time, the stiff's no lady."

Nita called Reuben's apartment and got his machine. Her call was likely the only one it had received in months.

"Reuben, where in God's name are you?" Nita kept her voice at its usual modulation. "Aren't you coming back? You're still on duty, you know. If you forgot and went home, please call and let me know. It's kind of busy."

And it would be. It always was after a killing.

The Ladykiller, indeed, she mused as she hung up the phone. What would they do about that?

Sometimes, Dave thought, you could see the killer in the victim's face. That's what his father had said. The last person the victim saw was the killer. In the glare of his flashlight, Dave tried to read the last face this victim had seen with his one remaining eye, which was flared open. In surprise?

Dave got up from his crouch and dusted off his knees. "No doubt about it. The same perp."

"Men now," Blake said.

"Two nights in a row," Wise said. "Perp is moving a lot faster."

"This crime scene is a residential neighborhood," Safir said. "That's different, too. Always before, we got a deserted area."

"This might as well be deserted," Blake said. "The neighbors who've come forward so far said they saw nothing. One heard a man shouting. Then a gunshot a little later. But he was in bed and half asleep. Everybody was asleep."

Jamie stood very close to Dave, close enough for him to smell her perfume. He didn't seem to notice. "What have you got, Dave?" she asked.

Dave was thumbing through the victim's wallet. "Name's Reuben Silver. He works at a place called the West Side Crisis Center. Not far from here."

"Still no pattern to the victims," Wise said.

"None," Safir said.

"No, that's it," Dillon said quietly, almost to himself. "That's got to be it. That's what we're looking for. That's the link."

"What?" asked Jamie.

"The missing link," Wise said.

"The Ladykiller's making a monkey out of us," Safir said. They both laughed.

Blake crinkled his forehead. "A middle-aged social worker?"

"The West Side Crisis Center," Dave said. "They deal with nut cases and street people, don't they. The hooker — I'll bet she went there."

"And the stockbroker?" Safir said with heavy irony. "Come on, Dave."

"Wait a minute," Jamie urged, thinking out loud. "If the hooker and the social worker both knew their killer from the crisis center, maybe there *is* a connection to the others, as well. Somebody at the brokerage house. A messenger. A guy in the mail room."

Dave nodded warmly at Jamie. "A pusher who worked the cheerleader's high school. The housewife's brother. I don't know, but it's there, all right. I feel it."

A tingle of excitement, like an electric charge, sizzled between them. Jamie felt a small shudder go down her spine.

Safir and Wise, not sharing Dave and Jamie's enthusiasm, looked at each other skeptically. Everyone turned to Blake, who paused thoughtfully before speaking.

"Right now," he said, "we need to interview neighbors before memories fade. Maybe one of them wasn't sleeping. Tomorrow, Dave, you go over to this crisis center and see what shakes. It'll be closed now. Personally, I have another press conference to worry about in the morning."

As the detectives dispersed to canvass the block, Jamie turned her best smile on Dave. "I'm sure you're right. I really am." She meant it.

Dave smiled back.

Nita had discovered the utility of the .45 at an early age. It was a sturdy weapon. You could throw the .45 on the ground and it wouldn't go off. The gun loaded easily, with a magazine of bullets shoved into the handle. Jams were cleared just as cleanly, by sliding the gun's carriage back and forth. Yet the .45's power was its best point. Nita admired her gun's ability to carve out half of a target's brain.

Her father had introduced her to the .45. As usual, he began with a history lecture. The United States at the turn of the century, he had told her with maddening pomp, needed a more powerful sidearm to put down an insurrection in the Philippines. Filipino rebels, hopped up on hemp and fanaticism, and protected by body armor of cane, laughed at the stopping power of American service revolvers. They weren't laughing after the .45 came on line.

Every weekend, her father would take her to the pistol range in the suburbs to practice with the .45, which he had brought home from the Korean War. He taught her how to take it apart, how to clean and oil it, how to align the front and rear sights, how to grip it with both hands, how to squeeze the trigger so gently that you weren't aware of squeezing it at all.

"I don't care how many twisted goons this godforsaken city turns out," he told Nita. "When you have a .45, no one can touch you."

Since the gun was too big to carry under his suit, Lars Bergstrom kept it in his briefcase. Her father carried that briefcase everywhere, even on the walks he took every Sunday. "This weapon," he told her, "is my best friend."

Looking back at the bitter, cold man that was her father, Nita thought to herself, "That I could believe."

Dave Dillon dragged into his apartment at an hour when only hungry cats were up. Dave's cat was affectionate only to its owner — and displayed that amply tonight. He rubbed Dave's ankles with a where-ya-been-when's-dinner insistence.

Dave opened a can of tuna and dumped it into the cat's dish, adding a sprinkling of crunchies. As he lowered the dish to the kitchen floor, the cat bobbed up to gobble a mid-air sample. Once the dish reached the floor, the cat attacked it with the zest of a ravenous lion.

"When you grow up into the king of the jungle, that's how you're gonna take care of the antelopes, huh?"

Dave tacked a picture of Lydia Daniels onto his wall, next to the other victims' photos. He would need a day or two to obtain a picture of Reuben Silver. Jimmy Conlon thought he was obsessed. "How can you put gruesome crime-scene pictures on your wall?"

"Maybe obsession is a good thing in a detective," Dave had told his friend. "Particularly one under a cloud."

Staring at the roster of victims, Dave tried to read their bloody, smashed faces.

Then he permitted himself to gaze on something else. Something pretty. For a minute. No longer. He kept the picture hidden in his dresser drawer. It was a glamorous, show-biz shot. Her smile was wide and electric. Her dark eyes had exotic power. And once, for a brief time, she had been his.

Safir and Wise went to Nita Bergstrom's apartment. A voice asked who they were and they identified themselves to a locked door. The woman who finally opened the door was a real looker, even in her bathrobe.

"Let me see your badges, please," she demanded in an uptown voice before removing the chain. She let them in but did not ask them to sit down.

"We're afraid we have some bad news for you, Miss Bergstrom," Safir said, trying to tell how nice her tits were beneath the bulky robe.

"Oh, and what is that?" A cool one, this chick.

"You were working the late shift on the hotline phone at the crisis center with a Reuben Silver last night?" Wise said.

"Yes. And he left abruptly about a half hour into the shift. Said he was going for a walk. Most unprofessional. Is he in trouble?"

The woman seemed more concerned that workplace rules had been broken than in the welfare of a co-worker.

"I'm afraid he's dead, Miss Bergstrom," Safir said. "He was shot in the head a few blocks from the crisis center. We believe by the same person responsible for the Ladykiller shootings."

She closed her eyes for a second. "Reuben? Murdered?" The detectives waited patiently while she absorbed the news. "Why Reuben?"

"That's what we're trying to figure out, Miss Bergstrom," Wise said. "Did he give you any indication that he was going to meet someone?"

"No. We weren't very close."

"Was he acting strangely?" Safir asked.

"Reuben was a bit of an odd duck. It's hard to say."

"Did he seem to be nervous or afraid?" Wise asked.

"Reuben wasn't afraid of anything," she said dryly. "Unless you count women."

"Did he—" Safir began.

"If you will excuse me, gentlemen," she said, "I'd like to be alone now. Although I admit I wasn't close to Reuben, we were colleagues and this is very upsetting. Perhaps we could talk later."

"No problem," Safir said. "A Detective Dillon is going to come by the crisis center later today. You can talk to him."

"That would be fine," the woman said.

On the way out, Safir said, "Woof. I wouldn't kick her out of bed."

"That bitch?" Wise said. "I wouldn't fuck her with your dick. She'd be nothing but trouble. I know women."

Blake called Dave early to ask him to fill in at the morning press conference at One Police Plaza on Reuben Silver's death. "I'll be tied up at the medical examiner's," he said.

Dave looked at the pictures of the dead on the wall. The cat worked his ankles, eager for breakfast. "Me and Mancuso?"

"Brief him. Answer any questions he throws you," Blake said. "And be nice."

Dillon set out for police headquarters resentfully. Mancuso? Dillon hated the sound of the man's name. But there was no use stewing about that. This morning had a spring snap to it: people going to work in the warm and sugary air, the clouds above the spires riding in puffy purity, the mirror-like windows of the shiny buildings reflecting the city's buzzing life. The weather was improving. The crisis center was a possible angle. Maybe things were pointing up.

Then he saw Chief of Detectives Richard Mancuso. Mancuso once had been a handsome man; Dave had seen pictures from his father's day. Years of politicking and plotting had worn grooves into Mancuso's noble Roman face. And into his immortal soul, as well. Time's cruel gravity had pulled the edges of his mouth downward in a permanent frown. Dave could hear Wise's taunt, safely delivered far from the chief's paranoid ears: "Big Dick Mancuso."

"Tell me what I don't know, Dillon," Mancuso said.

Dave meticulously covered every facet of the investigation into Reuben Silver's death. "And we think the link is the West Side Crisis Center," he concluded. "A lot of legwork needs to be done, though."

"Blake thinks or you think?" Mancuso asked nastily.

"I think, chief. And Lt. Blake thinks it's worth examining."

Mancuso swallowed, perhaps a dram of bile. "And this Silver is a man."

"That's right, chief. He was a man." Dave hoped he didn't sound too sarcastic.

"But the rest of the victims have been women."

"That's right. We think Silver may have stumbled onto the killer by accident. The site is a residential neighborhood, not the typical deserted places the perp prefers."

"And how," Mancuso almost snarled, "can you be sure this isn't a copycat killer?"

"As I indicated before," Dave said, holding the anger by a straining leash, "Silver was shot in the right eye. That information never has been released. No copycat could know that."

"Unless he's a copycat who got lucky."

"It's the same type of bullet, shot from the same distance, by a shooter who is expert at this. Someone who can pull a .45 up real quick and get one off before the victim can turn her — or in this case, his — head."

"Is that your theory?"

"Lt. Blake will back that up, chief," Dave said.

Chief Mancuso sighed. Dave followed him and his entourage into the elevator for the trip to the press conference.

"I hate these people — reporters," Mancuso said as the floors ticked by. "They're nothing but whores. Out to sell newspapers. They undermine citizens' faith in society. They want to destroy everything good — the family, religion, law and order, free enterprise. If it wasn't for them, we could just treat this shit like all the rest. There are 1,500 murders a year in this city, for God's sake. Now they are out needlessly scaring people."

The group rode in shoe-contemplating silence.

"They're all Jews, you know," Mancuso said.

The press conference was crowded. Hot TV lights baked the police officers as they filed in. Dave spotted Jimmy Conlon in the front row.

Dave half expected the press to start screaming and hyperventilating, as they did in the movies. Instead, after listening quietly to Mancuso's opening remarks, the reporters took turns asking calm, matter-of-fact questions.

Finally, Jimmy Conlon asked one: "Chief, I hear that the victims all are shot in the right eye, decimating that side of their skulls. Is that true?"

"I can't guess where you get your information, mister," Mancuso retorted. "But you don't know what you're talking about."

Dave flinched. Where could Jimmy have learned that?

"Is that a denial, chief?" Jimmy pressed on politely.

"Don't badger me. Are you running this investigation or is the police department?"

"I simply asked you a question, chief," Jimmy said, still keeping his tone steady.

"I've had my fill of your shit for today," Mancuso said. "You people figure you are better than anyone else. Well, I have a responsibility to the taxpayers of this city, who work for an honest living, not to you parasites."

Mancuso huffed off, followed by his retainers and Dave.

In the elevator, Mancuso angrily asked, "Who was that little kike in the front row, the one who is trying to tell me how to do my job?"

"For what it's worth," Dave said, "his name is Jimmy Conlon. And he's Irish."

"You a *friend* of his, Dillon?" Mancuso pounced, almost delighted to hear this. "Is that how he knew about the right eye?"

"No, chief. I disclosed nothing to Jimmy or anyone else."

"Sure, Dillon." Mancuso dripped sarcasm. "And if I ever find out you did, your ass is grass. And I'm the lawnmower."

•　　•　　•

The layer of dirt over Times Square, invisible in the gaudy neon night, was palpable in stark daylight. Ace kicked through it and talked to the sidewalk: "I'll show her — the bitch —"

He almost bumped into Martino and Blitzer.

"Talking to yourself is a sure sign of insanity, Ace," Martino said.

Ace never understood why women became cops. This one was a diesel dyke straight from the truck stop. "What?" Ace stammered. The two cops had Finesse and Falstaff up against the wall, their arms and legs spread.

"Let's go, Ace," Blitzer, the kid, said. Even the newest cops were cocky. "You know the drill."

Martino grabbed Ace by the collar and shoved him next to the other two. He reluctantly assumed the position. "What's this about?" he asked as Martino frisked him.

"It seems," said Falstaff, a fat ex-hippie with long, gray hair and an even grayer beard who had dedicated his life to the pursuit of cheap wine, "that there's been another murder."

"I can account for every second of my whereabouts," Finesse whined. "This is harassment."

"So," Ace said tauntingly over his shoulder while Martino worked her hands up his thighs, "I guess this means you assholes don't know shit about these murders."

The cop spun him around roughly and flattened him against the wall. "And I suppose you know shit, wise guy?" she said.

"Maybe I do."

"Christ, get a shower, Ace," Martino said. "You smell almost as bad as Falstaff here."

"Maybe I do know about the murders," Ace persisted.

"Maybe you're the one we're looking for, huh?" Blitzer the kid said.

"Maybe I am."

"Ace," Martino broke in, "you hustle tourists. You pick pockets. You roll bag ladies who can't fight back. You're scum, Ace. Not big scum. You're just scum."

She finished patting down the other two. "Now, listen up," she said. "All of you. If you hear anything on the street, anything at all, let us know. We'll be coming down hard on you till we get this sucker. So it's in your best interest to cooperate."

The men listened expressionlessly. The two cops strolled away.

Falstaff, the old wino, made a courtly bow to them. "Ladies, gentlemen."

Once the cops were out of earshot, Ace said, "Like hell. I'll tell them shit."

"Yeah," Finesse said, straightening the lapels of his green suit. "Police can suck my dick."

"You already suck their dicks, Finesse," Ace said. "How much they give you for snitching?"

"What you talkin' about?" Finesse said indignantly. "Watch your nasty mouth, boy. Don't go dissin' the man who buys you drinks."

Finesse minced away with all the dignity he could muster.

"A drink?" Falstaff said, brightening. "Sounds lovely."

Ace slunk after Falstaff as the wino retrieved a nearly empty bottle of Thunderbird from a recess beneath a loose grating. He followed him to a doorway where Falstaff upended the dirty bottle into his mouth.

"Fuck the police, huh?" Ace said excitedly. "Fuck them. I'll fix them."

"Absolutely," the wino said. "You'll fix them, Ace, my friend. You surely did throw a fright into them this time."

Instantly furious, Ace shoved Falstaff against the door. The bottle smashed to the pavement. Ace grabbed it and held the jagged glass to the derelict's fur-matted throat.

"Please — Ace, please," the wino begged, terrified.

Ace smirked, satisfied. He threw the broken bottle to the sidewalk, where it shattered into a hundred pieces. "You'll see. Some day, I'll surprise you. You'll see."

He sauntered toward the Deuce, remembering the night before. Plotting how to take advantage.

SEVEN

Dave Dillon stepped through the open doorway of the West Side Crisis Center into the ill-lit waiting room to hell. Tormented spirits, their minds short-circuited by alcohol, drugs, or grief, wandered about, apparently waiting to see the staff. A very old, very upset, black man sat near the door having mild hysterics. At his side, almost lost in the shadows, a striking-looking, dark-haired woman listened quietly.

"He was my brother," the old man moaned. "It's a bitter thing for a man to lose his brother."

"Why don't we start from the beginning?" the attentive woman said, calmly, totally in control.

Dave was reluctant to interrupt. He ventured farther into the lobby.

A young Rastafarian walked past with a clothespin in his nose, singing reggae: "Kill the white man. After he buy me record."

A seedy, wild-eyed white man rushed up to Dave. "Where," he cried urgently. "Where? Where?"

"Uh, excuse me?" Dave tried to disengage but the man stayed close, peering into Dave's face.

"Where? Where are you from?"

Dave reached for his badge but hesitated. "Well, I represent—"

"Where? Where are you *from*? Where?"

The man was getting more and more agitated. "I'm sorry. Where do I live?" Dave tried.

"Where are you from? Where? What *planet*?"

Two middle-aged women, linked arm in arm, stepped quickly

back and forth, careening into people, including the seeker after extra-terrestrial life, who ignored them and stayed in close proximity to Dave's face.

"Where? Where?"

An extraordinarily pretty, slightly disheveled young woman hurried up to Dave and touched his arm. "You must be from the police."

Dave pulled away, suspicious but fascinated, not knowing what to expect.

"It's okay," she gave a ragged laugh and pushed back an errant lock of strawberry blonde hair. "I work here."

"Detective Dave Dillon," he told her, hoping desperately that he hadn't offended her. "Could you direct me to Dr. Solomon?"

"Megan Morrison. Come this way." She led him across the lobby, pausing only to look back at the dark-haired staff person Dave had passed on the way in.

Dave turned and looked, too. The dark-haired woman, as if sensing their eyes on her, turned her attention from the old man and stared back.

"That's Nita Bergstrom," the young woman said simply. "She's the best we have." Nita turned back to her client.

The seedy man had followed Dave and pushed his face close to his again. "There's no life on Uranus, you know."

Dave caught Megan's eyes and they both laughed. Miffed, the old man turned away.

"What about you?" Dave asked her, quietly. "What planet are you from?"

Megan held his eyes for a moment as the confusion of the lobby swirled around them. Then she squared her shoulders and turned away.

"You're here about Reuben. Dr. Solomon is waiting."

He could see that her eyes had filled with tears. She led him past a glassed-in admitting desk, kindly but firmly fending off the clients. "Good morning, Howie. No, this is a visitor. This is not your breakfast."

Megan smiled and Dave gave a brief laugh as they passed the

large, disappointed man who rubbed his enormous belly. Megan glanced at Dave. He was watching her with interest. She reached up again to smooth her hair.

As they neared the stairs, Nita joined them. Megan introduced them and Dave shook her slim, cool hand.

"Today is more difficult than usual," Nita said. "They don't know what to make of Reuben's death. They're used to us being there for them. It's hard for them to grasp that we can have a crisis too."

Megan drew back automatically and let Nita take the lead.

Dave smiled back at her before turning his attention to Nita. "I'm sorry to be taking up your time," he said. "We need to develop some leads to find Mr. Silver's killer. You were working with him last night?"

"Yes. Reuben and I were on the hotline."

Megan sat anxiously checking out the reactions of the staff as they sat around the staff lounge. Grief and bewilderment held sway. Rose was sobbing softly. Tim looked scared. The other aides and part-time counselors were numb or nervous. Nita alone had not let the shocking news get to her. Megan admired her efforts this morning to soothe the clients and keep the center operating. She stood by the door, alert and vigilant, and, as always, coolly beautiful.

Dr. Solomon, more dazed than usual, had been saying, "Oh, dear," all morning to everyone. The good-looking detective was waiting for him to open the meeting.

Finally, Dave spoke himself. He went over the bare facts of Reuben's murder, at first relating no more than had been released to the media.

Then, when he had registered all their reactions, he leaned forward. "Mr. Silver's murder follows the pattern known as the Ladykiller slayings. His death may be one of a random series. However, we have a hunch. This is merely a hunch, but worth pursuing. It may be that the other four victims are linked to the crisis center, however remotely. If so, chances are the killer is too."

He paused to let that sink in, looking from face to face around the room.

"You know," Megan said tentatively, "it's funny, but Reuben sort of suggested the same thing. It was a joke really. He said we should start a counseling group for murders. Call it Assassins Anonymous or something. He had a whole routine."

After a moment of silence, Tim hooted with laughter, which he stifled in embarrassment. Dave seemed very thoughtful.

"Reuben had a highly developed sense of humor," Nita said. "But he often went too far."

"Reuben was a great kidder," Tim agreed. "He could beat a dead joke into the ground." He guffawed, then realized this was a tactless remark.

"Any observations about either Reuben or those he treated are helpful to us," Dave told Tim.

Megan noted with approval how Dave had deftly defused Tim's awkward comment. The detective was so broad-shouldered, strong, and sure of himself, yet with a rare warmth and kindness she didn't think possible in someone this physical.

"People come to you with their problems," Dave continued. "Addicts, crazies, victims of various forms of abuse. You're the experts, but I suspect sometimes it must be hard to tell whether someone is just a little unbalanced or whether he's seriously psychotic."

The staff glanced at one another, and Dave continued. "Dr. Solomon has told me a little about how each of you work here. Each of you leads one or more therapeutic groups for people with one type of problem or another. You also counsel people on the hotline phones. I'd like to show you some pictures of the other murder victims and have you —"

"We read the papers, Detective Dillon," Nita said mildly. "Don't you think that if our clients were being killed, we'd have noticed and come forward?"

"I don't know," Tim said. "Anything around here that reduces the caseload —" He failed to contain a hysterical giggle.

"Detective Dillon has asked us to cooperate and I'm asking all of you to help," Dr. Solomon said. "He'll be around here for several days looking at our files and —"

A storm of protest swept through the room. Amid the shouting, Dr. Solomon gestured ineffectually to restore order.

"We can't allow that," Rose insisted. "Our work here is confidential. Our clients can't be compromised."

"He can't do this," Tim whined. "We promise them that our records are strictly private. It's outrageous."

Megan had her mouth open to speak, but couldn't find the words.

"If necessary," Dave's voice carried over the melee, "I can get a court order. I'd rather do this with your help."

Nita strode into the center of the room and spoke quietly but with immense authority. Everyone fell silent at once.

"Perhaps if one of us goes through the records with him," Nita said, "we can help sift for whatever he needs without compromising our responsibilities."

"Yes," Dr. Solomon said gratefully. "Thank you, Nita. Detective Dillon, would that arrangement suit you?"

"Yes, doctor," Dave said. "Thanks."

"Nita," Dr. Solomon said, "I'd like you and Megan both to assist Detective Dillon in his examination of the files."

Megan felt a blush spreading involuntarily across her face. She turned to Nita, who watched her with narrowed eyes, unsmiling.

"Fine," Dave said. "And I'll also need help reinterviewing the other victims' loved ones and associates again. I think someone from the crisis center would know what to look for." He paused. "Perhaps Ms. Morrison would also give me a hand with that."

Surprised, Megan nodded at him dumbly.

"That wouldn't be possible," Nita said sharply. "We both have afternoon groups, detective. And we both work the phones at night."

"I'll take Megan's groups myself for a few days," Dr. Solomon said. "If this terrible thing does have anything to do with our clients——" He broke off helplessly.

"Poor Reuben," Rose said to Dave. "Don't you have any idea who could have done it?"

"I'm afraid we have very few leads," Dave said. "Whoever killed Reuben killed four other people, seemingly at random." He drew a breath and went on forcefully. "I'm trying to determine if there is a common element that links the five killings. I believe I'll find it here at the crisis center."

A minute of shocked silence passed.

"We do get some lulus,"Tim said. "But a Son of Sam type? I don't know about that."

"Our perpetrator may appear harmless," Dave said. "But make no mistake. He is a vicious killer. An animal. He glories in the taking of human life. He is twisted and sick."

Rose broke down again. Tim comforted her. Megan crossed the room to put an arm around Rose. Nita stood by the door, arms folded, thoughtful and aloof.

"If you're concerned about your safety," Dave said, "you should know that I'm assigning a uniformed officer to be on duty at the center around the clock until further notice."

As the meeting broke up, Dave approached Nita. "I need to talk to you about last night."

"Certainly, detective," Nita said. "But I don't have much to add to what I told your colleagues."

They sat down and Nita calmly answered questions. She took Dave back to Dr. Solomon's office and excused herself.

Dr. Solomon walked Dave out. "We'll do all we can to help you, Detective Dillon. Reuben may not have published regularly in the *Journal of American Sociology*, but he was a hard-working, decent man who really wanted to help people. He didn't deserve this."

Dave spent the rest of the day canvassing the neighborhood, interviewing possible witnesses in the Reuben Silver killing. As usual, nobody had seen a thing. "Why can't you catch this madman?" one elderly woman indignantly asked him.

"We're trying, lady. We're trying," Dave wearily replied.

As he marched from door to door, the image of the young woman at the crisis center kept returning to him. No woman had affected him this way for a long time. And Megan couldn't be more different. He thought even his mother would approve of Megan.

"What the hell do you want?"

Dave jolted into alertness. A sour old man, all lips and eyes, had answered his knock. Dave's father would have said, "The last face I saw that ugly had a hook in it."

"Police, Mr. Tucker. We wonder if you——?"

"About time you got here. I been dialing 911 all day. They keep saying someone will be over. Busy wolfing down doughnuts, weren't you?"

Dave wasn't surprised that he hadn't heard about Tucker calling 911. They were too busy with genuine emergencies to relay tips in a timely fashion. "Sorry, sir. I've been trying to get to you." Dave attempted an apologetic grin.

"There were three of them."

"I beg your pardon."

"Three of them on the street last night. I don't sleep good, nights. Never have. My wife, when she was alive, said it was because I had a guilty conscience. What have I got to be guilty about? People don't like me, I say, 'Fuck 'em.' Always have."

"What did you see, Mr. Tucker?"

"We're on the seventh floor now, remember." He led Dave to the window and pointed down to the taped-off murder scene diagonally across the street and down a building. "That's a ways down to the street. And my eyes aren't as good as they used to be, especially at night. When I was working, I managed an office. Used to be able to spot something wrong with someone desks and desks away. Old Eagle-eye Tucker, they called me. I straightened them all out. If they didn't like it, fuck 'em."

Dave nodded. "What did you see, sir?"

"Three people. One hit the other one, knocked him down. The one hit ran off, yelling. I couldn't hear what. The other two seemed to be talking. I figured this was some drug deal. Then there's this flash of light and a gunshot. Took me a moment to understand. The guy with the fists was shot."

Two persons involved in the slaying of Reuben Silver? "Could you identify any of them? Maybe pick out some kind of distinguishing characteristics?"

"Hell, no. Don't you listen? They were little dark stick figures from my window. The people who used to work for me asked stupid questions, like you do. I tried to fire them, every one of them. But they got me first. The bastards."

Dave nodded again. "The one who got hit, which direction did he run?"

"West. The guy with the gun, he went back that way, too. Only, he walked. Didn't even hurry, the son of a bitch."

At the task force meeting, Dave relayed Tucker's information.

"So we have two Ladykillers on our hands?" Blake asked.

Dave shook his head, puzzled. "Reuben Silver hit one guy and the other guy killed him. But we don't know how the three of them fit in."

Blake hadn't changed his expression. "Why?"

"Well, it's not that two-man teams of serial killers are unknown. Remember the Hillside Stranglers out in California? Two guys who committed murders together by strangling their female victims out of sexual rage. Here, though, the killer wants to execute his victims without touching them. A shooter is usually a loner."

"This gets weirder," said Jamie, who had spent the day interviewing Reuben Silver's grief-stricken daughters from the suburbs.

"Two people involved could be a break for us," Dave said. "Could be that one of them will crack and come forward. Or it may be that the guy who ran away is not an accomplice, but simply a witness too scared to come to us."

After the meeting broke up, Blake took Dave aside. "Mancuso is convinced you leaked the right-eye stuff to your reporter friend."

"Good for him," Dave said. "I didn't. Jimmy is my friend, but I'm not about to do that, and Jimmy knows it."

"Watch yourself. I'll do the best I can for you. But we've got to catch this bastard — or these bastards — and soon."

Jamie came up to Dave. "A bunch of us are going over to McSorley's. Want to come?"

"Thanks. I can't. Got some business to catch up on."

She gave a small, disappointed smile.

Dave went to a pay phone on the street to call Jimmy Conlon.

Jimmy knew at once. "You're in trouble, right?"

"They think I gave you that right-eye stuff."

"Well, you didn't. And don't say that now every copycat killer will do the same thing, so you won't be able to tell the difference. You guys have much more on the Ladykiller's MO than the right eye."

Jimmy was right. "I'm under a little pressure," Dave said.

"Me too. Listen, we both work for scumbags, but we'll come out okay. I gotta go and finish my story. Chip wants to see it before he leaves. He has a power squash game with the managing editor. That's following his power lunch with the executive editor. If the story isn't just right for him, he'll give it over for a rewrite to his latest favorite, this new reporter who was his younger brother's roomie at Andover."

Dave toyed with the idea of joining the others at the bar. But he decided to go for a walk: along the route Reuben Silver must have taken between the crisis center and the spot where he died.

Jamie sat with Safir and Wise at McSorley's and nursed a beer. "You guys know Dave pretty well."

They nodded in unison. "Know him," Safir said. "Knew his dad."

Wise signaled for another round. "A cop family. Irish. Queens. The usual."

"Dave had some kind of a problem," Jamie said. "No one will tell me what that is."

"Uh — shouldn't you ask Dave?" Wise suggested.

"I'm asking you."

Safir and Wise exchanged a look.

"Dillon was a rising star until six, seven, or so months ago," Wise said. "Then he fell in love with a... uh..."

"With his work," Safir said. "It didn't work out."

"Look, Jamie," Wise said, lowering his voice. "Can I ask a personal question, or should I just go fuck myself?"

Jamie bristled for a moment. Then she softened and gave a wary smile. "You can ask."

"I know you got a dose of the hots for Dave," Wise said. "But are you sure you know what you're getting into?"

"Hey, it's no big deal," Jamie answered, trying for a light tone. "I'm looking for a couple of smiles, that's all."

Wise nodded. "All I'm saying is: Dillon may not be Mr. Right, Jamie." He looked at Safir who took up the tale.

"He gets mixed up with the wrong kind of women. Like his old man. It caught up with him. He's a fallen angel —" Safir fell quiet and took a major swallow of beer.

"He didn't lose his shield, but he'll never get promoted," Wise said. "Like his old man."

"Unless he solves a big, splashy case," Safir amended.

"A real career-maker," Wise intoned.

Bewildered, Jamie signaled for another round. "But what happened?"

They exchanged a look and accepted the beer. Then they changed the subject and Jamie could not get another word out of them about the one topic that interested her.

The day had grown old and the last water colors of sundown were fading in the western sky when Dave reached the crime scene. The yellow police tape had already been ripped apart by tenants needing access to the apartment house door before which Reuben had died. His blood stained the sidewalk like a scarlet obscenity. Westward, where the array of looming buildings drank in the last of the day's blues and pinks, the shadows were coming out of their lairs.

The accomplice, if that's what he was, had run west. After the murder, the shooter had traveled west, as well. Were the shooter and the accomplice going to rendezvous?

Interestingly, Reuben must have been walking from the west to reach the site of his death. Coming from the West Side Crisis Center. Nita Bergstrom had said he simply left. Did he have an appointment to meet the shooter, the accomplice, or both?

Dave went west, toward the crisis center, staying on the same side of the street that the crisis center and the crime scene were on.

Chances were Reuben had stayed on that side. Alert for the stray detail, for the change in the psychic currents, Dave progressed slowly along the sidewalk.

Megan — on the same sidewalk, headed straight toward him. Did Dave see her first? Or did she see him? Or did they recognize each other at the same time?

He registered the paleness of her skin, the reddish-gold hair. Her eyes sparkled. She had put the cares of the day behind. "I didn't expect to see you till tomorrow," she said, clearly glad she was seeing him now.

He smiled back, perhaps his most genuine smile in months. "I've got a little work left. Feeling better?"

"A bit." Megan's smile dimmed. "It was a tough day at work. Everybody was out of it. Except for Nita. She's incredible. She's actually spelling Rose tomorrow night on the hotline because Rose is so upset."

"You admire Nita, don't you?"

"Everyone does. I've never met anyone like her." Megan shrugged awkwardly, showing the odd deference she had displayed earlier. "Well, I'd better get going. Got to finish picking my courses for next semester."

"Hunter School of Social Work, right?"

Her brow crinkled, her smile gone. "How did you know that?"

"Hey, I'm a detective, remember? Anyway, Dr. Solomon briefed me on the staff."

"Well, I'd better get going. See you tomorrow."

Megan walked on and turned and gave him a wave.

As men have done since the beginning of civilization, Dave examined the woman's walk. He sighed deeply. She had legs like a dancer.

➣ EIGHT ➣

A .45. That's what Ace needed. To make Nita his forever, he had to get one and show her that he could use it.

Ace's brains were a little scrambled from drugs, malnutrition, neglect, and general disuse, but he was far from stupid. When he heard about Reuben's death, he knew instantly what had happened. He put it together. It only made him love her more. With a woman like Nita, he could do anything. And to win her, he had to be strong.

The coolness with which she had blown that guy to hell and then walked away — Ace could only shake his head in admiration. This showed a kind of cool that Ace had only imagined or seen in movies. It was an attitude he always aspired to, but had seldom seen.

A .45. Ace had never fired one. In fact, Ace had never fired a gun in his life, except for the .22 pistol his pal Joey had boosted from a neighbor back in New Jersey.

Ace's father had been a brave and highly decorated soldier in Vietnam — or so Ace had heard, never having met the man. But Ace himself had inherited no firearms prowess, let alone bravery. Joey called him a pussy when Ace missed every one of the tin cans they lined up along the fence. He had winced with every shot.

Maybe Ace's mother, Doris, was to blame. A slatternly woman with a fondness for the bottle, she would not allow guns in their trailer home on the outskirts of Rahway. Even when she turned tricks for the local cops, she insisted that they take off their weapons before she would let them in. "I don't entertain anyone who's armed, no matter how good he's paying," she would say self-righteously in the small trailer, stinking of whiskey, cigarettes, and sex.

When Ace joined Joey in holding up a 7-Eleven, he had been too afraid to carry the .22 and merely stood lookout instead. That turned out to be a rare piece of good fortune for Ace.

When the cops caught them a half hour later with their pathetic take of fifty bucks, Joey drew the hard time. Five big years for armed robbery. Ace got probation as a first-time offender and accomplice. It also helped that Doris Cronen made the Rahway police chief holler every Wednesday night before he went home to his family.

Sitting outside the trailer, as he always did when his mother entertained, Ace had heard her tell the chief, "My boy ain't no master criminal. He ain't a leader. He's a follower. Give the kid a break."

A .45. Ace knew from the papers that a .45 was a powerful sidearm. Not the type of gun you would expect a woman to use. Nita, of course, was no ordinary woman.

"Can you get me a .45?" he asked Tony Topnut.

"A Colt .45?" Tony Topnut said from behind the bar. "We serve just Bud, Lowenbrau, and Michelob. And I gotta see your money before I give you anything."

"No, a gun," Ace whined, ignoring the insult as usual. "Finesse says you sell guns."

Tony Topnut put his fleshy face an inch from Ace's. "Maybe Finesse don't know fuck all."

"I need a .45," Ace persisted. "A good one. With bullets. Not like the one Billy Ray Battle had." He giggled. "His damn gun wasn't loaded."

"You know how to fire a .45?" Tony Topnut's breath reeked of onions.

"Sure. Used one lots of times."

Tony Topnut roared his onion laugh into Ace's face. His bulk jiggled beneath his Hawaiian shirt. "Let me guess. You're the Ladykiller, right? You and Billy Ray."

People were looking at them, now, and Ace snapped back, "I might surprise you someday, you fat piece of shit."

Tony Topnut grabbed Ace by the collar and pulled him halfway across the bar. He whispered in Ace's face, spraying sibilants and onion stench, "Listen, you little fuck. Show me three hundred dollars, and I might show you a gun. If I'm in a good mood. But right now, I'm not. I want your ass out of here before my mood gets any worse."

"Can't I stay and see the show?" Ace croaked.

Tony Topnut threw Ace back hard, sending him crashing to the sticky floor, tangled up in the barstool. "Get out."

Ace, his face on fire with humiliation, slunk out of the Foxy Lady with every eye watching.

The mocking guffaws followed him up the Deuce. Three hundred for a .45. Christ.

Dave picked up Megan in an unmarked car. She said nothing more than a nervous hello. As he pulled away from the West Side Crisis Center, he found himself tempted to stare. He allowed himself a quick glance. Megan sat primly with her hands on her lap and her knees together. Her short skirt showed off long, sleek thighs.

Then he noticed that she was actually watching him.

"Better buckle up," he said. "That's the law."

"We don't want to break the law," Megan said with a small, almost coquettish laugh.

He loved her laugh. It was high and musical, a brief, rich melody that hung in the air after she had finished. From the corner of his eye, he observed her pull the shoulder harness across her breasts and snap it in place.

"I appreciate your doing this," Dave said.

"I always want to support the police," she said. Teasing.

The farther they got from the crisis center, the more Megan seemed to loosen up.

"You like your work?" Dave asked.

"I love it. I love my job. Even though I'm going for my Master's, the crisis center is the best school. I get to work with terrific people. Seasoned professionals. Dr. Solomon is quite well known, or at least, he was in his day. And Nita — well, Nita is incredible. She knows everything, she can handle anything. She's taught me more than anyone I ever met."

The enthusiasm in her voice grew as she talked. Without knowing why, Dave was annoyed.

"I get the impression that she actually runs the place."

Megan laughed again. "The crisis center wouldn't function without Nita. Dr. Solomon needs a lot of backstopping and organizing. Nita takes care of that in her spare time."

Dave tried to stop himself from glancing at Megan's legs. "Sounds great," he said neutrally. "I appreciate the time I'm getting from you folks."

"May I ask you a question?" Again the teasing tone.

"Depends what it is."

"Detectives aren't the only ones who get to ask questions."

He hadn't figured her for a flirt. Some women were turned on by cops, but not social workers. They generally regarded the police as thugs in uniform.

"Ask away," Dave said genially.

"Why did you want me with you, and not Nita?"

Dave felt that a polite, white lie wasn't what Megan wanted or needed. "I don't think she likes me," he said truthfully.

"Nita can be intimidating," Megan said. "She's so dedicated to her work and so good at it that people sometimes are dazzled by her sheer professionalism."

"Good for her."

"So, why me?" More of the teasing tone.

"You're the first person I met at the center," he said lamely.

She sat quietly for a moment. "Who are we going to visit?"

"The parents of Lucy Cristides," Dave said, relieved to be off the hook. "She was the cheerleader from Queens — 16 years old when they found her body in the Meatpacking District. Lucy's parents run a coffee shop on the East Side."

"What have you found out about the girl?" Megan asked, clinically detached now.

"People will always say the deceased was a wonderful person, even if she was into bondage and devil worship. In her case, though, she seems to have been a genuinely nice kid. A cheerleader. Pretty, too. No troubles in school. Good grades. She wanted to go to college. Helped her parents out in the coffee shop."

"No boyfriends?"

"No."

"Was she a virgin?"

Dave cleared his throat. "Not according to the autopsy report."

"Were you a virgin at her age, detective?"

Dave chuckled. "No."

"I was." Megan said it matter-of-factly.

"Why do you ask?"

"These things are important to social workers."

"Are you going to ask me where I lost my virginity?"

"If it wasn't in a car, you owe me ten dollars."

"I don't owe you ten dollars."

"You're more predictable than you think, detective." The smile had returned to her voice.

Maybe he could get the hang of this badinage, after all. "I don't know. Sometimes, I surprise myself."

"Surprise me sometime."

"You're on." A big grin had stretched across Dave's face.

It was Nita's day at the shooting range. She caught the Long Island Rail Road out to Uniondale and walked the half-mile between the station and the range, the .45 in a gym bag. The spring sun felt good on her scalp. When the range was a mere twenty yards away, she suddenly felt someone's presence behind her, following her, footsteps in time with hers.

She spun around, hand pulling down the zipper of the bag. No one. Just a suburban street, empty as the beginning of the world.

Henry, the owner of the range, greeted Nita with a hug and asked after her health. The Fourth of July gunfire crackle sounded beyond his office.

"Never better. Busy today?"

"Unexpected. Bunch of cops here. Nassau County P.D. pistol team. Big match coming up. They were kind of last minute. But you can't turn away the cops."

"Now, Henry, are you trying to tell me that all the lanes are taken, and that I'll have to wait?"

Henry shrugged elaborately, palms outstretched like an Arab merchant. "What can I do?"

"Henry, I don't have the time. I've got to get back to the city. Let me take care of this."

She easily spotted the leader of the team. He wore that judgmental look, often seen on coaches at the sidelines or other macho places of worship. He fell for her challenge without hesitation. What man could deny a pretty woman's dare?

"How about a handicap?" the leader asked as he adjusted the earphone-like protectors around his meaty ears. His pals had stopped firing and were chortling among themselves and ogling her ass, which was covered by tight black leggings.

"Sure, lieutenant, if you think you need one." His cronies renewed their laughter, glancing nervously at their boss.

Novices think firing a .45 is like firing a blunderbuss. It is a heavy weapon with a kick. You have to hold the pistol steady, lining up the front and rear sights on the target, the silhouette of a man. Then ease the trigger gently, almost lovingly. You should be so intent on your target that pulling the trigger is virtually unconscious. Shooters who pull the trigger roughly or too soon always missed. Her father had told her: "There's this monkey on your shoulder, shouting, 'Fire.' You fire when you're ready, not when the monkey wants you to."

Over the years, Nita had gotten good enough that she didn't have to keep the monkey waiting long.

"Five rounds from a standing position," the lieutenant said.

"Lock and load," Nita said.

She pumped a clip of ammunition into the .45's handle. Then she stood facing the target downrange, her feet spread, her right hand wrapped around the weapon and extended before her, her left hand gripping her right, pulling back on it, stabilizing the sights.

At the command from the tower, they opened up. Brass shell casings flew out of their guns. Nita finished first.

At the tower's command, they trudged down to the targets. The coltish team members cavorted behind them.

The lieutenant had two bull's-eyes. Nita had five. The other cops exploded in mocking laughter. The lieutenant scowled at them.

"Boys, please," Nita said. "The lieutenant and I had an agreement: I'd fire at his target and he'd fire at mine."

They stopped laughing.

Nita took the lieutenant by the arm and led him back to the firing line. He was very flustered and looked at her with new admiration. "A lot of ladies are getting guns for self defense these days, but not many of them could—" He gestured lamely back at the range.

"Tell me, lieutenant," she said, lightly touching his bicep, "do you know a New York City homicide detective named Dave Dillon?"

Dave parked the car next to a fire hydrant outside the Cristides' coffee shop.

"Isn't this illegal?" Megan asked.

Dave put the Police Department identification on the dashboard. "Who's going to ticket me?"

She looked at him with coy amusement. "I can see you enjoy your work."

"My father was a cop. I come from a long line of cops. Grow up Irish in Queens, and you usually become a cop."

"What's the attraction?"

"I get to meet interesting people."

Lucy Cristides' father had a doughy face that drooped when he saw Dave's badge. "How can I help you, detective?" he said morosely.

He was mopping the counter with a dirty rag, and he didn't stop. His apron had grease stains. The place was empty, and the smell of frying had started to fade.

"Mr. Cristides, this is an associate of mine, Ms. Morrison," Dave said. "We'd like to ask you a few more questions." He felt Megan watching him, studying him.

Cristides sighed. "I don't know what more I can tell you. My Lucy, she went out to see her friends that night. Only her friends, they said later she never showed. She disappeared. Then they found her outside that meatpacking plant." He sighed again.

"And nothing had been bothering her at the time?"

Cristides talked as if the day had emptied him of energy. "She was a teenage girl. She had her ups and downs. Boys. Her friends. The schoolwork. The cheerleading. Clothes, looks, the usual things for girls."

"And she never went into Manhattan except to help you and your wife here at the coffee shop?"

"No. My Lucy stayed near home in Queens. When she went out, she went to her friends. Or to school things. She was not a wild girl. Not my Lucy."

A small, dark-haired woman charged out of the kitchen in the back. "What you want?" she demanded.

Cristides spoke to her in Greek, but she ignored him.

"You the police again, hah?" she said. She waved a finger at Dave. Her bare arms were covered with fine black hair. "What you want this time? When you gonna find the bastard who kill my daughter?"

"Mrs. Cristides, this takes a while," Dave said. "We're trying our best. The entire city wants us to find him, and we're on this night and day."

"What you asking my husband?"

"Well, Mrs. Cristides," Dave said, "I want to know if your daughter ever had any psychological problems."

"You mean sick in the head?" she shouted at Dave, and advanced toward him, making shooing motions with her hands. "Get out of here. Get out. Leave us alone."

"Mrs. Cristides —" Dave tried to calm her, but she kept shouting at him.

"Get out. Get out. Get out."

"We'd better go," Megan said.

Mrs. Cristides followed them out of the coffee shop, her arms flailing in all directions. "And don't come back here no more. Asking such questions. She was a good girl. Where were you when she was alive. No?" She spat on the sidewalk.

"Gina," her husband pleaded from the doorway. "Come back now. We must get ready for the lunch."

The dead girl's mother stomped back into the coffee shop, still muttering.

"She is upset," Cristides said.

Megan looked after her with concern.

"I'm sorry, sir," Dave said. "But I have to ask you one question. Did you ever hear your daughter mention the West Side Crisis Center?"

"The West Side Crisis Center? No, I don't think so."

"Thank you, Mr. Cristides." Dave shut his notebook.

"We're right across town," Megan said. "You can take a crosstown bus from here nearly to the Hudson River. The West Side Crisis Center."

Cristides shook his head sadly. "No. My Lucy was a good girl. She had no sickness in the head. She was in no crisis. Just a good teenage girl. Mixed-up about growing up, but just like all teenage girls."

Dave and Megan got back in the car.

"You blew it, detective," Megan said, with that teasing lilt.

"I don't have any other way of dealing with her," Dave said, slightly annoyed.

"There's was one way to get some answers."

"Yeah? How?"

"Quit the police force. The mother had a beef with the cops for not protecting her daughter, or at least for not finding the killer."

"Get serious."

"I am. Next time, let me ask some questions. And make sure they know I'm not a cop."

"You don't look like a cop," Dave said, and twisted the ignition key.

"What's a woman cop look like? Or aren't they real cops to you?"

"They're real cops. I'm not one of those guys on the force who won't accept female officers. My father wouldn't approve, but there you are." Dave pulled into traffic.

"Do they all look as good as that black detective who came by the center yesterday, the one who'd been out talking to Reuben's daughters? She's an attractive woman."

"Jamie Loud? Yeah, I guess she looks like a cop. And she's a good one too."

"I think she likes you."

Dave laughed in genuine astonishment. "Give me a break."

"She asked when you'd left. I could tell from how she said your name."

"You could, huh? Well, Ms. Detective, what could you tell from our little session with the Cristides?"

Megan said nothing for a moment. The car halted for a light, and the circus of Manhattan street life ambled past their front bumper. "There's something about Lucy that they're hiding. Probably something they consider shameful. I'll bet it's what we're searching for. But you'll have a hell of a time getting it out of them."

"Maybe. Want some lunch?"

They parked, once more at a hydrant, and he brought back food from a deli: a Coke and a roast beef on rye with Russian dressing for him, a Dr. Pepper and a BLT for her.

"I love how they do this sandwich," Dave said. The Russian dressing thrilled his tongue.

"Did you pay for the food?"

"Give it up. Of course I did."

"But you didn't have to."

He shrugged, his mouth full.

"I guess I'm struggling with the allure of being a cop. Park anywhere you want. Free food. I want to make sure I understand. Is it about power?"

"For some, yeah. Not for all. Like my father. He was a great man, a great cop, my father. And he never got off on being the big man with the badge. After he made detective, he told me — I was a kid then — he told me, 'It's great to find out what's wrong and fix it.' "

"That's what you're doing?"

"That's what I'm doing." He chomped into the soggy sandwich

and noticed, with satisfaction, that she ate hers with gusto.

"This case obsesses you, doesn't it?" she asked in a voice muffled by food.

"Yes. Every case obsesses me, but a big one is the worst. I have pictures of the victims on my wall at home." As soon as he had said that, he wished he hadn't. "Drives my cat crazy."

"Pictures of the victims. After they were murdered, detective?"

"I'm afraid so. And call me Dave."

"Why?" She scrunched up her face in mock distaste as she bit into the large pickle that came with her sandwich.

"Why what? It's my name."

"Why keep gory pictures on your wall?"

"To remind me that they're still waiting."

"What do the faces tell you?"

Dave wiped his hand on a napkin and picked up his Coke can and took a swig. "They were surprised."

"Isn't everybody surprised to see a gun aimed at them?"

"This is a different kind of surprise. The surprise of finding out that someone you trusted wants to kill you. See, I think the victims must have known the killer. And I believe they were surprised to see this person they trusted pulling a .45."

"Interesting," Megan said as she licked mayonnaise off her lips.

"Why are you a social worker?"

"Same reason you're a cop. To make things right. To save people, save the world."

"That's possible? You can fix some things, maybe, but the whole world?"

Megan nodded. "Nita thinks it's possible. It's our mission."

Dave swallowed a hard lump of roast beef. "I guess she ought to know."

Going through the crisis center's client files was a tedious process. Dave had decided to limit their inspection to active clients over the past half year.

Megan hoisted another pile of file folders onto the already

crowded conference table where Nita and Dave sat. Since returning to the crisis center, she had said little.

"You want to see the files on the staff too?" Megan asked.

"I'd like to take a look at them," Dave answered absently.

"I'll bring them up from Dr. Solomon's office."

"Thanks, Megan." He looked up and smiled at her and watched her leave the room. When he turned back to the conference table, he saw Nita regarding him with an ironic, tight-lipped expression.

"She interests you, detective?" Nita asked.

Dave found himself flustered at the question. He could understand the power Nita exercised over Megan and the others at the crisis center. "Megan's, uh, very nice."

"She's got the makings of a fine sociologist: intelligent, perceptive, intuitive, *dedicated*. Or aren't you interested in her professional qualifications, detective?"

"I'm interested in catching a serial killer, Ms. Bergstrom," he said with as much coolness as he could muster. "That's what *I'm* professionally qualified to do." He grabbed a yellow legal pad. "Let's get a system set up, shall we?"

He whipped out his pen and made neat columns on the legal pad, adding headings above them.

Megan returned with another stack of file folders. She put them down beside Dave and edged away. "The staff," she said.

"Thanks," Dave said. Without permission, he slapped the legal pad onto the photocopy machine and ran off a batch of reproductions. He gave a handful of them to each woman. "What we're after are patients who fit the profile of serial murderer."

"Clients," said Megan, exchanging a look with Nita. "We call them clients."

"Clients. It's not necessary that they were clients of Reuben Silver's. The killer, if he was indeed a client here, may have met Reuben simply in passing."

"The profile of a serial murderer," Nita said, rolling the words slowly and mockingly off her tongue. "And what, would you say, is that profile, detective?"

"Serial murderers tend to be in their twenties and thirties. Many had head injuries as small children or at birth. They are loners. Their parents abused them. They display symptoms of violence toward other people or animals. Sexual deviance, suicidal tendencies, and alcohol and drug problems are often present."

"Well, that certainly narrows the field," Nita said with a wry smile and selected a file from the pile closest to her.

They read for several minutes in silence. Dave noticed he was making faster progress than the two social workers. "The files aren't very conclusive about their identities, are they?" he said at last. "A lot don't give their proper names or even list addresses. This one says his name is the Cookie Monster, and that he lives 'around the corner.' Lotus, from the Lower East Side. Juke, Times Square. How many Fast Eddies are there, anyhow?"

"If they were willing to give us their names, and if they had addresses to give, they probably wouldn't be coming here, detective," Nita said. "Still, I'm sure the police are adept at finding people they want to. We have faith in your department's competence, detective."

"The people who come here trust us," Megan said simply, hoping Dave hadn't registered Nita's mocking tone.

"Do you know how many of these people have a sheet at headquarters?" Dave said.

"We aren't concerned with their criminal history," Nita said. "We're concerned with their future."

"I'm interested in the future, too. The future that five people already won't have."

"We can't exactly press for ID," Megan said, trying to be conciliatory. "If we press too hard for information, they just stop showing up. Then, we can't help them at all."

"Although that's not always possible," Nita said. "Some people simply can't be helped."

"I'd say that, when someone has killed five times, he probably fits into that category," Dave said nastily. Two could play this game.

"I wasn't particularly thinking about the killer," Nita replied.

Dave opened another folder.

Nita said without glancing up. "Say, here's one. White male. Age 29. Occupation: wino. Hobbies: Serial killing."

Dave kept reading and making notations, ignoring her. Megan glanced nervously at Dave, then at Nita, fascinated by the strange dynamics. She had the weird sense that they were fighting over her. She shook her head to clear it of the bizarre notion.

Nita selected another file and opened it. "Listen to this one. Schizophrenic. Age 25. Talks to angels and shoots people in the head."

Megan leaned over her shoulder and pretended to read. "Oops. No. Read the addendum. Kills only small children. For food."

Both women laughed. Megan's laugh failed to thrill Dave this time.

Dave didn't look up, but he stopped writing and spoke calmly. "I suppose you think I'm going to tell you this is not a game. That you haven't had to see them, lying on the ground, outlined in chalk, half their heads blown off." He put the folder down. "That there's a killer on the loose who won't stop until we stop him. And that until we do, nobody's safe."

The women had stopped laughing. Nita patted Megan's arm and glared at Dave.

"Tell me, detective," Nita said, her voice cold. "Aren't you afraid that this so-called Ladykiller is too smart for you?"

"A pattern exists, Ms. Bergstrom. We'll find it. Serial killers eventually get caught. They make mistakes. We outsmart them."

"Do you now? This city is a crucible of the unexpected."

"Is that what your studies have taught you, Ms. Bergstrom?"

"My studies have taught me that limited thinking cannot deal with this city and its problems, detective."

There was a silence and Megan winced inwardly at the level of dislike that sparked between the social worker and the detective.

"Let's get back to work, why don't we," Dave said.

They slogged through the files in silence. When they finished, Nita stood up and left without a word. Megan sat for a few seconds, then followed her.

Dave riffled through the notes. The two women had done a

thorough job listing several who fit the profile. As he scanned the lists, though, none seemed quite right. The violence in their pasts — bar fights, wife beating, child molesting — was almost always an un-premeditated eruption of rage, provoked by another's behavior. An insult here, a petty jealousy there. Not one had been arrested for an offense worse than assault and battery. The element of planning was missing. The smooth-clicking intellect of a master killer. And none showed any experience with firearms.

Then Dave got to the end of Nita's list.

The last name was Thomas Cronen. He once had been arrested in the armed robbery of a New Jersey convenience store. And he came from a dysfunctional family. His mother was a hooker, and he'd had a history of mental disturbance. Dave eagerly rooted through the pile in front of Nita's seat for the Cronen file.

Could this be "Ace" Cronen? The neatly typed reports suggested it was the same street punk whom Dave knew and loathed. They de-scribed a boyhood punctuated with capturing neighborhood dogs and cats, and torturing them to death. And although his partner in the rob-bery got convicted for carrying the gun, Ace boasted he actually had been the gunman and had planted it on the other guy. The reports were written by Reuben Silver.

Dave called the task force and got Jamie.

"Hey, Dave. How's your day been?" she asked cheerfully.

"Jamie, you know Ace Cronen. Real first name is Thomas. See what we have on him."

Dave closed the folder. "And I wonder if you could do some dig-ging for me," he added casually. "I'm sure Blake will okay it."

"Be glad to. What?"

"I'd like you to go into the backgrounds of all the social workers here at the crisis center. I doubt they'll have any criminal files, but I want you to find out about everything you can on them."

Jamie answered affirmatively but her heart sank. She knew in-stinctively that he only wanted information on one social worker, and she knew that his interest wasn't professional.

• • •

Nita stood stonily beside the fish tank and sprinkled food on the glowing water.

"It's getting dark out," Megan ventured.

Nita said nothing. The fish swooped on the descending flakes of food.

Megan gave a small cry. "Oh, God. You scared me."

A large cop had shambled into the room. His slack face resembled a doltish cartoon dog's. His waistline threatened to spill over the confining band of his gunbelt, which was on its last notch.

"Uh, sorry. Officer Sweeney. Detective Dillon assigned me here nights."

"Sweeney, is it?" Nita said with suspicious heartiness. "Wonderful to have you here, Officer Sweeney. Why don't you treat yourself to a cup of coffee? Over there." She pointed to the far end of the room.

Megan sat tentatively on the edge of Nita's desk. Nita leaned back in the chair and regarded Megan for a few long moments. Megan examined the floor. Finally, Nita smiled at her.

"So," Nita said, "how was it today, playing Nancy Drew with Son of Sam Spade?"

Relieved, Megan beamed back. "Great. It was great."

"Got any interesting leads on our Ladykiller?" Nita continued.

"We got nowhere," Megan said. "We grabbed a quick lunch from the deli and headed back here. He's kind of interesting."

"Our tax dollars at work." After a few seconds, Nita laughed. Megan joined in, only a little strained.

"Well," Megan asked tentatively, "what do you think of him?"

Nita considered for a minute, still smiling. "I think," she began slowly, "that policemen are to social workers what garbage men are to the great French chefs."

Megan's smile froze.

"I think," Nita went on, "that our job is to shape society. Theirs is to clean up after it."

"But you said we'd —"

"Oh, we'll help him with his investigation. But that's not what's important here. He only cares about catching killers. Putting them in jail. That's as far as he goes. What's interesting to us is what these crimes mean in context. What they're saying."

"The pattern?" Megan said.

"The pattern. The police are too stupid to see it. Society is re-shaping itself, and this killer, whom your detective is so preoccupied with, is simply the means."

Megan listened raptly.

Nita was getting uncharacteristically passionate. "Don't you see? We're the ones who can interpret these events. By watching these movements in the social fabric, and judiciously helping them along, we're sculptors. Artists. We're the ones who can mold the world."

Megan nodded, excited.

"We can create it," Nita said. "Polish it. Make it shine. The detective? He's a janitor. He'll sweep up the mess we leave." And in the dusk-shrouded streets outside the crisis center, the city's dark heart beat on.

Ace had tried everything to get the money he needed to buy Tony Top-nut's damn .45. He loped along the Deuce, asking all the people he knew.

"You shittin' me?" Finesse replied with a snort. "Motherfucker goes around dissin' me and he wants me to hand him two hundred big ones. You dumb? Or is you stupid?"

"This is a big deal, Finesse. I'll make it up to you. Look, I'm putting in a hundred of my own."

"What you need all this foldin' green for, my man?"

"Well —"

"You ain't into the white powder? Just say no, jack." Finesse chortled wickedly.

"It's, um, for a woman."

"Pussy? Listen to me and listen to me good. Ain't no pussy worth no motherfuckin' three hundred dollars. Understand what I'm sayin'?"

Finesse brushed the lapels of his electric-green suit. "Tell you what. Give your little Johnson a good handshake and save yourself the money, my man."

Billy Ray Battle, who had managed to pony up the ten thousand bucks for bail to get free pending trial, was no help, either. "You got shit for brains, boy," he said, as he sucked on a beer outside the grimy windowed off-track betting parlor. He wore a gauze pad over the eye that Dave Dillon had hit. "Why would I give money to a peckerwood like you?"

"I kind of figured that, since you had so much money to spend on bail, there'd be more where that came from. Shit, I'll pay you right back, Billy Ray. Trust me."

"Trust you? Fucked, if that don't beat ass all." The big man took another swig of beer. "The reason I got me the money for the bail is that I don't throw it away on every peckerwood what says he'll pay me right back."

"I figured you were my friend."

"I got me three friends in this life, boy. Me, myself, and I." Billy Ray took another gulp of beer and belched.

Ace ruled out begging. That earned only a quarter here, a quarter there. He settled upon a scam that had worked before: pretend to have been robbed a few minutes before and ask for nine-fifty for bus fare back home to New Jersey. A figure like that was more convincing than a round ten bucks.

But as he was going through his spiel for his first set of pigeons, a fat pair of tourists from the Midwest with Mongoloid-looking eyes, he attracted more interest than he bargained for.

Martino and her kid sidekick, Blitzer, sidled up. "What's this about you got robbed, Ace?" Martino asked.

Ace said nothing, and the tourist couple chimed in with how glad they were to see police officers and how awful that this poor young man had been robbed.

"Only thing he's missing is his brains," muttered Martino ominously.

"My mistake," Ace mumbled, and he shambled off.

Then he spotted Jackie Why chain-smoking his way up the street, greeting everybody with an upraised palm.

"Two hundred semolians, huh?" Jackie Why said, the cigarette bobbing in his lips as he spoke.

"Pay you back real quick. No shit. I'm good for it."

Jackie Why removed his billfold and counted out a wad of cash. He pulled it back as Ace grabbed for it.

"One little business proviso, Ace-hole," Jackie Why said. "You give me back this double by Saturday. That's four hundred, if you can't count. We got ourselves an understanding?"

"Anything you say. Hey, four hundred, no problem."

"I don't get that back in my hot hand by Saturday, Mr. Mouth, and you're dead meat. Hope I make my meaning clear."

Ace ran to the Foxy Lady. Tony Topnut made a strange face when he counted the money.

He disappeared in the back and emerged with a paper bag. Inside was a heavy object. "Point this in the right direction before you fire, dickhead," he said.

The night was warm, and Ace popped a good sweat running to the West Side Crisis Center.

The street outside lay silent. In Ace's sweaty grip, the receiver of the public phone felt slippery.

"Crisis center, can I help you?" came Nita's voice over the line, like a song from the starry sky.

He hung up without saying a word. She was there tonight. He would wait for her.

NINE

Officer Sweeney was snoring, a deep-lunged cycle of phlegmy breathing and snorting, zoned-out to the world. Nita knew the call would come about now, in the pit of the night when the bovine Sweeneys of this world nodded off.

"Crisis center," she said into the receiver. "Can I help you?"

"I've got to talk to you," came the jumpy voice on the line. He sounded as if he'd been hot-wired. "About what happened."

"You're outside, aren't you, Ace? You're nearby, waiting for me." She crooned to him, her voice at once sexy, maternal, soothing.

"How did you know?"

"I know you, Ace. I've known you for a while now. I know all your secrets, don't I, Ace?"

There was a silence and she heard his sharp intake of breath.

"I've been waiting for you. Your shift's supposed to be over. Where are you? I've got to talk to you."

"I'm working a double shift, Ace. Everyone is too upset to work."

"I've got to see you." Nita glanced at Sweeney, who had stirred and mumbled in his sleep. Breathe, snort.

"Please," Ace's voice was pleading.

She spoke even more quietly, her voice suggestive. "What are you going to do when you see me, Ace? Tell me."

"You're the one, aren't you?" he blurted out. "You did it. You did them all."

Nita checked out the sleeping policeman once more, a cunning smile creeping over her face, wicked and wise. "Always playing, aren't you?" she murmured into the phone. "Teasing. You see, I *know* that you did it."

Ace gasped, then laughed crazily. "Bullshit. I was there. And so were you. And so was that big, dumb bastard that got killed, Reuben."

"And when I last saw you, the two of you were both alive. I don't care, though. It just makes you more interesting. This was just the sort of thing you always said you would do, isn't it?"

Sweeney snorted himself awake, then yawned and stretched, looking over at Nita curiously.

Waiting, Nita could almost feel the flattering suggestion seep into Ace and swell his ego.

"Well, I could have —" Ace said.

Nita met Sweeney's porcine eyes. She sat up straight and her tone changed from insinuating to distantly professional. "If you think you or your friend saw a crime being committed, I'd advise you to go to the police."

Ace lacked the wit to pick up on Nita's predicament. "The police? Fuck the police. You think I'm nuts?"

"If you're worried about your sanity," Nita said, "I can give you the number of a very good doctor who —"

"Just meet me outside. Talk to me. I've got something to show you. Something important."

Sweeney lumbered over to Nita's desk.

"I'd love to," Nita said into the phone. "Well, if you decide to talk to someone, let us know. Any staff member here can help you. Good night." She hung up. The policeman loomed over her. Nita smiled up at him. "A kleptomaniac. His conscience is bothering him."

"I just wanted to know —" Sweeney said.

Nita's eyes narrowed. She reached for her purse and pulled it toward her.

"— if you wanted something," Sweeney continued. "I could go for a sandwich about now. I wouldn't mind going out to the all-night carry-out."

Nita smiled, relieved. "Great idea. I'd love a Greek salad." She put her hand in her bag. "Let me give you some money."

"My pleasure," he said with a grin, waving her away.

"How sweet," Nita said. Her fingers briefly touched the butt of her gun, where it lay hidden beneath an eighth-of-an-inch of leather, three feet from the law. She withdrew her hand into the light and favored Sweeney with her dazzling smile.

The cop nodded and turned away. He had a thought and turned back to her. "You don't mind if I go, do you? You'll be okay for a couple of minutes?"

"Go right ahead. I can take care of myself, you know."

The policeman grinned again. "Yes, ma'am."

Sweeney left. Nita waited for a few moments, then turned on the answering machine and grabbed her coat off the rack. The fish swam serenely in the glow of the glass tank. The street outside the crisis center had an even greater stillness.

The moment she stepped outside, she could sense the shadow that Ace was hidden in. He slinked out into the gray light, head jerking around in agitation, checking for cops, for ghosts, for demons.

Nita touched his scrawny arm, and his nerves jolted his face into a grimace, then subsided. "Let's take a walk," she said.

She steered him in the opposite direction from the one Sweeney had taken.

The feel of her hand upon him worked on Ace with the potency of a fine wine. "God," he babbled. "God, how I love you. I'd do any-thing for you."

"Anything, Ace?"

"I bought a gun. Just like the one you have. Let me show you."

He wanted to stop, to turn her to him, but she kept him march-ing, her neat shoes in rhythm with his boots on the gray concrete. "You know all about it, don't you?" she said. "You know all about the victims, their names, how they were killed, when they were killed. You met them at the crisis center. You know everything."

"Yeah, yeah. I saw the papers. I knew them all. Fucking Wall Street bitch looked at me like I was a piece of shit." He shook off the unwelcome memory.

And they walked and she told him, under the pure and lucent

stars, what to say and how to act and why it mattered. And she showed him the gun from her handbag. And he showed her his. And she exchanged guns with him. And when she had finished, she told him, "I love you, too."

After locking the crisis center door behind her, Nita called out Sweeney's name. No answer. Good. She had beaten him back. She climbed the stairs.

A man was silhouetted at the top. She started.

"Don't be afraid," Dave Dillon said.

"I don't scare easily, detective." She brushed past him. "How did you get inside here?"

"Dr. Solomon gave me a key. Where were you?"

No light was blinking on the answering machine. "I needed a breath of fresh air. We get a lot of calls between midnight and three." She indicated the clock on the wall. "But by four, they usually trail off."

"Even the crazies need their sleep, eh?"

"No one is crazy, detective." She sat at her desk and watched him.

"I'd say it's crazy to go out wandering at four in the morning."

She didn't reply.

"Where's Sweeney?"

"Out getting us something to eat. I asked him to go."

"You like ordering people around, don't you?"

"What I like is for you to tell me what brings you here at this hour, detective."

"I'm out searching for leads on the case."

"Well, well. So I *am* getting my tax-money's worth. The detective is still on the job. Don't you ever sleep?"

Dave had begun to pace. He prowled around the desks, circling Nita as they talked. "Not while a serial killer is out there, Ms. Bergstrom. Do you think the killer ever sleeps?"

"What did you want to talk to me about, detective?" Even though Dave was behind her now, Nita did not turn to address him, but spoke to the place he had occupied before he started to stalk her. "Did you really want to discuss the nocturnal habits of psychotics? Or are you working off the frustration that comes with drawing a blank during your visit to the Cristides family?"

"Megan told you that?"

Nita could tell she finally had the better of him. "We're close, you know. Very close."

Dave moved into her field of view, and he changed the subject. "Dr. Solomon says you are a top-flight sociologist, Ms. Bergstrom. And a very ambitious one."

"How kind of him. Yes, I want to make a mark in my profession. I won't deny that."

"Your credentials are impressive. And the number of hours you spend with your clients is amazing."

Nita locked her eyes onto his, as if willing him to stand still. But he kept moving, out of her line of vision.

"You had a good look at my file, it seems, detective. Yes, urban problems are my specialty. What better place to study them than at the grassroots level?"

"Exactly." His tone was ominous.

He moved into her view. "I came over tonight because I want you to help me."

She paused before answering. "I already am, detective. Didn't I go through the files for you this afternoon?"

"I don't mean that. You really run this place. I hoped that you could give me some insights about the people it attracts."

"I doubt you'd understand, detective. I'm sure you mean well, and I don't want to sound rude. But I don't think you understand what we do here."

"I'd like to."

When she didn't answer, he tried another approach. "You interest me, Nita," he said from behind her.

She noticed how he had shifted to using her first name. "Do I, Detective Dillon? And how is that?"

He walked around her, again, and sat down on a desk in front of her. Then he turned away and looked abstractedly off into the dark part of the room as he talked. "How is that?"

"Yes, detective. How is that?" She reached for her handbag.

"You figure you're immune somehow."

"Immune?" Nita opened the bag and slid her hand inside.

"You and Megan both. You seem to think that this city is your private laboratory and that urban problems are some kind of game. Like charades. For you to figure out."

Nita laughed and pulled a handkerchief out of her purse. She got up and began to prowl around the office as Dave had done, circling him. "I assure you that we're quite aware that the world is a dangerous place. And that anything can happen. Anything. Look what happened to Reuben."

Dave's eyes followed her as she walked. He shifted position on the desk, never letting her out of his sight. "Maybe you're aware. Careful. Is Megan, though? She's so —"

"Young, detective? Innocent? Unspoiled? Perhaps you'd like to be the one to teach her. Show her things."

"Maybe. Does that bother you, Nita?"

"Yes, it does bother me. I don't want Megan to get hurt."

"No one's going to hurt her. Least of all me."

Nita stood above him, her face hard. "That's wonderful. Then we'd better not tell her about your little problem."

"What 'little problem' is that?" Dave already knew the answer, and an icy finger seemed to run along his spine.

"I think you know."

It took Dave a few seconds to trust his voice to answer. "I was cleared. There was an investigation, and I was cleared."

"Yes. You were cleared."

He hesitated. He didn't want to sound defensive. "It's public knowledge. I don't have anything to hide." He hated the pleading tone that had crept into his voice.

Nita went back to her desk and sat down.

"It's all right. It's just between us. Our secret, detective. What do you say?"

Dave didn't have a word to say. A predator's smile lit Nita's face.

The phone rang, and she didn't drop the smile as she picked up the receiver.

"Crisis center. Can I help you?"

Dave walked down the stairs. He didn't acknowledge Sweeney, whom he encountered at the front door, Greek salad in hand. Or even hear his excuses for being away from his post.

Back home, the cat cuddled in his lap and purring, Dave sat transfixed by the bloody photos of the victims on his wall. He tried to picture them in the crisis center. But his thoughts kept returning to Nita and her hard smile — and how she now had a hold on him.

Then he thought about Megan and wondered how she looked sleeping. How she would look sleeping next to him. He stroked the cat like a woman.

He fell into an uneasy sleep where he chased a laughing Megan, her pretty legs flashing as she ran, beyond his grasp.

The cat woke him in the morning with its sandpaper tongue on his cheek. Time to eat. As he scooped cat food out of a can, the cat brushed his legs in gustatory anticipation. He remembered that Jimmy Conlon had to go in early today to work some kind of low-man-on-the-totem-pole news shift. So Dave would be running alone in the park this morning.

He was pulling on his running clothes when the phone rang. It was Mrs. Corrigan, his family's neighbor in Queens.

"I don't mean to be worrying you, Davey," said Mrs. Corrigan, who had spent a life worrying about everything. About money (too little of it), the passing years (too many of them), the steady deterioration of the neighborhood, other people's manners, and her own health. "But your mum's in the hospital."

"My God, what happened?"

"Well, the doctors don't know. The ambulance came last night. I didn't want to disturb you. You probably were with some girl. A young man like you. But —"

"Where is she? What hospital?"

He tooled the unmarked car over the river to Queens. His blaring siren and flashing dashboard strobe cleared the morning traffic out of the way. He spun between the iron legs of the el along Queens Boulevard and smacked the steering wheel with his palm, as if to make the car go faster through the rush-hour clog of inch-along commuters.

Within the hour, Dave was trotting down the sterile halls of the hospital. He pushed his badge into the nurses' faces and demanded to know where his mother was.

In a private room, sitting up in bed, wearing the sour expression of someone who had eaten a lemon.

"Ma, are you okay?" He clasped her bony hand in his.

"Of course I'm okay. I had a few chest pains, and old lady Corrigan dials 911. It's nothing. They're letting me out of here in an hour."

"Mrs. Corrigan had me worried."

"Well, if this is what it takes to get my son to visit me, I should have chest pains more often." His mother didn't smile. In fact, growing up, the only times he could remember having seen her smile was when she was hearing about the misfortunes of others.

"Ma, I've been on a case."

"Two months it's been since I saw you. I forgot what you looked like."

"Stop it, Ma. Listen. I'll take you home."

The old lady screwed up her mouth and pulled her hand from his. "Not necessary. Mrs. Corrigan is coming for me. You should get back to your case."

"Come on, Ma."

She sighed theatrically. "You're like your father. Police work, police work. That's all he cared about. That and running around with the wrong kind of woman."

"Ma, don't. Let's not talk about him."

"When I die, make sure she doesn't come to my funeral. The way she came to his. The cheap tramp."

"I don't have a clue where she is now. And what's all this nonsense about funerals? Really, Ma."

His mother licked her dry lips. "That cheap tramp ruined our marriage. And she killed him. If it weren't for her, he would be alive today. What is it with men?"

Dave didn't have an answer.

Unable to dissuade her from waiting for Mrs. Corrigan, he got back into the car and joined the slow morning parade into Manhattan. He tried to occupy himself with fantasies about Megan, but his father kept creeping in. Not his father, the teacher of police craft; his father, the strayer. The traffic's stately rhythms — move three feet, then stop, move three feet, then stop — lent itself to contemplation. The endless red string of brake lights ahead was mesmerizing.

His father was a jovial sort who loved to tell loud jokes and drink heartily and even sing a song or two in his rich Irish tenor down at the corner bar. That's where he met Cassie, the barmaid. She had teased hair and wore tight toreador pants with blouses that showed off her cleavage. A week after his father moved out of the house, his mother sent Dave to the bar with a message about some financial matter. "If he's not there, that cheap tramp will be able to find him," his mother said.

And so the bar was where Dave met Cassie too. His father wasn't there, but Cassie greeted Dave with an earthy warmth. "You're a fine-looking boy, just like Brian told me you was," Cassie said from somewhere above her breasts.

Weeks later, Dave sat on a barstool, a Coke in front of him, his father and a beer beside him, and his father's friends all around. Cassie had her back to them as she arranged newly cleaned glasses along the shelf. She bent down and the fabric stretched across the enticing globes of her butt. "That is a fine woman," his father told Dave. "My soul belongs to her, boy."

Detective Brian Dillon, to the dismay of his more conservative superiors and neighbors like Mrs. Corrigan, began openly living with Cassie. Mrs. Corrigan was the bearer of bad tidings and evil speculation: that Brian had bought that woman a new car, had paid for the new roof on her house, had spirited her off for an expensive vacation in Jamaica.

"Where is he getting all the money for this, do you suppose?" his mother groused to Mrs. Corrigan. "On a policeman's salary?"

Then the Knapp Commission on police corruption convened. The high spirits left Brian Dillon. When Dave came to see his father in the bar, he was hunched over a drink by himself or talking in a low voice to a somber Cassie. Years later, Dave read the evidence against his father. It was small stuff: petty payoffs from local merchants who were eager to help out local cops anyway. There was no extortion. Brian Dillon hadn't sold out to the Mob or anything really awful. But the day of his scheduled testimony before the Knapp Commission, Brian Dillon rested his service revolver's muzzle against the roof of his mouth and pulled the trigger.

Lt. Blake, then a sergeant, told Dave at the funeral: "Your father was a good detective. Smart, tough, hard-working. He couldn't stand being a disgrace to the force."

Dave thought it was more like he couldn't stand having his wife gloat over his disgrace.

As Dave's unmarked car passed over the iron grillwork of the 59th Street Bridge, it hummed an odd tune. And life ground on.

Megan lay on her bed, dressed and ready to go, reading the paper. Or trying to. Her neighbors were going at it above her head, their bed creaking like a freighter in a storm.

Megan had been trying without success to suppress indecent thoughts about Dave. She wondered whether he was noisy in bed. Robin had just blown a few short gusts of air out his nose when he came.

All was quiet upstairs now. Megan folded the paper on her lap. Her buzzer sounded.

"It's me," Dave said over the intercom. Familiar, as if they had been going together for ages.

"I'll be right down." Megan checked herself in the mirror for the tenth time since she emerged from the bathroom a half hour early, ready to go. She made sure her stockings were straight under her skirt, which was shorter than the one she had worn the day before.

Dave seemed tired, dark smudges hung below his eyes. But he seemed glad to see her, and smiled broadly. When he greeted her, the way he said her name had a pleasing sound. She shivered.

"I'm fine. How have you been? You look tired."

"I was up late working. And I didn't get much sleep. My mother went in the hospital last night with chest pains. I raced out to Queens early this morning."

"Is she okay?"

"She's fine. They're sending her home in a little while. A few chest pains. Nothing to be alarmed about. She's a tough, old Irish lady." They got in the car. "Are you Irish, by any chance?"

"A bit. The name is. We're mongrels really."

"Grow up Catholic?" he asked.

It was a prospective-boyfriend-type question. It didn't displease her. "Presbyterian. If we get married, though, I can convert."

They both laughed. She had no idea why she had blurted that out, but his evident pleasure over the remark dispelled her embarrassment.

"I'm glad you're not angry at me," he said. "Yesterday at the crisis center, it was, well, a little tense toward the end."

"Yeah. Nita can be like that sometimes. But she is really terrific. You have to get to know her. Everyone worships her."

Dave sped through a red light. "She have a guy?"

"Nita doesn't need men. There's just her work. That's her life."

"She's very attractive."

"You bet. Men meet her one time and fall madly in love with her. But she has no time for them." Megan noticed that Dave had been admiring her legs as he dodged in and out of traffic, speeding through red lights; she felt she was in strong, capable hands. "Unlike me."

He looked over sharply. "You must have a guy. A woman like you."

"Not at the moment. I've got the crisis center, my graduate work, and Nita. No fellas. What about you?"

"I don't have any fellas, either." They laughed, but he answered the question. "No. I'm unattached, too."

"I could have sworn that that detective —"

"No. Never shit where you eat —" He gulped, sorry that he had let the locker room vulgarity escape. "She's a good detective. And a great chick. But I work with her."

Megan smiled to herself. They drove in silence for a while. When Dave spoke his tone was darker.

"I was going out with someone for a while, but it ended badly."

She decided not to pursue it. "Where are we going?"

"The husband of Evelyn Hernandez works at a hotel in Midtown. She was the first victim."

"I thought Lucy Cristides was the first victim?"

"Lucy was the first we paid attention to. Maybe, I hate to say this, because she was white. Then we linked her to an earlier, unsolved case, that of Evelyn. The third was Kimberly Worth, the stockbroker. Then Lydia Daniels, the hooker. And of course, Reuben. You can tell from the list that, at least on the surface, they have nothing in common."

"Yes." Megan pondered for a moment. "I haven't seen any of them around the crisis center, but that doesn't mean much. They could have used aliases or dressed differently. Some people are awkward about coming to visit us."

"Do you know a client at the crisis center named Thomas Cronen? Goes by Ace?"

Megan nodded. "Sort of. He's some kind of scam artist, a petty criminal, right? I think I can place him. Maybe."

"He was a client of Reuben's. I know him from the precinct. You're right. He's not exactly a solid citizen."

"What was the story on Evelyn Hernandez?"

Dave turned onto Lexington Avenue. "She was the housewife. Had four kids, all of them disabled. She stayed home, in Spanish Harlem, caring for them. Her husband works the desk in a hotel."

"Where did she die?"

"In a vacant lot beside the SPCA. You can hear the dogs in the pound around the clock. Their howling must have drowned out the gunshot. Someone spotted the body at first light."

"They were all killed late at night?"

"Yes."

They parked in front of the Lexington Arms. The doorman started to object that they were blocking the taxi pickup area, but Dave waved him away by flashing his badge. As they climbed the red-carpeted steps to the plush lobby, Dave said, "The Hernandezes didn't have such a great marriage, according to their neighbors. She had bruises from where he beat her."

"Maybe it was the pressure from all those handicapped children. The money it costs to support them is one thing. The emotional toll on the parents can be harder."

"I guess," Dave said. "When she died, Evelyn was one month pregnant. That was too soon for the autopsy to tell whether this baby would have been handicapped or not."

"Her husband couldn't have been happy about another kid coming. Are you sure he didn't kill her?"

"Very sure. He was working the night shift when she got shot. A dozen witnesses confirmed that." Dave strode authoritatively up to the desk and displayed his badge. "Felix Hernandez, please."

Behind the desk, a woman dressed in the uniform of a nineteenth-century Prussian hussar, complete with gold epaulets, spoke quietly into the phone.

A burly man dressed in the identical getup emerged from the back. His thick moustache bristled at the sight of Dave.

"I'd like to ask you a few more questions, Mr. Hernandez," Dave said. "This is Ms. Morrison, a sociologist working with the police on this case."

Hernandez made no move to shake hands. "Let's go over to that corner so we don't disturb nobody," he said, pointing. As they crossed the lobby, he muttered to himself.

They sat on brocade covered chairs.

"I know you've answered a lot of questions about your wife, sir," Dave began. "We're sorry to bother you again."

Hernandez's moustache squirmed in irritation. "Now what?"

"How are your children doing, Mr. Hernandez?" Megan asked. "This must be an especially tough time for them."

"No kidding, lady," Hernandez said. "I got them all at relatives. Before Evelyn went and got herself killed, I had to work like a son of a bitch to support them. Now I got them with relatives but I got to pay them. I'm paying more now than ever before. My own damn relatives." He shook his head. "The kids can't feed themselves. Can't even go to the bathroom themselves."

"I know it must be difficult," Megan said, full of sympathy. She sensed Dave watching her. She was in charge of the interview.

Hernandez bristled. "Difficult? You don't know the half of it, lady. You got kids?"

"No, sir. I'm not married. Could you tell us if your wife had any interests outside the home?"

"Interests? Christ." He glared suspiciously at Megan. "Evelyn wasn't one of them feminists, if that's what you mean. It was all she could do to cope with being a good wife. You think caring for four retarded kids was easy? She didn't have the time for none of your 'interests outside the home.'"

"Then what was she doing in the middle of the night, miles from her apartment?"

Dave watched with interest as Megan put some steel in her voice.

"Look, I talked to the cops a million times." Hernandez was getting angry. "I don't know what she was doing. I was working. Here. Ask anybody. Maybe she was coming to see me. I don't know."

"Actually," Dave said, "we wanted to know if you ever heard Evelyn mention the West Side Crisis Center?"

Hernandez turned red and got up. "What's this?" he said, furious. "No. Listen, I'm getting tired of these questions —"

"We believe it might have something to do with your wife's death," Megan said forcefully.

Hernandez stood with fists clenched, eyes bulging, and moustache flared. "No, I never heard of it," he shouted, not caring that guests in the lobby turned to stare. "And if I ever caught Evelyn going there, I'd have —"

Megan stood up also, watching him carefully. "What?" she taunted him softly. "You'd have what?"

"I'd have —" Hernandez seemed about to detonate.

"Megan," Dave said in warning. He stood up.

She ignored Dave and leaned toward Hernandez. "What would you have done, tough guy? Or don't you have the guts?"

"I'd have killed her, you bitch," Hernandez screamed. He lunged for Megan, his fists enormous, his face swollen and red.

Dave intercepted him, grabbing his arm and twisting it, bringing the man hard to his knees. Dave with one hand held Hernandez's wrist between the man's shoulder blades. He grabbed the guy's neck with the other and forced it toward the floor. When Hernandez grew still, Dave said, "I'm going to release you now. One wrong move, and you'll get hurt."

Hernandez's face tilted up at them. His eyes were brimming. "She went to some bullshit psycho clinic. Telling all them about what a shit I was. Me who worked so hard to take care of her and the kids. She's the one kept having them idiot kids. It was killing me."

Megan nodded. She was shaken, but she stood her ground.

The lobby was at a standstill. People were like mannequins, immobile, limbs and heads freeze-framed, absorbed in the drama.

As they walked down the red-carpeted stairs, Dave said to Megan, "I thought you took the sympathetic approach."

"Sometimes, you need another way," Megan said.

"How's this for an approach?" Dave said. "Want to go out to dinner tonight?"

The detectives slouched around the table and reported their progress — or lack of same — to Blake.

"What about picking up that Cronen character?" Blake asked. "Where are we on that."

"We should bag him by tonight," Wise said. "He hasn't been to the SRO he calls home. Who knows what garbage can he's sleeping in? But he usually comes out to the Deuce after sundown, sort of like a mosquito."

"Buzzes out of hiding," Safir said.

"What about that background check on the staff at the crisis center, Jamie?" Blake went on.

Dave had felt her watching him, as he often did. The weight of her eyes shifted to Blake.

"Pretty nondescript bunch, Loo," Jamie said. She ran through the life stories of the do-gooding group that worked at the center. When she came to Nita, Dave sat up straight to listen. "A brilliant student. Working on her doctorate, but she's run into some kind of trouble with her adviser. The person I talked to would only hint. But the adviser seems to feel that she's gone off the deep end with her topic. Seems that she probably won't get her degree."

"Have you covered everybody at the crisis center, Jamie?" Dave found himself asking.

"Why, no, Dave," Jamie said with a wry twist of her mouth. "I don't want to leave out Megan Morrison."

"Tell us about Dillon's girlfriend," Wise said.

"Takes her for one interview a day," Safir chimed in.

"That's so he can stretch it out," said Wise.

Dave scowled. "Get off it. She can't afford the time to do all the interviews at once."

"I don't have much on Morrison," Jamie said. "Nice white girl — what can I tell you. Except..."

"Except?" Wise said.

"Except?" Safir said.

"She had an affair with this married professor at college. Robin Tolner. He busted it up. Broke her heart. I've got the report here." Jamie pushed the folder across the table to Dave. "Want to take a peek?"

"No, thanks," Dave said coldly.

Jamie looked at him searchingly, then pulled back the folder.

Blake leapt in. "One other item. This comes from the medical examiner's." He waited for all to turn their attention back to him and continued. "Lydia Daniels was HIV-positive, although she showed no symptoms, yet. The hooker had AIDS."

Dave nodded. "That makes sense. I bet she went to the crisis center because of it. Evelyn Hernandez because she had a bunch of crippled kids, with another en route, and an old man who beat her. Who knows why the cheerleader and the stockbroker went."

"If they went," Safir said.

"Remember that Bergstrom bitch" — Wise caught himself and made a semi-apologetic face at Jamie — "that Bergstrom woman told Dave they'd know if their loonie-tunes types ended up blown away by a .45. So how can any of them have gone to the crisis center?"

"Megan pointed out to me that they could have come in looking different, even in disguise," Dave said. "Besides, the center's records about their clients are pretty sparse. It'd be easy to use an alias. The staff is afraid of scaring away people by demanding too much identification."

"Megan?" Wise said. "That's Megan Morrison you're making the first-name-basis reference to at this point in time?"

"Megan, your interview pal?" Safir said.

"Knock it off," Blake said. "Listen, now, I —"

Chief of Detectives Mancuso blasted into the room, followed by his entourage. "They told me you were in here, Blake," he brayed. "Why aren't you people finding this damn killer?"

"It's getting bad," Jimmy Conlon said over the bar roar at McSorley's. "Chip is putting me under a load of pressure to produce something."

"Tell me about it," Dave said. He hoisted his beer. The bar light played through the mug. "Jimmy, I wish I could help you."

"Yeah," Jimmy said mournfully. They sucked on their beers and let the good cheer of the other drinkers wash over them. At last Jimmy said, "What you doing tonight?"

"I was going out to see my mother, but she's playing the martyr. Mrs. Corrigan will be buzzing around. I'll go out tomorrow."

"Knowing your mother, she'll be back on her feet tomorrow, kicking ass and taking names."

"Tonight, I've got a date," Dave announced.

"A date? With who?"

"This very nice girl I met the other day." Dave realized he had to watch what he said about Megan, lest he tip off his friend to the crisis center phase of the investigation.

"Pretty?"

"Very pretty. And very smart. Sexy, in a clean cut kind of way."

"What does she do?" Jimmy asked.

"Oh, she's a social worker. Name's Megan."

"Yeah? Where does she work?"

Dave said nothing and took a swig of beer.

Jimmy instantly knew he had struck a nerve. "What's the matter with asking where she works?"

"She works at the West Side Crisis Center," Dave told his friend.

"That's the same place Reuben Silver worked." Jimmy ran his thumb down the frost on his mug. "Are you guys focusing on the crisis center? Is it connected with the murders?"

"Jimmy I can't talk about this." Dave understood that he was as much as confirming Jimmy's suspicion. "Look, if any of that appears in the paper, Mancuso will cut my heart out. Already, he suspects I leak to you."

"Yeah," Jimmy said to his friend. He drank some beer. They ordered another round. Then Jimmy said, "So, you really like this girl?"

Dave found himself breaking into a smile. "I do. A lot. A whole lot."

Jimmy watched Dave shrewdly. "I haven't seen you this excited about a chick since — for a long time. I think you're on the road to recovery, my friend."

Dave nodded at the insight, which had not occurred to him until now. He took a long drink of beer, almost a toast to good fortune. "I think you're right," he said.

After Megan had finished with the last client, she stopped to see Nita, who was poring over the crisis center's books. "You do everything," Megan said. "If it weren't for you, this place would fall apart."

"I'm going to recommend to Dr. Solomon that we get new accountants," Nita said. "The firm we have now is far too slow. Would you take a minute and feed the fish?"

"I'd love to," Megan said.

"Let's have dinner tonight," Nita suggested.

"Dinner? Well, um, I ..."

Tim came breezing through. "Oh, what a horrid day. When *are* we going to replace Reuben? I'm so swamped I could die."

"Probably by next month, Tim," Nita said. "Our grant from the city should come unstuck by then. Meanwhile, you're doing a wonderful job coping. Everyone has noticed."

"They have?" Tim threw back his shoulders.

"Not everyone has been able to tough it out as well as you have," Nita said. "Poor Rose, for instance. Reuben's death has devastated her."

"I know," Tim said. "Poor thing. I called to ask what I could do. She wants to be alone."

"She told me you called. She's very touched." Nita picked up a piece of paper and examined it. "Incidentally, I realize you're shouldering a real burden, but could I ask you to take Rose's Wednesday morning group?"

"Which is that?"

"The homeless ladies?"

Tim blanched. "Lord, those horrible old —"

"If you'd rather not, I'm sure we can find someone else," Nita said.

"No, no, no," Tim burst, distressed to have disappointed Nita. "I'll be happy to. No problem."

"They're actually very nice women," Megan said, helping out.

Tim scanned Megan up and down. "My, my, my, you're looking hot tonight, my dear. Got a date?"

"Well, I —" Megan felt as if he had yanked the shower curtain back to reveal her shameful secret.

"I was standing by the window when that hunky detective let you out of his muscle car. He opened the door for you. Very gallant. And *you*. It was like you were walking on air."

"I better feed the fish," Megan managed.

Tim cleared his throat archly. "Bon appétit," he said, and wafted away.

Megan met Nita's half-closed eyes. Megan knew she must look guilty. What was Nita thinking?

After an eternity, Megan said, "What?"

"He won't be good to you," Nita said. Her tone was matter-of-fact, but there were steely barbs beneath the surface. "He's a cop. They're macho. They don't like women. They don't trust women. They only trust other cops. They aren't called pigs for nothing."

"Nita, it's only dinner," Megan said with an unconvincing laugh.

"Don't forget the fish. They're hungry."

Later, when Megan met him, she responded to Dave's welcoming smile with one of her own.

They walked silently down the block, the very picture of a perfect date.

"There's a great Italian restaurant I like," he offered. "You like Italian food?"

"That would be fine," she said in a tone that indicated anything would be fine.

"That's good. In Manhattan these days we have an infinite choice of restaurants. We have Italian. Then there's Italian. And in a pinch, there's always Italian."

She laughed.

As they turned a corner, Megan turned serious. "How's your mom?"

Over dinner, they talked about their families, their childhoods, and their friends. Nothing about the case or the crisis center. Nothing about Nita.

Dave watched approvingly as Megan ate with gusto. They finished two bottles of chianti.

When he drove her home, Megan turned to Dave to thank him. She meant to give him a quick kiss on the cheek and go home but somehow his lips trapped hers and held them. Only their mouths connected, he did not reach for her or hold her. She gave in to the kiss for a minute and was just about to pull away when Dave's hand reached up and found, through her blouse, through her bra, her nipple. He pinched it between his fingers, hard, hard enough to make her gasp, first with pain but instantly with the most exquisite pleasure. Her entire body flooded with sudden heat.

By unspoken agreement, they left the car and walked quickly into her building. Megan walked in front, breathing hard. She looked back once and smiled wantonly. She walked up the narrow stairs of her building ahead of him, and he watched her ass and her pretty legs climb. As she worked the keys in her door locks, her fingers trembled.

Inside, the door closed against the night, no light yet lit, crackling magnetism took over. They turned to each other and kissed again, softly at first, exploring, hesitating, then with abandon. Their open mouths crushed together and their hands roved over each other's bodies. Clothing was opened or removed. Megan found herself making small animal noises, as Dave sucked her breast.

"Know what I'd like to do?" Dave panted at her.

"What?" Megan gasped.

"Too dirty out loud. Better whisper." He put his lips against her ear and licked.

"God, yes," Megan said, moaning. "Please, yes."

When the phone first sounded, they were too busy on the bed to hear. Or to want to hear.

Most of their clothes were off. Dave was pinching her nipples again as his hot mouth worked its way down her squirming torso. Megan thought incoherently that if he didn't enter her soon, she would die. Her entire being seemed concentrated in the spot between her legs and she knew that when his lips touched her there she would explode.

Unnoticed, the phone rang several times, then the answering machine kicked in. Megan hadn't turned off the volume.

"Ms. Morrison, this is Detective Loud," came Jamie's voice. "I'm looking for Detective Dillon, and he signed out that he might be out with you tonight. If you could, please tell him —"

Dave jumped off the bed and grabbed the phone. He made an effort to control his breathing. "What is it, Jamie?" He felt for the volume control and turned it to zero.

"We've arrested Ace Cronen," Jamie told him. "A half hour ago on the Deuce. Looks like this is it. He's carrying a .45 that might be the murder weapon."

"I'll be right there." He hung up.

"What is it?" Megan panted.

"They arrested a suspect," Dave said, buttoning his shirt back up. "I have to go, Megan. I'm sorry."

"I'm sorry too," Megan said.

TEN

Jamie sat in front of the large one-way window that revealed the interrogation room, like a widescreen TV. Beside her, a man sat hunched over a video camera, recording the questioning. Inside the room, Ace was slouched in a hard-backed chair, a study in insolence. Safir sat in front of him, backward in a chair, his legs spread-eagled. Wise walked back and forth in his Florsheims, doing his caged tiger imitation.

When Dave came in he nodded to Jamie and stood beside her to watch. His clothes were disheveled and his hair mussed. He stood close enough for her to smell a woman's perfume on him, but not the scent of sex.

Dave pointed at Ace. "This hump is confessing?"

"Not only that. You'd think he'd won the lottery."

"You picked him up on the Deuce, huh?" Dave said.

"Yeah," Jamie said. "A couple of uniforms bagged him going into the Foxy Lady. He had a piece on him, a .45, but he offered no resistance. He's cocky, admits everything. Blake is really relieved. He's locked in a meeting now with Mancuso, figuring how to handle the media."

"Ballistics says it was the .45 that did the murders?"

"On a preliminary basis. They're studying the rifling on the barrel now, to make absolutely sure, but it looks like this is it. Congratulations, Dave."

Jamie grinned at him, as happy as Christmas morning. "Blake says it's your collar. Said he'd make sure Mancuso was informed."

"For what that's worth," Dave said skeptically.

The questioning came over the squawk box. Wise showed Ace an arrest dossier. "This your picture?"

Ace examined the arrest photo from his younger days in New Jersey. "Hey, that's cool. I'm looking pretty good there. They nailed me for armed robbery."

"You, a big-time armed robbery hard-ass?" Safir said. "Turns out, according to this, that all you ever did was stand lookout for the kid who was holding the iron."

"My mama was banging the top cop in town, so they did me a favor. What can I say? He got lucky and so did I."

Wise displayed another photo to Ace. "Who's she?"

"Evelyn Hernandez. She liked me. Thought I looked pretty good too."

"What did you do to her, Ace?" Safir asked.

"I broke her heart, then I blew her head off."

"So you killed Evelyn Hernandez?" Wise asked.

"Put one right through her right eye. Blam."

"These chicks were all over-the-top stupid to trust you," Safir said. "I mean, to come to these deserted locations with nobody around. I call that fucking stupid."

"You said it, my man. Stupid as whale shit. But they saw me around the crisis center and they liked my style."

"What were you doing going to the crisis center, Ace?" Safir asked. "You having a crisis?"

Ace had to ponder that. "Fuck, not me. I ain't no loonie. I went there to meet chicks. Chicks love me."

Dave read the preliminary ballistics report before he entered the interrogation room.

"Why, it's the great Detective Dillon," Ace said. "What an honor. You gonna hit me tonight, Dillon?"

"Where'd you get the .45, Ace?" Dave asked.

"Shit, I don't remember. It was years ago. Man needs to defend himself."

"All those arrests you racked up on the Deuce, each time you weren't armed. How do you explain that, Ace?" Dave stood over him, dangling the ballistics report.

"I ain't stupid, Dillon. If I'm lifting some poor fool's billfold, I ain't gonna be packing. In case you pricks collar my ass. Makes the sentence lighter, you understand." Ace smirked at Dave.

"This .45 is at least forty years old. Yet it has been very well maintained. How come we didn't find any gun-cleaning materials in your room?"

Ace pondered once more. "Guess I must've run out. I been busy, see?"

"But I hear you said earlier in the interrogation that you killed Reuben Silver because you confessed to him over the phone, then when he came out to meet you, you changed your mind," Dave said. He hunched down to eye level with Ace.

"Yeah, well, what's your point, Dillon?" Ace sneered.

"Why would a clever guy elude the police this successfully, and suddenly decide to confess to his social worker?"

"Beats the shit out of me, Dillon. Why don't you ask Reuben Silver?"

"I'm asking you, Ace."

"Maybe I had a momentary lapse, Dillon. Didn't you ever have a momentary lapse?" Ace jeered meaningfully.

Dave's hands curled into fists. He seemed ready to bite Ace's laughing face in two.

"Don't, Dave," Safir said.

"Not worth it," Wise said.

"Now that you dumb fucks finally got me," Ace said, "I might as well tell you what happened."

Dave stalked back into the adjoining room. Blake was there.

"Good news, Dave," the lieutenant said. "Ballistics has a positive match on the weapon. It definitely killed all four women and Mr. Silver." He smiled like a pennant winner. "Press conference in the morning, right before the arraignment."

"Something's wrong," Dave said.

Blake's smile dropped a kilowatt. "Dave, for Pete's sake. He has a thorough knowledge of the killings. Mentioned shooting through the right eye. And he was holding the murder weapon. It's U.S. Army-issue, during the Korean War."

"Long before Ace was born," Dave said.

Blake shrugged in exasperation and turned to Jamie as if for help.

Jamie put a hand on Dave's shoulder. "Listen, it's post-victory letdown or something. Why don't we get out of here and do a little celebrating?"

"Sorry, Jamie, I've got work to do."

"We don't need you for the interrogation, Dave," Blake said. "Why don't you two go tip a few wet ones?"

Dave scowled. "I'm not done yet."

Dave spent hours spooling through Ace's videotaped confession. Then he studied the ballistics report. He went over the notes from the crisis center files. He went out and walked the gaudy Deuce, back and forth in front of the Foxy Lady, where Ace had been collared.

Finally, he went home to his cat's complaining meows and opened up a tin of cat food.

"That's what you get for marrying a cop," he told the cat as he set its food dish on the floor. The cat sniffed at the food and peered up at Dave in indignation. "Oh, all right." He sprinkled some cat crunchies over the wet food in the bowl, and watched the cat attack the meal.

Dave stood in front of the victims' bloody pictures. He tried to see Ace in their eyes. If Ace pulled a gun on them, would they show that same surprise? What bothered Dave was that the victims had to have trusted their killer. Could anyone trust Ace? Ace said they were summoned to the traps under false pretenses.

Maybe the housewife and the hooker were dumb enough to go to a deserted place. And maybe the cheerleader was naïve enough. But the stockbroker? Kimberly Worth was a savvy, high-powered woman. Wall Street didn't teach trust. Why would she venture into a lonely park after dark with a lowlife like Ace?

Dave stood before Reuben's photo and tried to climb into his mind. Reuben knew Ace the best. The pain of death seemed almost eclipsed by the shock on what was left of his rubbery face. Would the transformation of big-talking Ace into an actual gunman bring on such an expression?

Near dawn, with the cat cradled in his arm, Dave fell into an exhausted sleep. Right before the alarm rang, he was dreaming not of gunmen and murder but of Megan and her bewitching smile.

He arrived at work just in time to join the Ladykiller task force gathered around the TV. Mancuso was holding a live press conference. All the chief of detective's toadies stood behind him proudly. The only person there who was part of the Ladykiller investigation, Blake, was off to the side, barely in camera range. He wasn't smiling.

But Mancuso was. "Ladies and gentlemen, we have arrested a suspect in the Ladykiller case," Mancuso announced solemnly. He went on to describe Ace's past, saying he had been arrested for armed robbery as a teenager. "This man is a vicious criminal. He has a long arrest record."

"Of course most of that record is for picking pockets," Wise said.

"Viciously picking pockets," Safir said.

Dave recognized Jimmy Conlon's voice asking how Ace had been apprehended. "My team assembled a personality profile of the perpetrator," Mancuso said, his distaste for the media overshadowed by his jubilation. "We distributed it to all uniformed patrols. Two alert officers on 42nd Street stopped Cronen for questioning and found a .45 on him. The weapon turned out to be the ballistics match of the murder weapon, and he confessed to everything."

A murmur of outrage from the Ladykiller task force swelled as Mancuso answered more questions.

After the press conference, the others stormed off. Dave sat and watched Ace being led into the courthouse for his arraignment on the murder charges. Although surrounded by big, thick-bodied officers, Ace could clearly be seen by the camera. His skinny frame and nervously grinning face gave him the appearance of a hyperactive child.

Someone managed to thrust a microphone through the phalanx of cops. "Why did you kill them?"

"They were stupid."

A cop shoved the correspondent's arm and mike out of their protective circle, and they moved on.

"He loves this," Dave murmured to himself.

Dave returned to his desk and phoned Dr. Solomon to make arrangements to examine Reuben's files. "I realize they may have used other names and worn disguises, but we'd like to try to establish that the victims were Reuben's clients."

"Oh, of course. If you need to," Dr. Solomon said distractedly. "We're overrun with the media. Thank goodness Nita is handling them. It's all most perplexing."

Dave phoned Jimmy from a phone booth outside, hoping he would be back in the newsroom. He was.

"Chip is ragging me for not getting this story ahead of the press conference," Jimmy said. "Told me one of his little Ivy League, squash-playing buddies could do a better job. I wanted to ask Mancuso about your contribution, but I figured that would just make trouble for you."

"That's for sure," Dave said. "Listen, with any luck, I'll have a big news break for you by day's end. I'll try to make it before your deadline. I just can't say anything yet."

"Give me a hint."

"Can't. But, Jimmy —"

"Yeah?"

"Don't go anywhere."

Like ancient evil, the tawdry filth of late morning hung about the Deuce: the neon glow of the nudie reviews was dim and ghastly in the full light, the people sallow and sunken instead of fluid and mysterious, the sun itself a broken yolk mess. Dave looked into each face he met until he found the right one.

Finesse nodded Dave into the dark, urine-soaked recess of a shuttered store's doorway. "Do you believe that shit?" Finesse said. "Our own little Ace is the Ladykiller himself. My, my, my, how the donkey does fly."

Dave leafed through a wad of bills. "Where did he get the gun?"

"Funny you should ask me that little thing," Finesse said, ogling the money as Dave's cat did its food dish. "Day before yesterday, I'd say, Ace was wanting to borrow some two hundred large. I wouldn't piss my hard-earned money away, but somebody did. Heard Ace used it to buy hisself a piece from Tony Topnut."

"The day before yesterday?"

"Sure as shit."

"Pleasure doing business with you, my man,"

Finesse gleefully pocketed the dollars. "But I ain't one to gossip, so you ain't heard it from me."

As the afternoon eased into its yellow home stretch, the reporters, photographers, and TV camera crews left, and the West Side Crisis Center began to return to normal. Clients, scared off by the commotion, came out of hiding. They needed heavy reassurance that, even though Ace had been a regular, they had been safe.

"I loved him like a son," the old man howled in the corner. "Do you know what it's like for a man to lose his son?"

"He wasn't your son," Nita told him firmly. "Now, we've arranged a small snack for you. Why don't you join the others?"

The clients soothed, Nita collapsed at her desk chair in exhaustion.

Dr. Solomon came dithering up to her and said, "Marvelous job today, Nita. Really first-rate. Do you know where I left my glasses? Sometimes I —"

"By your seat in the conference room."

Sweeney ambled into the room, adjusting his zipper. He gave Nita a big, friendly, reassuring smile. "So, they nailed that sucker, huh?"

"Sweeney, what are you doing here?" Nita asked, sitting up.

"I know I'm a little early, but I could use the overtime. The day guy's kid took sick and his wife had to work."

"I mean, we don't need protection anymore. They've arrested the killer."

"I do what I'm told, and nobody has told me not to come here to stand duty. It beats walking the beat."

Megan, nervous, floated into the room. She poured some coffee and approached Nita's desk. "What a day. No peace. I . . . I came by to see how you were."

Nita glanced at Sweeney, who was watching them both with interest. "You know, Sweeney, I could go for a sandwich about now."

Sweeney hitched up his belt. "Hey, there's an idea. Guess you two want to talk girl talk, huh?" After Nita gave him a sharp look, he continued, "Uh, women talk. People talk." He laughed.

"Corned beef on rye?" Nita said.

"You got it," Sweeney said. He looked questioningly at Megan, who was clenching and unclenching her hands.

"She'll share mine," Nita said.

Sweeney nodded and left.

Nita arched an eyebrow at Megan. "And they say one is never around when you need him. So. Your little investigation is concluded, it appears."

Megan sighed. "It appears."

"And how was your date with Inspector Clouseau?"

"He had to leave early. When they arrested that guy, Dave had to, well . . . leave."

"Too bad."

"I just don't know what to do," Megan said. "What's wrong with me?"

"Nothing's wrong with you. You're doing fine."

"I *was* doing fine, and now my life doesn't make any sense, somehow," Megan said.

"Maybe you simply need more time," Nita said. "That detective seems to be taking a lot of your time. Please don't tell me you're upset because he hasn't called."

Megan's eyes filled with tears. She dabbed at them. "You're right. He hasn't called."

Nita leaned across the desk and spoke firmly to the younger woman: "Megan, you've got to get your concentration back. You're falling apart."

"I haven't felt like this about anyone for a long time."

"And look what happened the time before. You want my advice, Megan?"

Megan said, "Yes," softly, her expression pleading.

Nita's face was as hard as New York pavement. "Dump him, Megan. I have a bad feeling about him."

Megan looked searchingly at her friend.

"You've got your career," Nita went on. "You've got your goals. He'll get in your way."

"Oh, no. He'd never —"

"Yes, he would. And let me tell you something else. He would never let you interfere with *his* work. He'll leave you at a moment's notice, day or night, since his work is more important than yours ever could be. If you're convenient for him, fine. If not, he'll forget you until he needs you again."

Megan blushed at the possibility.

"Listen," Nita said, "remember the Faust myth? He's tempting you with empty promises. He wants your soul."

As Megan listened, she began to cry. "It's awful. I don't know what to do."

In a rage, Nita exploded out of her chair and flew up to her young protégé. Megan cowered and shrunk before her. Nita pushed her into a seat, and she stood over the younger woman, powerful and dangerous.

"Stop this," she shouted at Megan. "Stop whining. If you want to throw yourself away on this cop, do it. If you want to fuck him, then fuck him. But stop whining. Christ, how I hate victims."

Megan stifled a sob. "You don't know him. He's a wonderful man. A kind man. A strong man. Nita —"

"I know him perfectly. And I know you." Nita put her hands on Megan's shoulders.

Megan lifted her water-streaked face up to Nita. "What?" she asked beseechingly, almost fearfully.

With her fingertips, Nita gently traced the line of Megan's cheek. Megan trembled slightly at her touch and her lips parted. Nita leaned closer and looked deep into her eyes. Megan thought, for an instant, that Nita was going to kiss her, but she did not. The startlingly intimate moment left both women breathless.

Dave waited across the street from the Foxy Lady until Tony Topnut sauntered through the front door. He came in every day in the late afternoon, ready for a night of peddling watery drinks and slippery sin.

Dave had just gotten back from seeing his mother in Queens. As ever, it had been a trying experience. Mrs. Corrigan had hovered around the bedside, complaining about hospitals and the sad state of the world. His mother lay in bed in a frilly, oddly girlish nightgown, bony and filled with weariness.

"I have one son, and he can't find himself a decent woman to give me a grandson," she told Mrs. Corrigan, as if Dave were invisible.

"Well, to tell the truth, Ma, I'm starting to see someone now," Dave said. "She's very nice."

"Not another hooker, I hope," Mrs. Corrigan said acidly.

Dave exhaled loudly. "She's a very nice girl, Ma. I'd like to bring her by when you're up to it. I'm sure you'd like her. Her name's Megan. Megan Morrison. She's part Irish."

"Part Irish," his mother said. "That woman of your father's was part Irish. When I die, don't you let her come to my funeral."

Dave crossed 42nd Street at the light. The traffic strained at the crosswalk, eager to lunge at every pedestrian and splatter him across their hoods. It would be a wild night on the Deuce, and the animals would howl.

Tony Topnut, his Hawaian shirt featuring bare-breasted hula girls, presided at the bar, where the lost souls clustered for their seamy communion. A woman in pasties and a G-string gyrated on stage, her sagging belly keeping time to the thumping music. Dave gave Tony Topnut a mock salute. Tony Topnut stopped his chore, wiping dirty glasses with a dirty rag.

"What do you want, Dillon?" Tony Topnut was smug and mean today, capable of facing down every cop in the city or every demon from hell.

"In the back," Dave said, and jerked his thumb.

"What the fuck for?" Tony growled.

"Because it's good for your health."

Tony Topnut threw his rag down on the bar in disgust and walked toward the back.

En route, Dave passed Billy Ray Battle, who sat at the bar over a beer. He glared at Dave, his eyepatch in place.

Dave stopped. "I heard you made bail."

Billy Ray muttered something obscene and inaudible. He turned away. Dave kept going.

In the back, among the mops and ladders, Tony Topnut crossed his arms across his bulk. "What, Dillon?"

"I got it on good authority that you sold a piece to Ace."

"Your authority is smoking the wacky weed, Dillon. I don't sell no guns. Not to nobody. You trying to haul me into the Ladykiller case, selling unlicensed weapons to murderers? No chance."

"Listen, you don't like me, and I don't like you. But you know I'll be straight with you and I'm telling you that I'm not aiming to charge you or anyone else with a weapons beef. I don't care if you sold Ace a warehouse full of crack. Your dealings with him stay in here."

"What's your question, Dillon?"

"Did you sell him a .45 day before yesterday?"

"Why should I tell you?"

Dave caught Tony Topnut by his fleshy throat and slammed him against the wall. "Because if you don't, I will kill you."

"I did, I did, I did," Tony Topnut croaked. Dave released him, and he rubbed his throat. "Brand-new .45. Got it off this Bolivian dude. No way Ace could've used that gun for any of his killings. Television said the gun he used was forty years old."

'"We haven't found a brand-new .45 in Ace's room," Dave said. "How do you explain that?"

"How the fuck should I know, Dillon? Jesus."

The West Side Crisis Center was bathed in the crimson light of the hamburger-pink sunset. There was an eerie, after-the-battle calm about the place. Dave used his key to let himself in. When he topped the stairs, Nita stood waiting for him. File folders lay in piles atop a creaky old table.

"Here are Reuben's files, detective," Nita said. "As you requested. I truly hope that this will be the end of it. You have your murderer. We'd like to get back to business as usual, if you don't mind."

"Where's Megan?"

"I have no idea. We've been busy here, thanks to you people. She must be tired."

"If you see her, please tell her I'll call her later."

Nita said nothing. She settled down at her desk to do her own paperwork, but Dave felt her watching him.

Dave couldn't find any files that remotely resembled the victims. No housewives with handicapped children, no cheerleaders with teen problems, no stockbrokers, no hookers with AIDS.

"No luck," Dave said to Nita. "I'd better examine the other files to see if they got mixed up with the other social workers'. Or maybe Ace was mistaken or lying about whose clients the victims were."

"You'll have to arrange that with Dr. Solomon, detective. This is outside my purview. I am sorry."

"The funny thing is," Dave said, "that I can't find Ace's file. It was here when we were going through the files together."

"I don't know about that, detective," Nita said. "You were the last one to touch it. We entrusted the files to you, and I do hope you haven't lost one."

"The file would have been helpful in Ace's prosecution, Nita," Dave said, ignoring her accusatory tone.

"That's not my concern."

"Ace murdered your colleague and, supposedly, four of your crisis center's clients — and this is not your concern?"

"Today has been a long day, detective. Please don't make it any more trying. I'll deal with my grief in my own way." Nita resumed reading.

"Something else is odd," Dave said.

She lowered the paper in front of her. "What is that?"

"Reuben's file on Ace was neatly typed. His other files here are a mess. Some are even handwritten. Why should Ace's file have been any different?"

"If you hadn't lost it, maybe we could find an answer," Nita said shortly. "Now, if you don't mind, would you please leave and let me get on with my work?"

"Your work isn't the only important work, Nita."

"Is that a fact?" Nita lay down the report she had been reading. "Your work is done, detective. Time for you to go out and get drunk with all your pals, slapping butts or whatever you do in your spare moments. You've caught your killer."

"Have we, Nita? Have we really?"

"You're the policeman. You tell me."

"I'm fascinated by serial killers," Dave said. "And this building has something to do with the Ladykiller that we still don't comprehend. It's interesting how it starts."

"How what starts?" Nita sat back in her chair in an attempt to be calm.

"Serial killings. With Henry Lee Lucas, Ted Bundy, practically all the infamous serial killers, the series started in the same manner. See, the first incident was an accident. Then they went through a panicked phase, fearful they would be caught. When nothing happened, they got cocky. They started to plan the murders. No accidents anymore. Method. Calculation. They began to think of themselves as God. No one could touch them. They were smarter than the police, than the victims. They didn't grasp the awful penalty of their actions, even if they never got caught."

"Penalty, detective?"

"They had lost their humanity. They'd descended into madness. They were lost to the world. They were lost to themselves and to whatever nobility they once aspired to."

"I'm not an expert on this subject, detective," Nita said, after a pause.

"I don't believe Ace Cronen is the Ladykiller," Dave said evenly. "I don't believe he has what it takes to kill another human being."

Nita stared at him. "How can you be sure, detective?"

Dave tapped his forehead. "Cop's intuition."

Clumping down the stairs, he met Megan. Dave brightened and reached to embrace her. But she shrank away from him.

"What's the matter?"

"Not here." She pushed past him on the stairs.

He caught her arm. "Look, I'm sorry I didn't call. I've been busy with the arrest and had to visit my mom. Please don't be mad. Maybe we could get a bite to eat."

"I can't. Not now. Nita is waiting for me."

"What's going on, Megan? I thought we —"

"Not now, Dave. Not here." She ran up the stairs.

"Megan," he called after her. She disappeared into Nita's territory at the top of the stairs. Dave slowly walked downstairs and out the door.

Nita took Megan out for dinner to a tiny French restaurant, where the waiters fussed over them and the food blessed the palate. She listened as Megan talked confusedly about men in general and Dave in particular.

"God, I wanted him," Megan said over coffee. "I wanted him so bad."

"Megan, please," Nita said with a small smile. "Hormonal urges are awfully trivial, aren't they? Your work is far more important than some man, no matter how sexy he seems."

"I know," admitted Megan, miserably.

The restaurant's owner brought over brandy and insisted they join him in a small drink. Nita thanked him and told him no.

"Let's go back to my apartment for a night cap."

At Nita's, they both threw down their bags and kicked off their shoes. Megan collapsed into a chair. Nita poured them cognacs. Then she noticed Megan staring past her. She turned around and saw that her bag was open and the butt of her new .45 was sticking out. How had she been this careless?

"Oh, my God," Megan exclaimed. Her eyes were as wide as headlights.

Megan charged out of her chair. But she sailed right past Nita's open bag to stand beside the fish tank, bent over in wonder. "Is that bright blue one new? I've never seen anything so beautiful."

"Do you like it?" Nita asked. She casually strolled over to the tank, making certain to close her bag on the way.

"I love it." Standing close together, they toasted the bright blue fish.

Once Megan had left, Nita sat in her window and gazed at the apartments across the street, imagining them to be Skinner boxes, compartments for rats in psychology experiments. One couple was arguing, their unheard invective fairly reddening the air. Another couple was reading, him a newspaper, her a paperback. And a lonely young woman was absorbed in television, mentally chewing her cud. The lonely young woman bore a resemblance to Megan.

She thought about what Dave Dillon had said about serial killers. Obviously, the man had read some foolish FBI pamphlet. She had been interested and had failed to take offense. Because the serial-killer genre did not apply to her. Nita also possessed some rudimentary knowledge about the breed. She had done some preliminary research to doctor Ace's file, to which she forged Reuben's signature. She had thrown in the part about Ace's violent youth and cruelty to animals to hook Dillon — and the ploy certainly had worked. She was actually pleased that Dillon was sharp enough to spot the difference between the cleanly typed, doctored file on Ace and Reuben's other files. But Nita remained convinced that, in the end, she had Dillon and the police fooled.

Still, she kept returning in her mind to his description of the first killing in a series. An accident? Well, Evelyn Hernandez was an accident, truth to tell. Nita remembered her frustration with the woman, who insisted on staying with her abusive husband, insisted on bringing handicapped children into the world — and was pregnant again.

"I don't care if my husband, he beats me," Evelyn said. "My babies, they love me."

"But you're bringing burdens into this world," Nita argued. "Say what you want about your husband, the man can't cope financially.

The children are often in pain. They contribute nothing to society. This makes no sense."

"My babies love me," Evelyn insisted, drawing the scarf around her head and looking about anxiously, as if someone she knew would recognize her.

And so it had gone. Over and over on continuous play. Nita tried every manuever she knew to shake the woman awake. To no avail. Finally, she arranged to meet Evelyn out of the crisis center. Nita figured a trip to the SPCA would work; she would let Evelyn listen to the cries of the doomed animals and make the point that her babies weren't much better off.

The lesson, though, didn't take. "My babies love me," Evelyn said over the dogs' barking.

"These animals are going to be put to sleep, you idiot," Nita shouted at her. "Can't you get that through your thick skull?"

"My babies love me," Evelyn repeated maddeningly.

Nita pulled out the .45, which she had always carried for protection. She pointed it at Evelyn's right eye, the one that fronted for the irrational, the emotional, the intuitive half of the brain — the half of the brain that should be brought under control in a well-functioning society.

She pointed the .45 at the startled Evelyn's right eye and said, "They put these troublesome animals to sleep."

Perhaps if Evelyn hadn't stubbornly repeated, "My babies love me," Nita would not have pulled the trigger. But she did, and half of Evelyn's head exploded. Nita stood over the woman's fallen body, not in shock, rather with a strange sense of triumph.

And just as Dillon had said, she went through a period of intense fright that she would be discovered. And when that didn't occur, she set about dispatching her other hopeless cases, cleansing the world of them. The cheerleader, the stockbroker, and the hooker — each brought more harm than good to society.

Descent into madness? No, Detective Dillon, that hadn't happened to Nita Bergstrom. If anything, she had descended into sanity.

What could that testosterone-dosed monkey with a badge understand? And with Ace taking the rap for her first set of removals, she could begin again in a different way, in peace until she had completed her work.

Nita smiled serenely at the Skinner boxes across the street, at the poor people ensnared in their anger, their alienation, their loneliness. Oh, what gorgeous alchemy she would perform.

Ace sauntered up to Dave as jauntily as if he were trolling the Deuce. Neat for once, garbed in jailhouse blues, he slid into a chair and burped. "Not bad eats you got in this place, Dillon. I like it here."

"None of the inmates given you an injection of hot beef yet, huh, Ace?"

Ace laughed. "Man, I'm a world-class prisoner. I don't mix with the other inmates. You assholes want to make sure your Ladykiller is fit to stand trial. I'm a fucking king."

"You're a fucking asshole, is what you are," Dave said. "I dropped by the crisis center to pull the files on your victims. They all were missing. I wonder why?"

Ace shrugged. "The place is a mess. Rueben couldn't find his ass with both hands. You accusing me of taking the files? Ooooo. That could draw me some serious prison time. I'm scared." He laughed again, enjoying himself.

"Tony Topnut told me he sold you a brand-new .45 a couple of days ago. That would be after you committed the murders."

"Tony said that?" Ace shrugged again. "So what? I wanted another .45 in case my old one broke down."

"Okay, smart ass, where is it?"

"I had it in my room. Maybe one of your thieving cop pals lifted it during their search. You bastards think you own the city." Ace belched once more.

Dave reached inside his jacket and produced a .45. He extended it to Ace, butt first. "You're right. Here it is. Take it. Go on. It's not loaded."

Ace was startled but said nothing. He reluctantly accepted the weapon. He held it with two fingers as though it were a bomb instead of a gun.

"I want you to show me how you field-strip the gun to clean it, Ace. That old .45, the murder weapon, was in mint condition. You really knew how to maintain it. You didn't want any jams when you cornered your victims. Go on. Show me."

Ace tried to hand the gun back to Dave. "I don't feel like playing your game, Dillon. Get the fuck out of my face."

"You don't know the first thing about this weapon, do you, Ace? Do you now?"

"Of course I do," Ace said. "I just don't want to let you jerk me around."

"Show me, Ace. Then I'll go. Break it down. Killer."

Ace fumbled with the L-shaped gun, moving the slide clumsily back and forth. But he couldn't get it to come apart. "The fucker's busted, Dillon. Jesus fucking Christ."

"You might try pressing the little button on the side."

"I did that, Dillon," Ace lied. "It's stuck. How do you expect me to —"

Dave grabbed the gun and removed the slide. He handed it back to Ace. "Try it now."

"Dillon, what are you —" Ace fiddled with the innards of the pistol, and it flew into pieces, the spring hitting the far wall. The rest fell on the floor.

"Very deft, Ace." Dave said. "Why don't you tackle putting the weapon back together again?"

"Why don't you fuck yourself, Dillon?" Ace jumped to his feet and pounded on the door for the guard to fetch him.

"You're not the Ladykiller, Ace," Dave said. "But I suspect you know who is. The night Reuben died, we have a witness who saw two people with him. I bet you were tagging along somehow. You aren't much for weapons, but you can tag along pretty well. Isn't that right, Ace?"

"Kiss my ass, Dillon."

"Oh, your ass is going to be out on the street, pal. Where it belongs."

Ace howled in panic.

"You don't have what it takes to be a killer," Dave told him as he left the room. "Sorry."

Ace pounded the wall. "No," he screamed. "No, no, no, no, no."

Dave made straight for an outside phone booth and called Jimmy Conlon. "Am I too late for deadline?"

⇒ ELEVEN ⇐

When Mancuso opened his late-edition morning paper, the sound from his office was like a soul cast into a fiery hell. He immediately summoned Blake.

The chief of detectives, his underlings fanned out behind his desk like centurions, waved the newspaper at the lieutenant.

"Where in God's name did this come from?" he demanded.

"Can't say, sir."

"Well I do know. Dillon filed a report saying Cronen is unfamiliar with the operation of a .45. No departmental decision was made about this yet. And I read it in the paper."

Blake said evenly, "Chief, it's very clear now that Cronen is not our killer. Unless we want to charge him with something else, we'll have to release him."

Mancuso threw the paper on his immaculate desk. "You are one terrific genius, Blake. My God, I'm going to look like a clown to the commissioner and the mayor."

"Cronen is not our man, chief. But he may know the real killer. Dillon proposes that we let Cronen go and put a tail on him. He'll lead us to our man and we'll all be heroes."

Mancuso's eyes narrowed in thought. Blake could almost see the wheels turning.

"Blake, I ought to bounce your ass off this case with a very bad black mark on your record. And I have a good mind to toss Dillon clear off the force. He doesn't belong in the NYPD. He's an accident waiting to happen."

"What about the plan, chief? It makes sense."

"Christ. All right. But one more fuck-up, one more nasty surprise, and you pukes are out the door."

Ace, his head hung so low his nose practically scraped the sidewalk, returned to the Deuce. He stopped in an electronics store and watched the TV news report on how a low-life scagball, Thomas Cronen, had been released. Turns out the no-good slug wasn't a killer after all.

The small Korean guy who ran the shop came to shoo Ace out. Then he recognized him. "You the big, bad Ladykiller." And he laughed, a deep belly laugh. The other customers joined in. Ace ran out of the store.

Maybe he should go back to his room, pack, and head for New Jersey. But he didn't belong there anymore either. They would laugh at him, too. His mother had vanished long ago. Even she would laugh at him now.

Up ahead on the street, Falstaff and his junkie pal were sprawled out against some steps. Ace slid up to them, preening. "You hear what the man called me? He called me the Ladykiller. The man, right?" Noticing his audience was inattentive, Ace sat down beside the old wino, who moved to make room. Very slowly, Ace leaned closer to the oblivious, daydreaming Falstaff.

"A killer," Ace screamed in his ear. "Me, man. I'm a killer."

Falstaff nearly had a seizure. He fell off the steps in his haste to get away from Ace. The junkie didn't budge.

"Hey, hey, hey," Falstaff said in confusion. He stumbled to his unsteady feet.

Ace leapt up, certain now that he had the wino's attention. "The man, right? The man called me a killer. What do you think about that, huh?"

The wino recovered his presence of mind and made a theatrical bow. "I'm deeply moved."

"Damn straight," Ace said. "A killer. With a .45. The fucking Ladykiller."

"How thrilling for you," Falstaff said, wiping his face with a large dirty handkerchief. Still wary of Ace, he sat back down beside the junkie.

Ace regarded Falstaff skeptically. "You jiving on me, man?"

"Heaven forfend."

Ace smiled slyly and slowly reached into the junkie's pocket. Falstaff was transfixed. Ace slowly pulled out a dirty cloth, which he unwrapped to reveal a used hypodermic needle. The wino stopped wiping his face and looked at him in fear. Ace very slowly made a fist around the hypodermic, raising the exposed needle aloft like a knife. The wino's attention was riveted to his every move. "I could do him," Ace whispered, "like I done all them others."

Falstaff watched, silent, horrified, fascinated, as Ace stood over the hapless junkie. Ace froze, his arm raised directly over his prey.

The big man collected his wits and lurched to his feet. "Ace, easy does it — don't — please." Falstaff backed away for a few feet, then he turned and ran awkwardly.

Ace stayed in his pose for a second, smiling. He dropped the needle and called after the retreating wino, "But I ain't got my gun with me."

Flushed with the gratifying response to his demonstration of mastery, Ace set forth down 42nd Street with some of his old swagger. Until Jackie Why jumped out in front of him and ran him into a doorway.

Holding Ace against the wall by his throat, the pimp reached down with his other hand and grabbed Ace's balls and gave them a cruel squeeze. Ace squeaked like a mouse.

"Today's Saturday, babes," Jackie snarled. "You owe me a chunk of change, I do recall. Where the fuck is it?"

"The cops screwed me up, Jackie," Ace said in a tight voice. "I can get it next week. Don't hurt me."

"Ordinarily, Ace-hole, I would hurt you real bad." Jackie released him. "But on account of you're a celebrity, I'll give you the time. One catch: You owe me double." He smoothed Ace's ratty jacket. "But a vicious killer like you ought to have no problem arranging the green."

He chortled and left Ace there, holding his crotch.

Ace wheezed up to a pay phone and pumped in a quarter. When they answered at the crisis center, he asked for Nita Bergstrom.

"You heard?"

Nita was not in a good humor. "Don't call me here. Are you totally stupid?"

"I have to see you," Ace whined.

"Tonight." She hung up.

For Nita, concentration was virtually impossible. The staff meetings and client counseling sessions and paperwork all blurred by her. What did Ace's release mean? It had been negligent of her not to instruct Ace in the operation and maintenance of the .45. There simply had been no time.

Her real mistake, she knew, was underestimating Dillon.

Dave Dillon was waiting in the conference room with Dr. Solomon. The black woman detective was there too. The staff assembled slowly.

"I'm afraid that since the murderer is still at large," Dr. Solomon said, "that we must continue to help the police with their investigation. Megan, you are requested to accompany Detective Dillon on more of his interviews. And Nita, we'll need you to help Detective Loud here go through the rest of the files to see if we can find any mention of the victims."

"Dr. Solomon, I protest," Nita said. "We don't have time to go off on all these paper chases and Chinese fire drills. Our clients have suffered enough from this charade."

Dr. Solomon's resolve withered before her. "Well, um, perhaps you have a point, Nita. Uh, maybe next week. Or —"

"No way," Dave said forcefully. "I can get a court order in a half hour. And the publicity stemming from your reluctance to help us catch this killer will do your crisis center no good, I assure you."

"Oh, my," Dr. Solomon said. "How awkward —"

"Fine," Nita said. "If the detective won't admit he was wrong about the crisis center, we'll indulge him."

"Megan, let's go," Dave snapped.

The staff trudged out. Nita led Jamie to the file cabinets. "Here. I don't have time to help right now. Please leave everything in order, and please do not lose any of the files. We've had some trouble in that regard with you people."

"You got a pretty high opinion of yourself, don't you?" Jamie said.

"Detective, I have no idea what a woman of your obvious intelligence is doing on the police force." Jamie raised her eyebrows and Nita watched her appraisingly. She took a deep breath and decided to take a flyer. "But I wish you'd put your talents to work on Detective Dillon. He's making an ass of himself with my vulnerable young friend."

Jamie, prepared to lash into Nita, brought herself up short. "What do you know about Dave and me?"

"Only what I see."

"It's that obvious?"

"What's obvious is that you're a better woman for him than poor little Megan ever could be. I'd like to see you get him."

Jamie laughed, partly at the sharpness of Nita's insight, partly at how rapidly the social worker had disarmed her. "Girl, I tried every trick in the book on him. But he's wrapped up in the case. And when that's not going on, he's wrapped up in your friend. I can't fight it. Time to move on."

"You're wrong. If she doesn't suffer a relapse, I believe Megan is cured. He'll want a woman to bounce back with." She gave Jamie a sly, why-not smile.

"Better buckle up," Dave said as Megan settled beside him in the unmarked car. He started the car. "We're meeting a friend of Lydia Daniels. Another hooker, named Carla. What struck me was that Lydia was wearing a coat much too long for her the night she died. Her pimp, a nasty piece of work called Jackie Why, said Lydia had no other friends, but we asked around and found this woman, Carla. A tall woman. Carla is no fan of the police, which is one reason you can be a big help here."

Megan nodded. "I'll try."

The dark blonde hooker sat waiting for them in a booth at a seedy coffee shop. There were only a few other patrons, hunched over their coffee or sleeping on the Formica counter. The counterman, who showed hair sprouting from every orifice and patch of skin, was busy reading the racing form.

Even seated, Carla was tall. "You got my coat?"

Dave handed her a bundle as he slid along the cracked Naugahyde seat all the way to the window. "We don't need this anymore. It's been dry-cleaned." Megan sat down beside Dave.

"Any blood on it?" Carla asked as she ripped open the paper package.

"Not now," Dave said. "Dry cleaner did a good job."

Carla swiped the package onto the floor. "Ick. I don't need no coat been doused in blood. Uh-huh. I'll get me a new coat."

"You're aware that she tested positive for HIV?" Dave said.

"Lover, are you paying me for my time?" Carla said. "Time is money, honey, and Jackie likes us girls to keep up the cash flow."

Dave grimaced. "Not in the budget, Carla. Sorry. We hoped you'd help us out because Lydia was your friend."

"Sweetcakes, the only friend I got is named Jack Daniels," Carla said. She started sliding out of the booth. "If you'll excuse me, I must be moving along."

"Sit down," Dave growled.

"Darling, unless you're arresting me, I don't have to talk to you," Carla said. "So, toodles."

"She went to the West Side Crisis Center, didn't she?" Megan asked.

Carla jerked a thumb at Megan. "Who's this, Dillon? Little Bo-Peep?"

"I'm a caseworker at the crisis center," Megan said. "Apparently, this killer is preying on our people. We've got to stop him. He killed Lydia. He killed a friend of mine, and he'll go on butchering innocent people if we don't find him."

Dave, surprised as much by what Megan said as by the passion with which she said it, stared at her.

Carla stopped sliding out of the booth. She sat opposite Megan now. "Did you know her? Lydia?"

"I don't think I did. We get a lot of clients. And we suspect that she wore a disguise anyhow. Many people are ashamed to be seen coming there."

"She did," Carla said. "Put on this funny Tina Turner wig. She was scared that Jackie would find out. Jackie, he don't like nobody messing with his girls' heads. If he heard that Lydia was bitching about him to somebody, that girl would be dead meat."

Dave started to ask a question, but Megan held up a hand to silence him. Then she asked exactly what Dave wanted to know: "What social worker did she see at the crisis center?"

"She never told me. She was real secretive. Whoever, this person had a real hold over her. Lydia thought this caseworker was God. Lydia did a lot of her tricks raw — like, without the condom — and this caseworker told her she was spreading AIDS. Lydia didn't believe the test, so she kept accepting the hot shots. Guys like it better, see?"

"Did Lydia say who she was going to meet the night she died, Carla?" Megan asked.

"She said she had an important date. And it was no trick. That's all I know."

Outside the coffee shop, the hooker moved her tall frame into the spring afternoon. Dave smiled at Megan in admiration. "You did great in there. Thanks."

"You're welcome." Megan smiled. "It pays to be nice to people."

"Hey, Megan, I'm crazy about you. I want to be really nice to you."

"I'd like that."

"Do you like music?"

She nodded.

"There's some great music I want you to hear. With me." He ripped a piece of paper out of his notebook and scribbled an address. "Tonight. Eight o'clock. Meet me on this corner and we'll walk. How about it? Then I'll fix you dinner. You like steak?" He seemed boyishly eager, needy. She couldn't stop smiling. "Please come."

Megan accepted the notebook paper and put it in her purse. "I don't know," she said with a small laugh, "I'm not sure I should be alone with you in your apartment."

"My cat will chaperone."

Megan caught herself giggling like a schoolgirl. And as she walked off into the skipping beat of the avenue, she felt the warmth of Dave's eyes on her. She thought it was just as well that she had the afternoon off — she had to register for courses at Hunter — and wouldn't encounter Nita.

Ace slunk into the Foxy Lady. Tony Topnut spotted him and bellowed, "Take cover, it's the Ladykiller." A few of the regulars erupted in a maelstrom of hoots and catcalls. They pelted Ace with bar coasters and wadded-up napkins.

But Ace found who he was after. Billy Ray Battle sat at the far end of the bar, wearing his eyepatch and sipping his beer.

"What the fuck do you want, dickbrain?" Billy Ray said.

"Billy Ray," Ace said, at a loss for words.

"You and me got the distinction of being Ladykiller-for-a-day," Billy Ray said. "Ain't that sweet shit?"

"I need your advice."

"If I ever cross paths with that Dillon again, I'll boil his ass for breakfast. That's a natural fact."

"You're good at handling women," Ace went on. "Guy like you, the chicks go nuts. Listen, I got this, like, problem. I been seeing this real crazy bitch. And I mean, nuts. Fact is, she scares the shit out of me. She wanted me to do something, and I fucked up. Now she wants me to meet her tonight."

"Simple." Billy Ray burped. "Don't show up."

"Not that simple," Ace said. "I got a real thing for her. I got to go. I got to hear what she says."

"You fucking this bitch?"

"Well, uh, sure. But she's crazy, man. I never can predict what crazy, wild-ass shit she'll pull."

"Let me guess," Billy Ray said. "You want me to be your bodyguard. That it?"

"Yeah, uh, I guess you could, sort of — Uh-huh."

"She pretty?"

"Pretty?" Ace said. "She's a walking wet dream."

Billy Ray licked his lips. "Good. I like them pretty."

Nita had a while between the end of her long day at the crisis center and the start of her shift on the hotline. Tim would be her partner tonight. She realized she hadn't heard from Megan and wondered how her friend had fared with Detective Dillon. Nita called Megan's home and got her machine.

"Called to say hi. Nothing important. Wanted to hear how course registration went today. And of course, how your gumshoe work went with the red-light district's favorite dick. Why don't we have dinner tonight before my shift?"

Realizing she needed some air, Nita went for a walk. Evening was about to settle in. The street moved at an underwater pace. She passed the building where she had shot Reuben. Bloodstains were still visible. If only that fool hadn't disrupted her plans, how much easier her progress would be. And she never should have used Ace for a deceptive ploy. She could almost hear her father telling her that she wasn't as good as she thought.

The weight of the .45 seemed extra heavy in her bag. Tonight would be the first time firing this weapon. She had taken it apart, cleaned and oiled it, inspected every part, and dry-fired it — no bullets — repeatedly. Tonight, she would set matters right. Her feet clicked resolutely along the sidewalk.

Then, once again, she heard the steps behind her. Right behind her. Keeping time with her. Mocking her.

She whirled around.

Nobody. Down the street, a dust devil of spring air whirled scraps of paper about in a teasing spiral.

Megan couldn't help herself. She walked up to the designated corner feeling heady, both guilty and excited at the same time. Dave was waiting for her, leaning against his illegally parked car and watching her approach with frank admiration. She noted with relief that he wasn't wearing a tie. She had agonized over what to wear and decided on a simple but stylish sweater dress that could go to a concert or a jazz club with equal aplomb.

Dave kissed her quickly. The glint in his eye was enough to make her tingle as the memory of that night flooded her senses. She shook her head to clear it, sending her reddish curls bouncing.

"Well, where are we going?"

"Right here," Dave replied teasingly and bowed and stretched out his hand to usher her down a subway entrance.

"But you said we were going to walk there," Megan said, confused. "And your car's right here."

"We are going to walk. Trust me."

Megan marched obediently down the dank concrete stairway. Dave followed her. He was clearly enjoying his little game.

A train was roaring through the local station on the express tracks, and without trying to talk over the deafening roar, Dave handed Megan a token with a small flourish. She accepted it with a puzzled look and went through the turnstile onto the platform.

There was a small knot of patrons clustered at one end of the platform. Dave touched her elbow to steer her toward them. The sound of the express train's noisy passage died away in the distance and was replaced by the sweetest sound Megan thought she had ever heard. She forgot her problems. She forgot the rank smells and crude graffiti-strewn walls of her immediate environs. She walked toward the voice.

When she reached the small crowd, she saw a short, fat black woman in African dress and lots of colorful jewelry singing a sad French song a cappella. The lovely voice in the natural echo chamber of the subway took on a rich, vibrant quality. The hairs stood up on the back of Megan's neck. She barely breathed. The only coherent thought that crossed her mind was that this was what Edith Piaf must have sounded like.

Without interrupting her song the woman smiled and nodded at Dave who gave a small wave. Megan was brought back to her surroundings and took his arm and gave it a squeeze of gratitude. The slightly mournful song ended just as a train pulled into the station.

A few of the listeners got on the train, several of them pausing to put money in a basket at the singer's feet. At least one was wiping away a tear. Much of the audience did not budge and Megan realized that they must be regulars. Dave too. The singer came up to Dave and put her hands on his face to pull him down and kissed him warmly on both cheeks. She smiled at Megan, who blushed as if she had been introduced to an angel.

As the train roared away, the singer returned to the center of the circle of her fans and spoke in a lilting island patois. "I'd like to dedicate this song to my friends and to lovers everywhere."

She began to sing again, an achingly beautiful French love song. Megan leaned against Dave when he put his arm around her and listened, her eyes brimming.

When Dave unlocked his door, Megan produced a bottle of Chianti from her large shoulder bag and handed it to him.

"Great. Thanks. But first, let me introduce my roommate."

But the cat already had sashayed up to Megan and rubbed her legs. Delighted, she picked it up and cuddled it. The cat purred with engine-room-level happiness.

"A cat person," Dave smiled approvingly.

"And a music person," Megan said warmly.

"My mother didn't like either, so I'm making up for it," Dave said. He uncorked the wine, which gave a merry pop.

"How is your mom?" Megan asked as she rubbed cheeks with the cat.

"Better. She cursed the mailman from her bedroom window today. Always a good sign. I marinated the steaks to a fare-thee-well. How do you like yours?"

"Bloody," she said.

He smiled widely. "Me too." As if their concurrence on cooking beef portended other, more delicious, similarities.

They sat on the couch and drank Megan's wine. The cat sat between them and they took turns stroking it. Their conversation was fun and lively. Sometimes, they just smiled at each other for no good reason.

Then Dave got up to put the steaks in the broiler and toss the salad. Megan wandered about his apartment, impressed by its neatness and the solid, manly but tasteful furniture.

She went into the wrong room.

"Jesus," Megan said, spilling her wine. She stumbled back out holding her hand to her mouth.

Dave rushed to her side and held her shoulders. "God, I'm sorry," he said. "I forgot to take the pictures down. They're a part of my life now, and well —"

"It's so gruesome. And poor Reuben. My God."

"I told you that I — Well — Why don't you sit down? I'll get you more wine."

"Where's the bathroom?" she asked in a choked voice.

He pointed, and Megan ran inside, shutting the door after her. Dave poured more wine and watched the door, troubled. He shouldn't have left the pictures up but he hadn't figured her for quite so squeamish.

When she emerged, her pallor was corpse-like. "I'm okay," she said weakly. "I'd better go."

"Please stay," Dave begged. "Let me take care of you."

"I need to make a phone call." Megan picked up the phone and stabbed out a number. No one answered and she hung up.

"That was to Nita, wasn't it?" Dave said.

"She wasn't home. She's doing the hotline later tonight. I'd feel better if I talked to her."

"You're so very loyal, aren't you?" Dave blurted angrily, and instantly wished he had shut up.

The color came back to Megan's cheeks at the mention of her

friend's name. "Absolutely. She cares about me. Why, do you have a problem with that?"

Dave knew he should be conciliatory, yet some gremlin inside kept driving him on. "Cares about you. Like Robin Tolner, your professor?"

"What?"

"I did some checking on the crisis center staff."

"Dr. Tolner was my adviser," Megan said.

"And your lover."

"Checking on the staff? More like snooping. My relationship with Robin is none of your business."

"I was curious what was behind your obsessive relationship with Nita. I guess you always get hung up on your mentor, don't you, Megan?"

"Don't play amateur psychologist. You're no good at it." Megan shook her head. "I don't believe this. I'm proud that Nita takes so much time with me. I've learned a lot from her."

"Is that why you don't make a move without consulting her?"

"Who are you to point a finger at me? You, the one who had a hooker for a girlfriend. You who killed her pimp out of jealousy. Who do you think you are?" Megan stormed past Dave and out the door.

The cat, no fool, had gone into hiding.

With deadline over, Jimmy Conlon worked the phones. The news-room, a cavernous expanse of computers and well-clipped heads, had hunkered down to an early-evening buzz. It would be at least an hour before Jimmy's story went through the copydesk. Tonight's effort, which would appear in the next morning's paper, wasn't spectacular: a recounting of the pressure on the police to catch the Ladykiller, now that Ace Cronen had proved to be inconveniently innocent. But his story last night, about police doubts of Ace's guilt, had set the city afire today.

Chip, resplendent in his power tie, summoned Jimmy over to the city desk with an imperious wave of the hand. He gestured disparagingly at Jimmy's story, which was gracing his computer screen. "Can't you do any better than this, Conlon?"

"Chip, I'm glad you're reading my stories. Did you, by chance, happen to read the one in today's paper?"

"Conlon, a story like that was overdue from you. To me, it only illustrated how far behind you've been on the Ladykiller beat."

"Chip, while I realize I should have solved the case by now for the cops, could you please show me who else in this city has beaten me on Ladykiller stories?

"That's not the point, Conlon —"

"No, the facts are never the point, Chip."

"What is the point, Conlon," Chip said, "is that we're giving Laird Caruthers the job as lead reporter on the Ladykiller story. We need someone a little more aggressive."

Jimmy felt as though someone was shoving a glacier down his throat. "Laird Caruthers? You mean, your younger brother's room-mate at Andover?"

"I mean, someone who can deliver. We'll allow you to backstop him, doing sidebars and day-to-day routine stuff. I expect you to give him access to all your sources."

Jimmy wanted to say much. His mouth no longer worked.

"If you'll excuse me," Chip said, "I have a dinner engagement."

Jimmy watched him sling his suit jacket jauntily over his shoulder and cross the newsroom to the managing editor's office. The managing editor stood there talking to Laird Caruthers. The three of them headed off for dinner.

Dave cooked the two steaks, regardless. Maybe Megan would return. Or maybe, he figured, he would recover his appetite and then some. He piled the steaks onto one plate and plunked it on the table.

"Is steak good for you?" he asked the cat.

The cat replied by about-facing and showing him its ass.

The buzzer went off. Without using the intercom, he pushed the button to let his visitor in the front door below. He mentally timed how long it would take her to ride the elevator. And when his doorbell rang, he threw the door open.

To Jamie. She wore a marvelous clingy blouse, pleated pants, and carried a bottle of wine.

Dave blinked. "What are you doing here?"

"Nice greeting. I'm dropping by. You busy?"

"No, I was just fixing dinner and — Come on in. You hungry?"

"You always set your table for two with flowers and a candle?" She swept by him in a cloud of sexy perfume.

"Every day." He watched her put the wine on the table, circle the room, taking in the posters and bookshelves, ducking her head into the kitchen.

"You know," he told her when she came back to him, "I'm really glad to see you." He was surprised to find that he meant it.

Jamie gave him a dazzling smile, a quick peck on the cheek, and a squeeze of the hand.

"Let's eat."

They had a pleasant meal, ate the food, drank the wine, talked, and laughed. Dave felt much better. The only work talk was Jamie's recitation about her findings in the crisis center files: nothing. They quickly moved on to other subjects.

After dinner, he poured two glasses of good port. When he sat down on the couch, Jamie surprised him by sitting down close to him. Very close.

"You don't mind, do you?"

"I, well —"

She set aside her glass and kissed him. He let himself open his lips. Her mouth moved against his, gentle but hungry. He could lose himself in a kiss like this.

But a few moments later, he broke from her and eased away from her down the couch.

"Jamie, I can't."

"What's the matter, Dave?"

"You're extremely attractive. I like you, but I can't."

"Talk to me."

"Megan was here a while ago. We had a fight and she left. I'm just incredibly hung up on her. I can't help it."

Jamie compressed her lips and got up. Dave looked up at her unhappily, but did not ask her to stay. She picked up her purse and stood looking down at him.

"Is she good for you, Dave? Will she give you what you need?"

"I don't know. I think so," Dave said helplessly, sounding less than convinced.

"God help you, my love."

When Ace met Billy Ray outside the Foxy Lady, where midnight's bone-crunching music refused to end, he had one question for the big man: "You packing?"

"What?" Billy Ray cupped his ear over the racket. The later the hour, the louder Tony Topnut turned up the music out on the sidewalk to attract roaming wastrels too far gone to discriminate between rotten and bad.

"You packing? You armed?"

"Fuck no." Billy Ray guffawed. "Cops took my .45 same as they took yours. I don't need no gun to go meet some pussy."

"I told you. She's nuts. She's got one. She can use it, too."

"Can't tell you how scared I am. I'm shaking like a fucking leaf." Billy Ray punched Ace's shoulder hard enough to make him stagger. "Let's move out. Show me this girl who got you so scared."

As they walked away from the Deuce, the streets took on a graveyard quiet. Ace wished he had Billy Ray's bravado. Ace's lips were dry. A manic butterfly was trapped in his throat. The only people they passed on the street were solitary and spectral.

"This lady," Ace said nervously, "she's something else."

Their shift over, the hotline torments of the late hours dealt with, Nita and Tim finished their logbooks.

Tim broke into a chorus of Paul Simon's "Still Crazy After All

These Years." He giggled. "This guy called who said his pee-pee was missing. I asked him where it went. He said the cat took it. I suggested he get some catnip. To ransom it."

Nita didn't respond. "You're tired. Go home and get some sleep. We have a long day tomorrow."

"Walk home?"

"No, thanks. I have to stay here for a while and catch up on the paperwork."

"No, I meant, walk *me* home," Tim said. "This time of night I get scared." He giggled some more.

Nita waited a few minutes after Tim slammed the front door. Sweeney was deeply asleep, sitting in a chair tipped back.

Midway down the stairs, she took the .45 out of her bag and checked the action.

Tailing Ace in the night was not what Safir and Wise had in mind as sweet duty.

"Where they going?" Wise asked.

"They're crossing that parking lot," Safir said.

"Shit. If we follow them across they'll make us."

"No sweat. Hang back a bit."

"We could radio for somebody till we can close the distance."

"And have some snot-nosed uniform ragging us that we can't do a tail by ourselves? I ain't ready for that tonight."

Wise considered the alternative. "At least they aren't moving fast. When it's our turn to cross the lot, let's not run, okay?" His new Florsheims felt like iron. "Not tonight."

Safir peered at Ace's and Billy Ray's departing backs. "This is where the Ladykiller iced the hooker."

"Yeah. One of my favorite tourist spots."

As soon as Ace and Billy Ray disappeared, the two detectives marched across the lot. When they got to the other side, they had a dilemma.

"Fucking A," Safir said. "Where did they go?"

*   *   *

"There she is," Ace said. Nita, a shadow under the faint stars, was locking the heavy metal door to the crisis center.

"Hey, ain't this the psycho house you go to?" Billy Ray said. "And ain't that the gorgeous piece of pussy what was on the news after they arrested your sorry ass? She was talking about this here loony bin and how it took care of sorry fuckers like you."

Ace gave him a look, but prudently did not say anything.

Billy Ray did not notice the look in the dark. "But I'll tell you this. You're right about one thing. She's a walking wet dream."

"Let me alone with her," Ace said. "You stay here."

"Fuck no. I want to meet me this little lady." Billy Ray hitched up his pants.

"Please give me a minute, Billy Ray. I'll pay you a hundred."

"You ain't good for no hundred."

"Please."

"You pathetic sack of shit." Billy Ray said disgustedly. "Go talk to the bitch. But then I get introduced."

Ace climbed out of the dense purple umbra and into the uncertain light of the street. He wished he had drunk more. But his throat was so tight that he doubted he could force one more drop down.

"Good evening," he said to her, trying for debonair. The result was more like strangled chicken.

"Walk with me," she said, all business.

They walked in silence.

"Have you ever followed me?" she asked.

"Me?"

"Like this afternoon on the street. Was that you, Ace? Was it?"

"I don't know what you're talking about. Can we talk about important stuff? Can we —?"

"In a moment. Did you mention me to the police?"

"What? You kidding? Me?"

"If you did, Ace," she said, "I'll find out. I'll know."

"No. Never. I'd never betray you."

"Good. That's good, Ace. You realize you let me down?"

"It ain't my fault," he whined. "Honest. I tried."

They reached the playground, whose slides and jungle gyms were weird, otherworldly shapes in the pit-deep night.

"Ace, sit on the end of that slide."

He did as bidden. "Shit, a slide," he said with nervous laughter. "I never had no slide when I was a kid."

"I'm glad you're having fun, now," Nita said. She reached in her handbag.

The constellations above threw a glint off her gun.

"Oh, no," Ace exclaimed, frozen to the spot. "Hey, wait. I love you. Please."

"It's necessary, Ace," she said. "The truth is I don't need you anymore. Sorry." She aimed carefully.

"Hey! What the fuck you doing, lady?" Billy Ray bellowed from the edge of the playground.

Nita turned her gun in the direction of the outburst. Ace used the opportunity to scramble off the slide and rat-run amid the equipment.

She fired at his flitting shadow. Missed. Then she couldn't see him.

She ran after Ace toward the street, where she heard a scurry of boots racing into the sanctuary of the night.

⇒ TWELVE ⇐

Dave's words echoed cruelly through Megan's mind all night, spoiling her sleep, and into the day, distracting her. When she bought coffee at the doughnut shop, she forgot to scoop up her change.

"Troubles, Megan?" asked the kindly old storekeeper after he'd called her back.

"Sorry," she murmured and picked up the coins.

She went back to her apartment and tried to read the paper. But the news columns were an inky jumble. The coffee cooled, untouched, as she stared through the newsprint and into the past.

Megan wished she had close friends to talk to. Or a mother. Or even a father. Both her parents were dead. And her old friends, the ones to whom secrets should be told, were years gone — married or in business school or law school, none of them near New York. What was she supposed to do? Pick up the phone and say, "Hi, remember me? My life is falling apart."

She shook her head ruefully. She only had one friend, but she realized she couldn't talk to Nita about this.

When she was younger, Megan expected that the coming years would make her more assertive and that her success was assured. She would be able to carve a career, a marriage, a family, and a boatload of happiness out of the future's glittering raw material.

Maybe she still expected that. Megan had obsessed about Dave and Nita all night. And now, thoughts of Robin kept assaulting her. She remembered sitting in his study, pretending to be reading her textbooks, and watching him write. He had seemed to glow, iridescent.

How could she have been so stupid? So blind? And was she doing it again?

She wanted Dave with a kind of physical craving. She also felt the kind of romantic longing for him that she had felt for Robin. She wasn't sure if she wanted to swoon in his arms or fuck him — hard.

She shook her head violently, laughing bitterly at her own distress. No. Enough. Maybe a walk would do her good.

She emerged into the day and noticed what she hadn't on her earlier coffee foray: How wonderfully spring-like the weather was. Then, as she strolled along, she noticed how many couples were out and about, holding hands, kissing. She resolutely suppressed a pang of envy and shook her head to clear it.

She marveled at how different her neighborhood was during the day, when the sunshine rendered it benign. She looked around with pleasure and the bounce came back into her walk.

She was smiling at a dog walker who had eight dogs of various sizes and breeds on leashes and was bopping along briskly, his charges well behaved and in perfect harmony, when she thought of Dave's cat. Why was it that every thought seemed to lead her back to him?

Then she heard her name.

Dave pulled up alongside her in his unmarked car. He was doing his best at a welcoming smile. Her heart skipped a beat.

"I'm sorry for what I said last night."

"Me too."

Without a word, Dave let Megan take the lead. He trailed her into the Cristides' coffee shop. They sat down at a small table.

Lucy Cristides' mother stalked over to them. "What you want?" she fairly snarled at Dave.

"Two gyros," Megan said. "And two Cokes."

Mrs. Cristides nodded tersely and left.

"You do the ordering often?" Dave said.

"Today I do." When the woman returned with the sodas, Megan said, "Let me ask you one question before we eat, and we'll leave you alone."

Mrs. Cristides sighed. "What you want?"

"The food here, I'll bet, is great."

"Is good. So what?"

"About Lucy," Megan said. "Did she like to eat this food?"

"Sometimes." The woman appeared to be warring with herself whether to walk away or stay.

"I understand she was pretty thin," Megan said.

"You want me to say bad things about my daughter, my Lucy? That what you want?" Mrs. Cristides wasn't belligerent now, but softer, even sorrowful.

"Tell me what bothered her," Megan said. "Tell me that, and we'll catch the man who killed her."

Her husband came out of the back and said, "Gina?"

His wife waved him away. "My Lucy —" She wiped a tear that had tumbled down her cheek. She pulled herself together with a visible effort. "My husband and I make people food. Sometimes Lucy served the food here for us. On weekends a lot, when we were very busy."

"And?" Megan gently prompted.

"My Lucy stopped eating the food. She said she was fat. She was not fat. She wanted to be thin. She got too thin. Like bones, my Lucy."

Her husband stood by mutely.

Gina Cristides brushed at another tear. "We worry. We make her eat. She make herself throw up. We read articles. We sent her to doctors. Nothing worked. She said she would deal with problem herself. Said she was getting help."

"Who —?" Dave blurted until Megan motioned for him to shut up. He did.

"We afraid she would starve to death," the girl's mother said. "No. She shot to death."

"Whom was she getting help from, Mrs. Cristides?" Megan asked, barely audible.

"She never told us."

"What did she say about this person, Mrs. Cristides?"

The woman's lips quivered. "She worshipped this person. This person was like a god to my Lucy. But my Lucy, she wouldn't tell us anything."

"I try to get Lucy to tell me," the father said. "I was worried about who my little girl was seeing. I said to Lucy, I said this person wasn't doing her any good. Lucy not get rid of the anorexia."

"Mr. and Mrs. Cristides," Dave broke in, "does the name Reuben Silver mean something to you?"

"Of course," the father said. "He the last one to die, right?"

"I mean, did Lucy ever mention him?" Dave asked.

Both parents shook their heads.

As they left, Dave said thoughtfully, "It's a funny thing. Carla said almost the exact same thing about Lydia. She was seeing someone she worshipped. Was Reuben capable of inspiring worship in his clients?"

"No. Reuben was a plodder. An old-fashioned paint-by-numbers social worker. His lack of inspiration, imagination, and commitment to the clientele drove Nita nuts. The best you can say is that he did his job adequately."

"What I can't understand is how Ace knew all the victims were clients of Reuben. We let Ace go before we asked him about that." Dave opened the car door for her.

"Can't you bring him back in?"

"I'm going to." Dave circled around the car and got in on the driver's side. "We assumed there would be files at the crisis center on the victims. That they were disguised, yet recognizable. Maybe we just didn't focus on them. So Jamie is going to go through them again. Jamie is very thorough."

"Is she?" Megan said, eyes straight ahead.

Dave was glad she didn't look at him because he knew he was blushing.

The Wall Street area, situated between a church graveyard and the river, was quiet on a Sunday. Long, stray shrouds of computer paper bounced in the quiet wind along the narrow streets lined by the discreet gray facades of the financial temples.

"Nobody's working today," Megan said. "The markets are closed."

"The people we're interviewing work today. And every day. Around the clock."

A bored guard with a gold earring let them into the lobby of a building after Dave flashed his badge. "Mr. Corson of Corson & Worth is expecting us," Dave told him.

"Give him my regards," the guard said. "Only don't give him none of my money. Go to the 14th floor."

Corson & Worth had a stark, white-on-white reception area. No one sat at the front desk. Dave knocked on the inner door. Then he tried to open it. Locked.

"Why don't you shoot it open?" Megan said with a laugh.

The door swung back on its hinges. A stout fellow in a gaudy tie and bold suspenders stood inside. The suspenders had a skull-and-crossbones insignia. Behind him were rows and rows of men in shirtsleeves, talking on telephones. "Are you the detective?"

Dave introduced himself and Megan. "You're Mr. Corson?"

"Sammy Corson. Yeah, that's me. Here, let's have a seat in the reception area. We don't exactly like to have outsiders on our floor. Information is money and all that." He spoke with the orotund assurance of someone keeping the secrets of the universe.

Dave and Megan sank into opposite ends of a chalk-white sofa. Corson leaned his fat butt against the empty receptionist's desk and fired up a cigar. "Hope nobody minds my smoke," he said. "Personally hand-rolled for me by the best British tobacconist in New York."

Megan made a face but said not a word.

"Today's busy, and I got to get back on the floor," Corson said. "What can I do for you?"

"Your partner was Kimberly Worth, right?" Dave said.

"Yeah, and did she ever know the market. And fearless. For a woman, she sure had a pair of brass balls." When Corson laughed, plumes of cigar smoke escaped his mouth like volcanic emissions. He waved the cigar at Megan. "No disrespect intended for your lady friend."

"Did Ms. Worth ever mention the West Side Crisis Center?" Megan asked.

Corson spread his hands, and a heavy chunk of cigar ash fell to the floor. "Nope. She gave to a bunch of charities. Could be this was one. Beats the hell out of me."

"Did she ever receive counseling of any kind?"

"From our lawyers? You bet."

"That's not what I meant," Megan said. "I was referring to psychological counseling."

"Kimberly? Nah. She was a woman, but she wasn't a pussy. She didn't need some damn shrink. Oh, we have a lot of stress in this business, all right. The stock market is war. Kimberly could stand on her own two feet, though."

"What does your firm do, Mr. Corson?" Megan asked.

"We trade common stocks, mostly. Nothing too exotic. No derivatives. No international issues. Just plain old common that the average Joe can understand."

"Uh-huh," Megan said. "Mainly blue chip stocks?"

"No, no. Penny stocks, really. From companies too small or young to be listed on a major exchange." Corson drew a circle in the air with his cigar. "We raise the money to fund the companies that will be the Microsofts of tomorrow."

"Well, with the exchanges closed today, how much trading could you be doing?"

"Today?" Corson took a savage puff on the cigar, whose tip glowed like the most wicked plutonium. He exhaled and the smoke wreathed his head. "Oh, today we're servicing accounts. Our staff works very hard. Money's a garden. You have to tend it constantly or it'll die."

As they headed into the elevator, Dave said admiringly, "You're up on the stock market."

"My father was a broker. He left me stock in his will. I play the market now and then."

"What do you make of this operation?"

"It doesn't smell right," Megan said. "It smells like a bucket shop. They peddle lousy small stocks to poor suckers they enlist over the phone. If you have any contacts with the Securities and Exchange Commission, I suggest you ask about Corson & Worth."

"As a matter of fact, I do," Dave said.

Ace and Reuben. Reuben and Ace. Damn, damn, damn.

Fate had a bad effect on over-confidence. Nita realized this now. She hadn't been able to dupe the cops with Ace. And she hadn't been able to position Ace so she could dispose of him. Nita had spent the night in her apartment, transfixed by the fish tank, charting her next moves. Panic would be fatal. A well-thought-out strategy, based on logical assumptions, was her best course.

The new blue fish swam slowly about, large-eyed and flat, almost two-dimensional. With transparent feathers of fins, it idly moved the water. Its deliberate motions had a certain majesty. The other fish, unsure of their place or purpose in a glass-bounded universe, darted around like unstable molecules. Nita thought irrelevantly that if the blue fish were a carnivore, it very quickly would be well fed and lonely.

First, Nita drew up the logical assumptions. Ace was very afraid of her — and probably still moonstruck, as well. But he would not go to the police because he hated them and knew they wouldn't believe him. He also likely had not left the city. From their counseling sessions, Nita was certain that he felt at home nowhere else and fancied that he was able to hide in the city's corners and crevices until danger passed. And judging from his delusions and intellectual vacuity, he undoubtedly had forgotten how much of his routine he had told Nita.

Next, Nita turned to the strategy. Ace must die and very soon. Although the cops probably wouldn't credit any of his stories, there was no sense letting them or anyone else hear about her doings. As a result, she should hunt him down, searching his various haunts. Before their encounter at the playground, she had considered switching weapons, confusing the cops about who Ace's killer was and giving her time to map out the second phase of her removals. But she planned to stay with the trusty .45: This was her gun, and she worked best with it. Big deal if the cops labeled Ace another Ladykiller homicide.

She wrapped a kerchief around her head, just as Evelyn Hernandez used to do, and popped on a pair of mirrored sunglasses. No one could see her eyes. It was a simple but effective disguise. Most people were very unobservant, and this would serve her well.

The .45 secure in her handbag, Nita set out into the buoyant Sunday. The initial stop was the sleazy rooming house off the Deuce that Ace called home. The entrance was guarded by a desk clerk, a slimy fellow with pockmarked skin and a cigarette dangling from his lips like a spent penis. He regarded her sullenly from behind his bullet-proof glass.

"I need the key to Thomas Cronen's room, please," she announced confidently.

"Who the fuck is that?"

"Ace."

"Oh, that hump. What you want in his room, lady? He owe you money, too?" The clerk gave a painfully dry laugh that wagged his cigarette, which seemed glued to his lower lip.

She slipped a fifty dollar bill halfway into the narrow slot at the base of the glass. "Please."

"Shit," the clerk said. "You got it, lady."

"Is he up there?"

"Fucked if I know." The clerk shoved a key through the opening and snatched the bill.

"If he comes in behind me, please don't tell him I'm here. I want to surprise him."

"No sweat. It's first floor, up that flight of stairs. Number of the room is on the key."

Ace's hallway was a tour through one of hell's grimmer precincts. Only one solitary bulb hung from the ceiling, an obscene appendage that shed meager light. The entire span smelled of the most pungent urine, as though minutes before, a band of extremely ill men had hosed it down. Crude drawings of enormous genitals decorated the walls. Behind one door, someone was laughing hysterically and nonstop. Behind another, two men were arguing in high-pitched voices.

"He's mine, you faggoty little bitch."

"Why don't you lick my lower intestine, like you do your daddy?"

The two men started smashing against furniture and screaming. The laughing person laughed louder. Nita felt her heart pounding.

Ace's rusty lock gave way with difficulty. He wasn't inside. His unmade bed was a tangle of gray, yellow-stained sheets. Empty beer and soda cans and fast-food containers littered the floor. Large roaches skittered among the debris.

"I can't wait for him here," Nita said aloud. Later, she knew, he could be found at the Foxy Lady, but not yet. She had some time to kill.

Everyone has a place they go to in times of stress. Some retreat to their homes, to bed or a favorite chair. Others head to a park, take a certain walk, sit under a favorite tree.

When Nita emerged from the elevator lobby onto the windswept open platform, she breathed in the brisk, clean, cold air with a sigh of relief. She had never told anyone, even Megan, how often she came here. It was her place and here she could think.

Ignoring the knots of tourists who mostly clustered around the coin-operated viewing machines set at intervals around the deck, Nita climbed a narrow metal ladder set into the wall. It led to another platform above, this one not screened in by chicken wire fencing.

She approached the waist-high railing. The day was clear and she could see for miles across the crowded city from her vantage point atop one of its most famous buildings. She removed her sunglasses and scarf and let her hair blow in the wind. She tipped her face to the late afternoon sun.

She had no need for binoculars. She disdained the fools who came all the way up to the top of the Empire State Building and then squinted through a tiny aperture to get a close-up view of something down below. And, she marveled, they paid for the privilege.

She bent forward to look over the rail. Where she had come up, the platform looked onto the main observation deck. On this side, the drop was vertiginous, all the way to the street, a dizzying distance below.

She straightened and closed her eyes briefly, feeling the sun and the wind. For the first time in days she felt good, the knot of anxiety loosening, confidence in her ability to cope surging back, filling her with peace as she filled her lungs with deep breaths of cold, clean air.

"Show you the sights, lady?"

Nita stiffened and turned. The short, wiry man who had come up behind her had the dark curly hair and swarthy good looks of a young Arab. His dirty suit and stained white shirt, open at the neck to show a cheap gold chain, proclaimed him to be a street hustler. Nita gave him a cold once-over and turned back to the railing.

"Where you from? You speak English? I can show you the city, Broadway, the Bronx, New Jersey. You name it."

Nita continued to ignore him. They usually went away if you failed to engage.

"No kidding. I show you. Where you from? Europe? France, maybe?"

When he put his nicotine-stained fingers on her arm, Nita turned slowly, looking down at his hand where it touched her. Not taking the hint, he gestured expansively with his other hand.

"No kidding. I show you. Take you shopping. Take you to a club. You like to dance? I show you."

"No," said Nita, "I'll show *you*." Grabbing his gesturing arm with one hand she swung it around behind him and reached up with her free hand to grab a handful of his collar. She bent him forward over the railing until she felt his feet go out from under him.

The Arab teetered precariously over the railing which caught him at the waist. His left arm was twisted painfully behind his back and her hold on his wrist and on his collar were all that kept him from plunging to the street hundreds of feet below. Helplessly he rocked forward and back, making small, high-pitched sounds in his throat, his eyes bulging wildly as his view swooped from sky to surrounding buildings to the street with its yellow cabs and blue buses the size of ants.

"Take a good look," Nita said. "Look at the whole thing. The big picture. How do you like it?"

After a few seconds that seemed like an eternity during which he had forgotten everything, even prayer, Nita released him.

He backed away, suppressing an urge to vomit, wanting only to get out of there, get off this roof, out of this building. He backed away, rubbing his throat where his shirt had nearly strangled him, staggering a little.

Nita did not turn around. She was gazing serenely over the city again. Her city.

Ace looked longingly at Billy Ray's beer, but lacked the gumption to ask the big man to buy him one. "She's one crazy bitch, man. I'm telling you."

"Well, now, crazy is how I like them. They taste better that way," Billy Ray drawled and rewarded his oratorical effort with a long glug of suds.

"The cops took my piece," Ace said. "I'm unarmed."

"Little farthole like you never gonna shoot nobody," Billy Ray said. He drank again.

"I'm serious. I done them bitches and that Reuben guy, but the cops ain't smart enough to pin it all on me. So I'm out." The cold beer in Billy Ray's mug was amber ambrosia.

"Sure as shit," Billy Ray said. "You're one vicious, goddamn motherfucker, is what you is." He laughed and drank some more. "What's the bitch's name?"

"Nita Bergstrom. Billy Ray, I can't afford to leave town. I got no money."

"I am totally aware of that fact. You falling in love with my beer? You keep fucking mooning over it." Billy Ray finished his draft and signaled Tony Topnut for a refill. "She a social worker lady, right?"

Ace nodded vigorously. "West Side Crisis Center. Shit, you saw her. She was shooting at my ass."

"Well, well. A person of the female persuasion is scaring little you to death. You are one sorry turdball."

"She may be a woman, but she's got a gun. And she's real good at using it. No fucking fooling, Billy Ray. What would you do, if you was me?"

"I'd grab her popgun, rip off her fucking fancy clothes, and fuck the bejesus out of her, is what I'd do." Billy Ray reached for the mug that Tony Topnut plopped in front of him.

Ace laughed mirthlessly. "Shit. She'd blow you away before you got near her."

Billy Ray's big hand grabbed him by the chin and scrunched up his lips and cheeks so Ace resembled a stricken fish. "Watch your mouth around me, boy," Billy Ray growled. Ace made pained sounds, and Billy Ray released him. "Can't stand no disrespect."

Ace rubbed his jaw. "Wasn't no disrespect, Billy Ray," he whined. "It's just that she scares me."

"Scares you?" Billy Ray said derisively.

Ace saw the woman in the scarf and sunglasses at the other end of the bar. Sunglasses even in the pit-dimness of the bar. "Holy shit," he breathed. "It's her."

"Huh?"

"Christ," Ace yelped. He shoved off the barstool, which went clattering to the floor. With legs and arms flailing, he raced out the back.

With growing annoyance, Nita strode through the sleazy girlie joint, past the lowlifes lining the bar, into the back with its ladders and buckets and mops. Never taking off the sunglasses. Tripping over a box. Almost falling. Catching the fire door as it closed after Ace.

Ace was hopping and dodging as much as running. But Bergstroms were strong. Her footsteps kept pace with his along the lurid maelstrom of the Deuce. In and out of the gaggles of people. Around their slow-moving clusters. Ace up ahead, all elbows and lurching. Past the peep shows and porno movie palaces.

He skipped twice beneath a marquee advertising its double feature in blood-crimson letters: *Pussy Whipped* and *Hot Hooters from Hell*. Ace dodged into the theater's dank mouth, bolting past the ticket window.

The large-pawed ticket collector made a swipe at Ace and missed. "Hey, asshole. You got to pay."

The ticket collector did a double take when Nita swerved around him and charged through the closing door into the auditorium.

"Hey," he called in vain. "Get back here." Yet because it was too much aggravation, he gave up the chase and went back to his post, where a half-eaten meatball sandwich awaited him.

Panting from the run and the adrenaline, Nita pulled off the sunglasses. She had to find Ace in here, and no one could identify her in the flickering darkness. Thanks to the shades, her eyes quickly adjusted. On the screen, a demonically leering farmer had pinned a naked woman to the barn floor and was pumping into her with his remarkable anatomy. Solitary male heads were scattered throughout the theater. No one was running down the aisles toward the exit signs.

Thrusting her hand into her bag and gripping the good steel, Nita stalked down the center aisle. The men sat as still as mummies. Except for one who was busy pulling at his lap. The whole bunch of them should be exterminated.

Nita was very deliberate in her search. Ace could be crouched among the seats, low to the sticky floor.

Then Nita heard the slapping of feet behind her. Somehow, Ace was crashing through the door they had just come in. She doubled back after him. Ace squirted past the ticket collector, who sat on a stool clutching his dripping sandwich.

When Nita reached the door to the street, the ticket collector was half out of his cage and managed to snag her left arm. She gasped at the pain in her shoulder socket.

"Okay, lady," the ticket collector fog horned. "None of your fucking games. You owe me seven-fifty." He put down the sandwich. One of its meatballs had plopped out onto the filthy floor.

Nita's free right hand pulled out the .45 and stuck it in the man's flaccid face. "Let go of me, you piece of scum," she yelled. The ticket collector did as ordered. He held up his meaty hands in supplication. "Hey, no problemo. I'm cool."

Nita jammed the gun back into her bag and slapped the sunglasses in place. It was easy to find Ace in the bobbing, throbbing mass.

He was the only one running. He almost had the length of a block on her.

Nita pounded after her quarry, twisting through the thicket of hips that separated them. Then Ace made a mistake. He looked behind him for Nita and collided with a bag lady's heavily laden shopping cart of rags, bundles, bottles, and cans. Ace and the cart toppled onto the sidewalk. Bottles smashed.

Ace lay there, dazed. The old woman hovered over him, flapping her arms hen-like and nattering her outrage. Passing pedestrians gathered for a drama. A gang of teenage boys in turned-backward baseball caps emerged from a subway station and broke into laughter at the sight.

Shaking the shock out of his head, Ace focused on Nita as she bore down on him. He struggled to his feet and sent bottles and cans flying.

"Ace, you clumsy bastard," the bag lady howled.

"Fuck you, Stinky," Ace yelled. He threaded through the knot of teenagers and catapulted himself down the subway stairs.

Nita neatly skirted the bag lady's debris on the sidewalk and pounded after him. She threaded through the teenagers and loped down the steps. Ace was limping — *limping* — ahead in a long, lonely tunnel.

The boys, however, suddenly ran past Nita with their turbocharged youthful energy, turned around, and formed a line in front of her. She came to an abrupt stop.

"Where you going, pretty momma?" the largest one said. He had a ring through his nose and a cocky grin. The boys circled around her. The large one stepped close, ogled her breasts and said, "What's a fine-looking thing like you doing hiding herself behind them shades?"

Nita pulled out her .45 and jammed it it into his waistband, pointing downward. "I'll blow your balls off, you worthless parasite," she told him, an inch from his instantly slack face.

"Sh-sh-sh-sh-shit," he stammered.

In a squeak of sneaker rubber, the other boys took off for the street.

"You're no damn good and you deserve to die," she said.

"Oh, fuck," he said. "Please, God, n-n-n-n-n-no."

Nita noted with pleasure that he had wet his pants. She withdrew the gun and aimed it at his right eye. "I ought to," she said. But then she lowered the gun. "There will be time. Believe me."

She ran after Ace's hobbling form.

The boy sank to his knees and sobbed.

The blood lust pounded its savage tattoo in Nita's temples.

To Ace, the pain was an anklet of fire. Every step with his left leg shot shafts of agony up to his hip and into his groin. He made little sobs of hurt and fear as he chugged up to the subway turnstiles. He had no token. So he hoisted himself up and slid his butt along the turnstile's metal casing. On the other side, he came down hard on his left foot and howled in torment.

He was on the subway platform, an empty wilderness of stained concrete and girders that offered no sanctuary, no hiding, no salvation. The trench for the subway tracks ran either way, damp and relentless as the River Styx, into tunnels of final darkness. He peered desperately down the tracks for some inspiration. No one was there to help him.

"Turn around, Ace," Nita said, slightly out of breath but thoroughly in control.

He turned slowly, the boiling air whooshing in and out of his lungs, to confront the dark zero of the gun barrel's opening. "Why?"

"It's for the best, Ace," she said. "You'll be better off."

"Bullshit," he whined. "I don't deserve to die."

"I'll be the judge of that."

"Hold on a minute," he pleaded. His entire body was shaking.

She tensed her arms to fire.

Tears slalomed down Ace's cheeks, into his scraggly half-beard, and dripped onto the platform. "I love you, Nita," he said. "How can you do this to me?"

"It's not hard," she said. Her finger began pulling the trigger back.

"Billy Ray Battle knows about you," Ace blurted.

Nita stopped. "Who?"

"My friend Billy. I was sitting with him in the Foxy Lady when you came in."

"Is he the one Dillon arrested first?" Nita asked, lowering the gun slightly. Ace nodded, and she said, "And is he the one who shouted at me on the playground?" Ace nodded again. "What does he know about me?"

"That you want to kill me."

"Well, he sounds like another candidate for removal," she said, and she raised the gun again, prepared to fire.

A train roared into the station in a metallic clatter and a gust of foul wind. Surprised, Nita momentarily froze. The subway doors parted and a walrus-moustached transit cop sauntered out onto the platform.

"Help. Police. She's gonna kill me," Ace shouted.

Nita quickly stashed the gun into her purse before the cop turned. She walked briskly toward the turnstiles.

"She's getting away," Ace cried.

"What's your noise, scumbag?" the cop said to Ace.

Ace stood wordlessly and watched Nita's head kerchief recede into the dank distance. When the suspicious cop pushed him against the wall to frisk him, Ace smiled gratefully. He could have kissed him.

⇛ *THIRTEEN* ⇚

Dave met Don Cole for a late afternoon beer at McSorley's. They sat far from the TV, where the Sunday football game drew the other patrons, bugs to the light. Dave had met Cole when the two were rookies in the 19th Precinct. Cole left the force to go to St. John's Law School and then joined the Securities and Exchange Commission as an investigator.

Dave came right to the point. "I need information about an investigation."

Cole inspected the foam on his beer. "Dave, I can't tell you about any ongoing stuff. Maybe if Mancuso formally —"

"Forget Mancuso. And forget formally. This is about a dead woman. Name of Kimberly Worth."

"One of the Ladykiller victims."

"Uh-huh."

"Of Corson & Worth."

"You got that right."

Cole downed some brew and pursed his lips in thought. "I guess she can't sue us for defamation of character. But you haven't heard a word from me."

"Fine."

"Kimberly Worth was a real classy girl. Went to Stanford Business School. Had a hot rep as a young broker at one of the best firms on the Street. Along came the 1987 stock market crash. She got caught doing all kinds of unethical shit to save her hide. Traded from her own account and ignored her customers. Whatever it took to come out ahead. Her license got revoked."

"So how did she end up heading an outfit that had her name on the door?"

Cole lit a cigarette and sent dragon plumes of smoke shooting out his nostrils. "She got a temporary injunction. Sued everbody in sight. Since nobody legit would hire her, she went into business with this major sleaze, Corson. They started a bucket shop. And it's still pretty profitable."

"Tell me how a bucket shop works, exactly," Dave said.

"Specializes in penny stocks," Cole said. "That's anything less than five bucks a share, usually. Their brokers work the phones, night and day, doing cold calls. They love a retiree with a little money to burn, but not a lot of market sophistication. They dangle riches in front of the poor slob. Tell him the stock will take off any day now. When it does move up—from the demand generated by the bucket shop, as often as not—they persuade the pigeon to sell and roll his gains into another hot number. Every time there's a sale, the brokerage gets a commission. This goes on and on. The customer never can cash out and go home."

"Not good," Dave said.

"It gets worse. Lots of times, the broker will make sales without the client's permission. More commissions roll in. That was the specialty of Corson & Worth. These sleazeballs convinced retirees to pledge their homes as collateral for loans to buy more stock. Unreal. We have documented cases where their shenanigans cleaned out several old people. They lost their houses, everything. At least two I know wound up homeless. One poor widow died of overexposure. She used to give bridge parties, for Christ's sake." He shook his head and took a drink. "Corson & Worth—they're pigs. We'll get them sooner or later. Corson won't budge and throws up a smokescreen of legal crap to stop us."

"How about Kimberly Worth? Did she feel guilty? Maybe want to quit? Get help or something?"

"Are you kidding? That bitch was cold. All she cared about was how much long green she was raking in. I mean, she had a nice place in the Hamptons, a swanky condo on the Upper East Side, the works."

"Any clue if she ever sought psychological counseling for anything?"

"Nothing that I know of. Unless she was worried about her habit."

"Her habit? What habit?"

Cole looked startled, then laughed. "Hey, I thought you cops knew everything. Kimberly Worth had a horse habit. Big time."

"No she didn't. There was an autopsy. It would have come out. Besides, I examined the body myself and there were no track marks. Nothing."

Cole shook his head, grinning. "Are you living in the fifties? Track marks? She didn't shoot it, she inhaled it. It was designer horse. Actually, it was probably some synthetic. Probably got it from Mexico or Belgium or something. Maybe it didn't show up in the blood, but she was doing it and it could be she was worried about it. Other than that, I don't think she had a care in the world."

"Until she faced that .45," Dave said thoughtfully.

"Until then."

Billy Ray Battle spent the early evening pacing back and forth on the other side of the street from Nita's apartment building. A big man like him was conspicuous. If he simply stood there and waited for her, someone would notice. So he had to keep moving. But where the fuck was she? He spied a pay phone in a Korean grocery. He dialed directory assistance and asked for the number of the West Side Crisis Center.

"The hotline?" the operator asked.

"Hotline, coldline, whatever fucking line you got."

An electronic female voice, which was vaguely seductive, chirped out the number.

"Just one damn minute," Billy Ray said. "You got a pen?" he called to the Korean counterman. Snatching the pen from him, Billy Ray copied the number onto his palm when the voice repeated it.

An older woman answered the hotline. "Crisis center, may I help you?" She sounded Jewish, whiny, motherly.

"Looking for Nita. This here's an old friend of hers."

"I'm sure you are, dear. Nita stopped by for a minute, but she's off today. Is there anything I can help you with?"

"She go home?" Billy Ray demanded.

"I don't know where she goes. If you have a problem —"

"Don't got no fucking problem." Billy Ray slammed the receiver home and quickly returned to the street. Could he have missed her?

He could taste her already. Then he saw her approaching, her legs in snug jeans, her ripe breasts in a nice pullover, the hair, the face. His fingers and crotch tingled.

Nita needed time to plan. She studied the sidewalk as she headed home. Megan wanted to have dinner, but she couldn't spare the time tonight. The younger woman's eagerness to please was more than Nita could handle now. Life had become entirely too complicated. Planning was the answer.

She was sorting out her keys at the front door to her building when she felt the looming presence behind her.

"Open the door, darlin'," came the man's drawl from behind and above. "Got us some things to do."

She stifled the yelp that shot up from her heart. And she froze, gripping the keys.

"Open the door, darlin'."

Nita's hand slid toward her bag. But the man's massive paw was there already, clamping it shut. He slid it off her shoulder.

"Don't want no trouble, do we? Trouble gets in the way of loving, every time." His voice had the low, honey menace of a tiger's purr.

Her own voice came out surprisingly steady. "If you don't leave me alone and drop my bag, I'll yell for the police."

His broad fingers slid across her throat. "You try that, and you won't make no more noise, ever again." He squeezed gently.

She took a tortured sip of air, and said nothing.

"Now, let that key in, nice and easy," he urged.

Her key zigzagged toward the lock, slid in, and turned. The door opened with a disheartening snap.

She felt his erection against her behind.

"See how nice that key went in?" His lips were near her ear.

She trudged up the stairs, his hand still around her throat. At her apartment door, she dropped the keys. She bent to retrieve them, and as she did, he bent over with her, his hand still at her throat, his bulge bumping against her ass. Nita opened the door and they entered the apartment, which was dark except for the fish tank, lit by an eerie inner glow. The door closed.

His hand moved from her throat to the collar of her pullover. "Let's take them clothes off.

"You were with Ace at the playground, weren't you?" she asked. The dead calm in her tone remained.

"Maybe I was, little darlin'." The large hand roughly fondled her breasts. "That was then. Tonight is now."

"Let me turn around and look at you," Nita said, spicing the words with a flirtatious lilt. "You seem big and strong."

The hand went to one of her shoulders and turned her to face him. He stood there in dark immensity, the lusty grin catching the light from the fish tank.

"You have an eye patch," she said. "I like men with eye patches. They're so — manly."

"You do?" His grin widened.

"Yes. Like an old shirt ad."

The grin dropped a few watts. "What you say?"

"I wish you weren't carrying a purse." She gestured at her bag, which he had clamped in his other hand. "A man like you wouldn't want that, would he?"

He delved inside the bag. "Well, well, lookie here. Got ourselves that piece you was shooting at poor little Ace. You got the fire in you, girl. I like my women wild." He threw the bag behind him, where it lay at the foot of the door, the gun inside and too far from her.

"Why don't we turn on the light, so we can see each other better?" she suggested.

He flicked the wall switch. Totally visible, he appeared less terrifying. It was a good sign that he had obeyed her.

"Strip off them clothes, darling," he said.

"I need a drink of water first," Nita said.

"You can drink all you want after," he said.

"Let me get my drink of water, Billy Ray," she said. Her knowing
his name jolted across his face. Before he could respond, she turned,
and walked into the kitchen.

He followed her. "You make it a short drink. Hear?"

Good. Nita had won another psychological point. She picked up
her coffee cup, where it sat upside-down in the dish drainer, right beside the toaster oven and the butcher block full of carving knives. She
rinsed out the cup and filled it with water. She forced herself to down
the entire thing.

"I'm sorry about what Dillon did to your eye," she said.

A storm gathered about his mouth and remaining eye. "What you
say, woman? You mocking me?"

Careful. She had to work this just right. "No, no, no, Billy Ray.
He's a terrible man. I'm sure you would have demolished him if it
were a fair fight. But cops don't fight fair."

"You damn straight." He pulled back his shoulders. "Now, take
them fucking clothes off."

"Billy Ray, do you know what would be really exciting?"

His lips puckered like a little boy's. "What?"

"Why don't you take your clothes off first? Then you could take
mine off."

"Well —"

"Oh, please. For me, Billy Ray."

Somewhere inside the most brutal, woman-hating rapist lurked a
desire to be bossed around in sex by a woman. The grin returned.
"That turn you on, huh?"

"Like you wouldn't believe. Oh, please."

"Okay, then. Anything for a lady." With tripping, almost silly
alacrity, he pulled off his boots and yanked at his clothes. In seconds,

he stood before her, an overfed, oversized version of Michelangelo's *David*. His erection curled out aggressively from under his slag-bag of a gut.

"Come to me, my love," Nita said, and held out her arms.

Grinning ferociously, he crossed the kitchen tile. She reached for his genitals. "Yeah, baby," he said.

Billy Ray's balls rested in Nita's palm, tight, bulbous prizes. With every erg of strength she had, she squeezed them hard. Crushed them like rotten pears.

The man jackknifed forward and roared in exquisite agony. Nita backed off quickly to get clear of his arms, which flailed around before they clamped around his crotch. He made gagging sounds. His face had turned sunset red.

Nita, losing not a moment, pulled a large knife out of the butcher block. When Billy Ray could look up from his intense pain to croak his curses at her, he saw the knife zooming at his bad eye. It went through the eye patch and sliced deep into his skull. For a moment that seemed like forever he stood there, staring at her from his one good eye, then he slipped down, slid down the knife blade, and slowly eased down onto the floor.

Nita stood over him as he twitched in death. When he was still, she took the knife and washed it carefully in the kitchen sink. Fortunately, little blood leaked out his eye onto her floor. She would clean that up later.

In Manhattan, even on a Sunday night, you can get any items you want. Delivered too. In an hour, a moving company had delivered a crate and hand truck to her door. She bought industrial-strength trash bags from the deli. And she picked up the van from the 24-hour car rental herself. Happily, there was a parking place right in front of her apartment house door when she drove the van back.

Now came the hard part. Billy Ray lay on her linoleum, a twisted lump of meat with overly large joints shooting in all directions. He had started to stiffen. She had to push hard to get his arms to his sides and his knees tucked up to his chest. He had started to smell, too.

Dark ooze, from where his bowels had given way, puddled the floor beneath him. She would clean that up later, as well. His waxen face was wrenched into the wretched gorgon's snarl of sudden death.

Previously, she never had to bother with her victims after she dispatched them. Just walked away. She unfolded the trash bags. Billy Ray would need at least three.

Nita struggled the big man into the black plastic. He was like a bag of rocks, inert and muscle-strainingly heavy.

Next came the hard part: shoving him into the crate. She had chosen a sturdy one whose top and bottom could be removed without the sides collapsing. She braced a corner of the crate against her kitchen door jamb to prevent it from moving backward, and dragged Billy Ray's bulk into the crate. It took a long frustrating half hour. Even though she had the advantage of being able to pull him through the far, open end of the crate, the damn box kept shifting from side to side. And God, was he the deadest of deadweight?

At last, he was safely inside. Nita sat wearily down on the floor, soaked with sweat, muscles on fire.

Her buzzer sounded. Nita struggled to her feet and hit the intercom switch. "Who is it?"

"It's me," came Megan's perky greeting over the tinny speaker. "Ready for dinner?"

"Dinner."

"Come on. Let's celebrate. One of your neighbors let me in. Be right up."

In a frenzy, Nita sealed up the top of the crate, which had a latch. The bottom, though, needed to be nailed shut. No time for that. She leaned the bottom panel across the opening, hiding the plastic-sheathed mass inside. With a fistful of paper towels and a blast of Ajax, she cleaned up the soiled linoleum.

Her doorbell chimed. Megan had on smart slacks and a light sweater. She carried a bottle of champagne. "I'm really in control," she gushed. "I went on another call with Dave today, and I really have my emotions where I want them. I don't need him. I proved that to myself today. You'd have been proud of me."

"That's great, but —"

Megan stepped inside, holding the champagne by its neck. The handbag with the .45 still sat beside the door where Billy Ray had flung it. "I saw today that you're right. He wants to steal my soul. But he's weak. I can be stronger than him. I can tell him no. And I can mean it. I wish you could have seen me."

"Megan, please —"

At last, her young friend realized she was intruding. Then she noticed Nita's appearance. "Oh, you look —" Yet Megan couldn't bring herself to say that Nita looked any less than perfect. "You're not ready."

"I've been a little busy," Nita said with heavy irony, suppressing the urge to laugh. She recognized incipient hysteria when she saw it. She sat down and pushed back her damp hair.

"What's that crate?"

"I've been doing a little spring cleaning."

"Can I help?"

"No. That's okay. Why don't I give you a rain check? This is dirty work."

Megan walked over to the crate, pulled the bottom panel away from where it leaned, and peered inside. Nita tensed. Her eyes darted to the handbag in the corner, where the lump of the .45 showed clearly.

"What is this?" Megan asked.

"You wouldn't want to know."

"Woo, it smells." Megan jostled the side of the crate. "My God, it weighs a ton."

"You wouldn't believe the trash I have to throw out." Nita got up and slowly walked across the room and picked up her bag.

The two women looked at each other as the night gathered itself together beyond the window. And they seemed to find some elusive something behind each other's eyes, some sturdy spiderweb of trust that bound them together for all their seasons.

Megan exhaled and said in a small voice, "The box is very heavy. I can help."

Nita stood quietly for a moment, then nodded. She fit the bottom panel squarely against the crate and nailed it shut. "There," she said.

Megan helped her upend the crate and shove it onto the handcart. Then Megan went first down the stairs, holding the cargo steady as they bumped the crate down to the street. The two women strained to push the crate into the van. Without Megan, Nita doubted she could have managed. The burden must have weighed 250 pounds.

"Let me go with you," Megan said. "It will be just as heavy — wherever you're going."

"You've done enough," Nita said. "I can take it from here."

"I'll do anything for you, Nita."

"I know."

As Megan left, Nita called after her, "Remember. A rain check on dinner."

Nita decided on New Jersey. She could have unloaded the body on some deserted back street in Lower Manhattan. But in the city, there was no telling who would happen along as she struggled with the crate.

She drove through the back streets to the Lincoln Tunnel, which sat at the end of the Deuce like a giant drain for all the human sewage that sluiced along that putrid street. As she sped into the dirty, white-tiled tunnel, lit in a sickly yellow glow, Nita felt the triumph begin to swell.

She went quickly past the evil-smelling New Jersey towns that wadded up against the nether end of the tunnel. Without too much searching, she found a lonely road threading through the sewage pools of the Hackensack Meadowlands. She pulled the van over beside a shallow ditch and waited. No other car came along. She killed the headlights and got out.

Over the reedy horizon, Manhattan's towers stood waist high against the night sky, incredible statements of pure light where the world's work got done. Gearhouses that ran the machinery of society. And the Billy Rays and Aces and Reubens and Lydias and Kimberlys and Lucys and Evelyns were nothing but sand in those gears. Off to the west rose the arenas of the Meadowlands sports complex. The soft breath of air that rattled through the reeds carried faint cheering.

"Thank you," Nita said, making a mock bow to the ghost applause.

Inside the van, she braced her shoulder against the crate and inched it out the back. It fell hard to the ground, but didn't break open. Nita popped open the top and squinted into the crate. The trash bags might rip and break if she tried to pull the body out. Instead, she hammered the sides of the crate loose. And she rolled the stinking plastic load into the ditch. The shards of the crate went back into the van, so no one could trace it back to her. She turned once more to the luminous Manhattan skyline.

There was another burst of distant cheering and triumph swelled out of her. She laughed and laughed. To think that removing scum like this was against the law. Her laughter mounted to a manic crescendo. Well, how fitting that the law was easily outsmarted. The laughing tripped into a fit of coughing and gagging.

"I'll save the bad news for later," Blake told the morning meeting of his task force. "Cops in East Rutherford found a body around dawn tentatively identified as Billy Ray Battle."

"Where's East Rutherford?" Safir asked.

"I never heard of East Rutherford," Wise said.

"It's in New Jersey," Jamie said. "Where the Meadowlands sports complex is. You know, Giants Stadium and all."

"Oh, that East Rutherford," Safir said.

"The one in Jersey," Wise said.

"Was he shot in the right eye?" Dave asked. He didn't bring up his head to speak, merely kept glowering at the coffee cup that sat before him on the table. He had been staring at that cup since they all had sat down. Jamie glanced at him, then looked away, remembering.

"Stabbed in the eye with a knife," Blake said. "The right eye. The one where Dave, uh, zapped him. Large blade, like a kitchen carving knife. No evidence of firearms damage on him. Severe damage to his testicles, as if somebody had squeezed them."

"Got him by the balls," Safir said.

"The hearts and minds follow," Wise said.

"We can't say it was a Ladykiller homicide," Blake said. "But because it was his right eye and because he is peripherally involved, well, I want someone here to examine the body. Seems like the local Jersey cops are in a snit over something to do with interstate flight policy. So they aren't being cooperative. Maybe you can charm them into access to the body, Jamie."

"None of the male detectives are as charming, Loo?" Jamie said. "Safir and Wise can speak suburban."

"Who me?" Safir said. "All that crabgrass gives me allergies. If it was up to me, I'd pave over Central Park."

"Put up a few parking garages," Wise said. "Make it useful."

"Billy Ray was seen with Ace yesterday in the Foxy Lady," Dave said. "There's got to be a connection."

"Maybe, maybe not." Blake shrugged. "Worth Jamie taking a good look. No luck finding Ace?"

"Martino and Blitzer say he was seen running into the Times Square subway station," Dave said. "He acted like he was being chased. He knocked over an old bag lady's shopping cart. The bag lady was afraid of cops, but a transit cop in the station says he saw someone who resembled Ace. He couldn't be sure, though."

Blake clapped his hands onto the table. "Folks, we're getting nowhere here."

"The link is the West Side Crisis Center," Dave insisted. "Listen, Ace said all the victims were clients there. Trouble is, the center's files show no sign of the victims. Not even under fake names, as far as we can tell."

"Nothing matched," Jamie added.

"If we find Ace, it will fall into place," Dave said.

"Will it, Dave?" Blake said. "Will it? We've been down too many blind alleys." He was uncharacteristically angry, almost shouting. "We're getting absolutely nowhere. Jesus." He stopped himself, then rubbed his temples with his fingers.

"What's the bad news, Loo?" Jamie asked softly.

"Mancuso," Blake said. "He's given us till the end of this week. To-day is Monday. If we haven't collared the perp — the right one this time — the task force is disbanded. And that will have bad conse-quences for a lot of people in this room." He scanned their faces and locked his gaze on Dave.

"Me, I'll retire," Safir said.

"Yeah, time to hang it up," Wise said.

Dave stood and left the room without a word. The group sat in silence. Jamie scraped her chair back and followed him.

She caught him as he was heading out the front. "Dave, about the other night —"

"I'm sorry, Jamie," Dave said, not looking at her. "I mean it but —"

"No. Don't. Forget that. What I want to say is, you can count on me to help you with this case. Together we can nail this asshole."

Dave looked up and gave her a tight smile. "Sure we can."

"Where are you going?"

"The West Side Crisis Center."

The first morning counseling session behind her, Nita fed the fish. The flakes drifted in equal portions all over the tank. No fish went hungry. They didn't fight over the manna. They were smooth and beautiful.

Once she disposed of Ace, she could start over. Obviously, re-moving any more clients of the crisis center was too dangerous. And just as obviously, shooting them in the right eye was too much of a sig-nature. In the heart, or anywhere else in the head would have to do, although she regretted the loss of the right eye as a target. It had such poetry.

Sated, the fish swam in their smooth, orderly currents.

The next phase. The trick was to avoid mistakes. The police had gotten too close to the crisis center, although Nita appeared to have stopped them. No one knew that the victims all saw Nita Bergstrom or even that they came to the crisis center.

No one other than Ace, that is. Always trying to hang around Nita, he had probably met every one of her clients. He actually attempted to hit on Kimberly Worth, of all people. Nita should have realized that Ace would catch on to her. She simply never thought about him.

Nita remembered the frustration of dealing with poor Lucy. The girl was starving herself and, by her own account, driving her parents mad with guilt and grief and worry. Nita completely lost it professionally with Lucy, yelling at her to wake up and get a life. The girl kept whimpering, "I'm so fat." Typical of the cops, no one ever picked up on the irony of Lucy's dying outside a meatpacking plant.

Kimberly was a study in exasperating behavior. The woman, a spoiled brat from a rich family, was an addict, as pathetic as the lowest junkie on the street.

"How can I help you when you won't admit that you're hurting yourself? Just as you won't admit that your work involves hurting others?" Nita asked her.

"Caveat emptor — 'Let the buyer beware' — is at the heart of the capitalist system," Kimberly said breezily.

"I think your problem is guilt. And that you can't bring yourself to stop hurting others."

"My problem is that I don't understand what my problem is."

When the .45 was pointed at Kimberly, in Carl Schurz Park, the woman's reaction was superbly in character: "Whatever do you think you're doing?"

Lydia Daniels' behavior displayed a more deadly form of denial. She showed Nita the HIV diagnosis only to laugh at it. "They think I'm a drag queen queer or something? Shit. This piece of paper is as phony as a three-dollar bill. They just disapprove of my lifestyle, is all."

"I'd take this seriously," Nita told her. "Maybe the men you infect deserve it, but they go on to infect innocent women. How can you live with that?"

"Sure, sure, sure. Hey, if I'm Typhoid Mary, cure me."

"All right," Nita said, "I will."

The fish swam in their perfect world.

•   •   •

Dave opened the heavy door of the crisis center. Inside, the usual bedlam reigned. The seedy, wild-eyed man ran up to Dave once more. "What planet are you from?"

"Did you know Reuben Silver?" Dave asked.

"Reuben lives on another planet now. With all the early saints. A lot of the early saints were Jewish."

"Were you a client of Reuben?"

"Hell, no. He used to call me crazy. Ha-ha. If he was so great, how come he's dead?" The man roared. "Ever ask yourself that?"

Megan hurried over. "Dave, what's going on?"

"Talking to this man."

"Well, have you?" the man bellowed.

"Why?" Megan said.

"Two items on my agenda. The first is a chat with Dr. Solomon," Dave said.

"Guess what?" the man proclaimed with a cackle. "She's real sweet on you."

"What's the second item?"

"An invitation to dinner." Dave smiled. "Not at my place this time. And we won't talk about Nita. We'll just have a nice meal."

Megan looked up into his eyes. She briefly touched his shoulder. She could feel the heat. "When?"

"Tomorrow night. Pick you up at seven?"

"All right," Megan said. "I don't have to work the hotline tomorrow night. But please, if you see Nita, don't —"

Dave put a finger to her lips. "I won't say a word." He smiled and went upstairs.

Rose disturbed Nita's reverie. "Dr. Solomon wishes to see you, dear. It's must be important." She seemed worried.

"What's the matter, Rose?"

"That detective is here again. Dr. Solomon is in quite a state." Rose waved vaguely. "Will this ever end?"

Nita swallowed hard and stalked into Solomon's office. He

slumped behind his desk, as if he'd been deboned. Dillon sat upright in the chair opposite him, brimming with grim force.

"Nita, Detective Dillon has a proposal that, well, I frankly need your input on," Dr. Solomon said. "Apparently, the investigation to find Reuben's killer hasn't exactly progressed to the point of satisfaction. And, well —"

"What do you want with us now, detective?" Nita asked.

"Why don't you sit down, Nita?" Dave said.

"I prefer to stand, thank you very much. Well?"

"Certain aspects of this case don't add up," Dave said. "We have established links between the first four Ladykiller victims and the crisis center. And yet no record exists of their ever being here. The files show no one close to them in age, appearance, what have you. That's odd. I'd say someone yanked their files."

"What are you driving at?" Nita asked.

"Do any clients have access to the area where the files are kept, Nita?"

"Only crisis center professionals are allowed access to the files," Nita said.

"Yes, but are any clients allowed near the filing cabinets where they are kept?"

"We have some clients who help out around the office. The less seriously disturbed, of course."

"Another curious thing is that the victims were all Reuben's. At least, that's what Ace said." Dave folded his arms. "Now, the victims were said to be very enthusiastic about the person they saw here. That's what their loved ones and friends told us. Trouble is, Reuben was not known around here as someone to inspire much fervor among his clients. Quite the contrary."

"How dare you," Nita said angrily. "Reuben was dedicated. He worked hard. You're talking to the wrong people."

"Um, I have to corroborate the detective's assertion, Nita," Dr. Solomon said apologetically.

"At long last, detective," Nita said, her voice cold, "please tell me what you are getting at."

"I want to interview your clients," Dave said.

"What did you say?"

"You have some seriously disturbed people here," Dave said. "You admit that some could have gotten near the filing cabinets. Perhaps the files contained clues to who the killer is. The files might explain the relationship that Reuben had with these clients — which I frankly don't understand — and that might shed even more light on who our perpetrator is."

"Never," Nita said.

"Nita, aren't we being a little hasty?" Dr. Solomon said.

"Never in a million years," Nita said. "Those clients trust us. We're not going to set them up for another of the detective's fishing expeditions, endangering their therapy."

Dave jumped to his feet. "Endangering their therapy? What about the lives this weirdo has snuffed out? What about the innocent people he is going to kill if we don't stop him?"

"Never," Nita told him. "Never, never, never."

"The odds are that one of your loonies is the killer," Dave thundered back at her.

Nita shouted loud enough to echo through the building. "The odds are that you can't do your job right and are recklessly trying to find someone to pin the blame on to save your ass."

Dave shook with rage. The cords stood out on his neck. "I can get a court order," he said through clenched teeth.

"You do that," Nita shot back. "We'll fight it in any courtroom you want."

"Oh, my," Dr. Solomon said. "We can't afford a legal battle, Nita. Oh, my."

"We don't need to afford it," Nita said. "I know a good lawyer who will work for nothing to tie them up in knots for weeks, months, years. Watch me do it."

Dave marched out of the office. The social workers stared at him. Megan was nowhere to be seen.

Nita had called his bluff. He didn't have the time to wage a court fight. And even if there was more time, Mancuso would never go for it. He had to apply some other pressure to gain quick compliance.

Another thought nagged him: At a time like this, was it wise to romance Megan?

It didn't matter. He needed to. That part of his life was separate and precious.

At the pay phone outside the center, he stabbed out Jimmy Conlon's number.

⇒ *FOURTEEN* ⇐

"Incredible," Jimmy Conlon said as he read the newspaper story for the fifth time. "In-fucking-credible." It was a front-page story by Laird Caruthers on the lack of progress in the Ladykiller investigation: most of it regurgitated clips from stories Jimmy had written. To freshen it up, there were only three new quotes, saying the obvious.

Then it got worse. Laird was lounging at his desk, which was two away from Jimmy's, when Chip traipsed up.

"Great work on the Ladykiller piece," Chip told him. "Keep that stuff coming."

"The most original reporting I've read all year," Jimmy called to them. They ignored him.

"Thanks, Chip," Laird said with the practiced boyish grin that had ingratiated him to elders his entire life.

After Chip went away, Jimmy approached Laird. "Anything I can do for you on this story? Other than give you more of my clips to rewrite, that is."

Laird's grin took on the mean edge of a poker player about to lay out his winning hand. "Just go on being you, champ."

"Uh-huh. How do you do it?"

"Do what?"

"Make Chip and those assholes love you."

Laird smirked. "I don't call them assholes, for one thing."

"I hear they're grooming you for the Washington bureau." Jimmy's arm swept toward Chip's office. "How do you do it?"

"Hard work, champ."

"I can see that. Say, do you even know any cops?"

"Some reporters know cops a little too well. They actually think they are cops. That stops them from digging hard. Not mentioning any names, of course."

Jimmy balled his fists against his elbows. "You have no idea what you're talking about. I grew up with guys who became cops. Where did you grow up?" He added sardonically, "Laird?"

"That's not the point."

"What is the point?"

"The point is that I grew up."

Verbally outgunned, Jimmy was grateful when his phone rang. Glowering at Laird, he moved back to his desk and unholstered the receiver.

"I got something for you," Dave said. "Big."

Jimmy felt the insistent heat at his temples. "What?" He grabbed for a pen and notepad.

"All the victims were definitely clients at the West Side Crisis Center. A source told us they were Reuben Silver's. Problem is that we can't find files on any of them. We suspect that the killer is one of the clients. Looks like whoever it was removed the files from the cabinet. We're betting that the files contain clues to the killer's identity. We want to start interrogating the clients."

"But the caseworkers don't want you to, right?"

"Ta-da. Remember how, after Reuben Silver died, they used this woman as a spokesperson? Nita Bergstrom?"

"Yeah. A real looker, in a sort of frosty way." Jimmy scribbled madly.

"She really runs the place," Dave said. Jimmy could hear the traffic behind him. Pay phone, as usual. "On paper the chief is this Dr. Solomon. He's a real space cadet."

"So I better talk to Bergstrom," Jimmy said.

"Don't say I sent you."

"She can stonewall you in court, no matter what we print."

"It'll be tougher against public outrage that she's sheltering the Ladykiller. This should greatly accelerate the process." Dave added, "Run tomorrow morning?"

"No. I better be in early for this. I'll be lucky to get to see this Bergstrom woman today. I remember what a bitch she was. She'll try to put me off too, no doubt. I don't want to tell Chip what I'm doing or he'll give the story to his favorite. How about tonight at McSorley's?"

"Nope. Gotta visit my mother. Then go home and spend some quality time with the cat. How about tomorrow night? Early, though. I got a date."

"With the —"

"Yeah, with her. Now go win a Pulitzer." Dave hung up.

Jimmy called the crisis center and asked for Nita, making sure to identify himself as a reporter. A gay-sounding fellow named Tim, who cupped his hand over the phone when soliciting Nita's availability, came back to say she was in conference and could he take Jimmy's number.

Jimmy gave it, knowing she wouldn't vouchsafe the courtesy of a reply. With a lead as sensitive as this, you followed polite protocols at the outset. Then you barged in uninvited.

Laird, feet up on desk, was chortling over the phone to an old school chum and planning a weekend outing to the Cape.

Jimmy imagined him in a gun sight. "Champ," he said.

Ace hunched over, palms outstretched, the classic hapless beggar. "Please, Finesse, I got to have it."

Finesse, who leaned against a grafitti-blotched wall, served up a rich laugh. "Name me one time you did one thing for me."

"I'm your friend. Please, Finesse. I got to get out of this town. I'm dead meat if I don't."

"You're tellin' me you're dead meat," Finesse said. "Jackie Why been searchin' all over for you. You owe him a fortune, is how I hear it."

Ace smacked his forehead. "Jackie Why. I forgot that shit."

"You are crazy, boy. You forget about a debt you owe Jackie Why, you done forgot your brains. Who else is after your sorry ass? I know it ain't the police."

"That's a long story," Ace said. "I need money for a bus. It's a matter of life and death."

"Afraid you end up like Billy Ray Battle?"

"What?"

Finesse cocked his head to the side. "You ain't heard? You on the wicked weed again? Everybody on the Deuce knows about old Billy Ray."

"What happened?"

"Cracker got hisself killed, is what happened. Somebody stuck a knife in his eye, dumped him over in Jersey."

"A knife," Ace said hollowly. "In Jersey."

"Yes, indeed. There an echo around here?"

Ace spun away and limped along the Deuce, his head bent over, watching the cracks on the sidewalk flip past like a TV picture with the vertical hold gone wrong. God, it hurt to walk, but he had to keep moving. He had wanted to try Billy Ray for money. That was out.

In the gaudy dimness of the Foxy Lady, Tony Topnut was no more helpful than a dead Billy Ray. "Get the fuck out of here."

"Only a little money. I'll repay it. Honest. I'm good for it. Honest."

"Go piss up a rope, Ace," Tony said. The exploding Hawaian volcanoes on his shirt resembled penises. Hula girls greeted the lava joyously. "When Jackie Why gets done with you, the only thing you'll be good for is piloting a pine box."

"I got to get out of town."

"Tough shit," Tony Topnut said.

Ace said nothing. A customer called out to Tony Topnut with a question about when the skin was coming on. After Tony moved down the bar to talk to him, Ace hit the open lever on the cash register. The till popped open. He grabbed a fistful of cash, reaching underneath the cash tray where the big bills were kept. As Tony Topnut yelled, Ace bolted out of the bar. A couple of stools went flying when he bumped into them. His leg didn't even hurt as he ran for his life into the daylight of the Deuce.

Sitting on the sofa against a mound of pillows, Dave's mother had on her usual sour expression.

Mrs. Corrigan sat beside her, pretending to read a thick paperback with a picture on the cover of a bosomy Southern belle in the arms of a Rhett Butler clone. A prime-time cop show flickered on the huge screen of the Sony that Dave had bought his mother once for her birthday — a gift she never had thanked him for.

"Jimmy Conlon's mother came by to check on me today," his mother said. "Said you were taken up with some girl."

"I told you about her, Ma. Megan."

"Catholic?"

"No, Ma."

"But Irish?"

"Sort of, Ma."

"You going to marry this girl?"

Dave considered. "Maybe. I am crazy about her. That's for sure."

"Not Catholic," his mother said. "That woman of your father's wasn't Catholic, either. There's one who deserves to burn in hell. Break up a man's family."

"Megan is a nice girl, Ma," Dave said. "Very smart."

His mother frowned deeper. "The day a Dillon man gets himself a good woman is the day I'll never see."

"Dad got you, Ma."

Mrs. Corrigan did her best to stifle a titter.

"I'm glad I'm seeing you lately," his mother said with a sniff. "For a change. I ought to go to the hospital more often."

"Ma, I swear. When this case is over — and I feel it's going to be real soon — I'll be here more."

"If I had a nickel for every time I heard your father say that, I'd be a rich woman. And you know who he spent all his money on, don't you?"

*   *   *

Megan felt as if she were being ripped apart. All day long, she watched Nita move through the crisis center, directing people, motivating them, a dauntless helmsman. Megan didn't dare speak to her for fear that Nita could tell about Dave. Then she thought about Dave and the way he looked at her. She clamped her knees together.

"Nita isn't herself today," Tim said.

"She isn't?" Megan said. "I haven't noticed."

"That business about the detective. We can't let them in here like that."

"Like what?"

Tim told her. "It was such a scene. I wouldn't have missed it for the world. But we can't have them giving our clients the third degree."

"Oh." After she had agreed to the date with Dave, Megan had left the crisis center for a short walk to try to reconcile her growing attraction to Dave with her fierce loyalty to Nita. It hadn't worked. "I guess I was out of the building."

"I hate to say this," Tim said, "but that detective is one gorgeous hunk. He really starts my engine." Tim giggled. "And I *know* he starts yours."

"Excuse me," Megan said. "I have to go to the ladies' room." En route, she encountered Nita at a clerk's desk, listening to WCBS Newsradio.

"How are you?" Nita asked brusquely.

"Terrific." Megan mustered a smile.

"You seem a little frazzled."

"Well, it's been a tough day."

"Tell me about it," Nita said. "You heard about the encounter we had with Sherlock Holmes?"

Megan nodded, perhaps too vigorously.

"No chance he's going to disrupt our therapy," Nita said. "And to top it off, I just got off the phone with this obnoxious reporter, who wants an interview. Who do those people think they are, anyway?"

"Are you going to talk to him?" Megan asked.

"Certainly not. I have more important things to do than to cater to his prurient interests. The gall of him. He says he's heard that the murderer is one of our clients."

"We don't want that in the paper," Megan said. "What does Dr. Solomon say?"

"I'm not going to bother Dr. Solomon with this. He has enough on his mind."

"What about the reporter, Nita?"

"Ignore him. He'll get sick of this and go off to do an article about flying saucers or whatever people want to read about these days. I hate reporters. There ought to be laws to control them. Other societies are better at that than ours."

"I've got an idea," Megan said. "Why don't I cook dinner for you tonight?"

"That would be lovely," Nita said. "However, I have something to do right after work."

"That's okay. I can wait. It would be fun."

"As long as you're willing." Nita favored her with a faint smile and headed toward her next group session.

Megan made straight for the ladies' room. She locked herself in a stall and leaned against the wall, hugging herself. Maybe seeing Nita and then Dave would let her sort out the jumble in her mind.

Sweeney showed up, and Nita went to work on him quickly. "Officer Sweeney, I need your help on a confidential matter."

Sweeney hauled himself to his feet and adopted an eager expression. "How can I help?"

"Detective Dillon has been to see me professionally about his problems. With the prostitute and the pimp he killed."

"Wow." Sweeney's eyes widened and he ran his big hand over his face, as if to wash it.

"But he's a little on edge and won't tell me about his difficulties right now on the police force. I want to help him, but it's difficult. I felt that, as a fellow officer —"

Looking delighted to be told some dirt about a detective, Sweeney said, "Is it okay for you to talk about him to me?"

"Perfectly acceptable. I'm not going into the details of his therapy, of course. Sometimes, however, a trained therapist needs to reach out to others concerning treatment."

"Well, it's no secret that the Ladykiller task force has until Friday to find the perp. If not, Chief Mancuso folds it."

"Ah, that's the pressure he's been under."

"Yeah. And if the task force goes, Mancuso will nail Dillon. He may bounce him off the force."

"Thank you, Officer Sweeney."

Nita donned her sunglasses and head kerchief, and slipped down to the Deuce. Even through the tinted lenses, she could make out every face she passed in the 42nd Street glare. She had to be thorough —as thorough as she had been disposing of Billy Ray's body.

Passing the Foxy Lady, she saw the bloated slug of a man who she had seen inside the bar on Sunday. He was braying come-ons to male pedestrians.

"Our girls got the biggest hooters this side of the New York Phil-harmonic," he cried. "Check it out." He was wearing a disgusting Hawaiian shirt.

"Excuse me, sir. Have you seen Ace lately?"

The fellow leered at her. "What's with the shades, honey? Afraid I'll fall in love with your beautiful eyes?"

"I need to find Ace."

"I seen you before, baby. You was in there yesterday."

Nita peered into the bar's darkness. "Where's Ace now?"

"Heard about Billy Ray?"

Nita forced herself not to flinch. "Who?"

"Friend of Ace got stabbed and unloaded over in Jersey."

"Really?" Nita remained composed.

The man laughed until the phelgm collected in his throat. He spat an oyster-size wad onto the sidewalk. "Humps like Billy Ray get iced every day." He shrugged philosophically.

"Where's Ace?"

"Oh, I seen the little bastard all right. Said he needed money 'cuz he had to get out of town quick. So what does he do? He grabbed a couple hundred from my cash register when my back was turned. Wasn't too long ago. I imagine he already hopped a bus."

"Really?" The Port Authority bus terminal lay a mere block away. She felt the lump of the .45 in her bag.

"What you want with Ace, anyway? Don't tell me he knocked you up." He guffawed evilly.

"Hardly." Nita strode along the sidewalk to the bus depot. Port Authority was a remarkably clean palace of ramps and concessions, despite the riffraff that slithered all around her. And then Nita saw him.

Ace saw her, too. He swung his game leg around and hobbled into the crowd.

Think now. Think. Nita went after him. She slid a hand in her bag and gripped the reassuring steel cool of the gun butt. Think. She had to get him alone, but the terminal was packed with humanity. Any cops around? No. Think. If she shot Ace in public, people probably would be shocked enough that she could get away before the police showed up. Maybe. Yet she was on unfamiliar turf. What if she fled in the wrong direction and trapped herself in some cul-de-sac corridor, as the cops swarmed behind? Think.

With everyone up to Reuben and Billy Ray, she had had time to plan. With Reuben and Billy Ray, she had improvised out of necessity. And it had worked. Maybe she should trust her instincts now.

Ace's head bobbed ahead. She was closing on him, threading through the baggage-laden crowd. She bumped her knees on luggage and kept gripping the .45 in her bag. Then Ace, five people ahead, broke free and dodged to the left. Nita swiveled to follow, and a soft, huge mountain of flesh sent her staggering against someone else's back.

"Watch where you going, girl," said the mountainous woman who had bumped into Nita.

Over there. Ace had mounted an escalator crammed with people. Nita stepped onto the rising grillwork. She and Ace watched each other, unable to move. When the escalator disgorged him at the top, Ace disappeared.

When she reached the top, Nita turned about in a helpless circle, trying to find him. Ah. She spotted his narrow shoulders popping through a doorway.

Nita sprinted over to the door. On the other side was a loading platform and a bus bearing the legend, NJ Transit. A last passenger — a feeble old man — was climbing onto the bus. A conductor helped him up.

Nita impatiently waited behind the old codger, craning her neck to see past the dark glass of the bus. When at last the old man had negotiated the bus stairs, she tried to follow.

"Excuse me, m'am," the conductor said. "Ticket?"

"I don't have one," she said, striving to maintain control when she wanted to scream at him to get out of the way. "I'll buy one on the bus."

"I'm sorry," the conductor said. "This run is sold out. Next bus leaves in an hour."

"I'll stand."

"Not allowed. Sorry." He started to get aboard the bus.

"I have to get on the damn bus," Nita shouted at him.

The conductor paused. "If you have a problem, why don't you discuss the matter with them." He gestured at two cops who lounged against a nearby wall.

Frustrated and furious, Nita stood on the concrete platform as the door sighed shut and the bus rumbled away.

At the rear window, Ace's face swam. The tinted glass removed the sallow cast of his skin. And pain showed on his bony face. He looked like a lonely youth whose only love had left him.

If the cops weren't there, Nita could have put a bullet right through his maggot-filled skull. She went back into the terminal. The sign beside the door to the loading platform said the bus was bound for Rahway. That's where Ace came from, she remembered. Rahway.

Nita, adrift in thought, headed for home through the darkened spring streets. A few others flitted past, flying empty flags of faces and hair, living their mundane lives. Think.

Face it. Not every contingency could be planned for. Nita adjusted the strap of the bag on her shoulder. Perhaps she was better off than she thought. There was no chance the cops could connect Billy Ray to the Ladykiller series. And Ace — well, he had left town, likely for good. His haunted expression in the bus window of thwarted love seemed like solid insurance he would stay silent, wherever he went. So she had time to track him down and take appropriate action.

The steps sounded behind her. Right behind her. Just a few paces behind. Clip, clip, clip — in tandem with her gait. She speeded up. The steps increased their pace.

Nita yanked the .45 out of her bag and whirled around.

No one.

She squinted into the shadows collected in the nearby doorways. No one.

But someone *had* been there. She had always thought Ace was trailing her. He was on a bus to Rahway, though.

Uneasily, she resumed walking. No steps now.

At her apartment, the answering machine flashed one message. It was Megan: "Hi, it's me. It's about seven. I've got everything ready. Tell me when you're coming over. Can't wait." Her good humor seemed forced.

Nita considered backing out after the day she had had. But she smiled at the sound of Megan's voice. She turned on the shower and stripped off her clothes.

Nita had dressed up and put on make-up and a skirt. Megan greeted her at the door with a nervous smile. Her small table was set romantically, with roses and a candle. Megan was dressed up herself, and her strawberry hair shone in the candle's moody flicker.

"Wine?" Megan offered.

"Please. This day has been hell."

Megan nodded, "I seldom hear you complain —" She cut herself off and said, "I'll get the wine."

As Megan busied herself with the cork, Nita glanced around the small apartment. Nita noted with distaste the many stuffed animals on this grown woman's bed. "You appear to have even more teddy bears than I remember."

"Oh, this guy at the doughnut shop down the street gave me the white one. Out of the blue, tonight when I was going past. I go in there a lot for coffee." As she poured the wine, Nita noticed that Megan's hands were trembling, and she missed the glass. Red wine stained the tablecloth like blood.

"How interesting," Nita said. "Who is he?"

"A lawyer. On Wall Street. He's very nice." Megan finished pouring and clasped the bottle to her chest.

"A lawyer," Nita said. "That's a higher rung than a cop on the social scale, I grant you." Nita drank half her glass in one swallow. "A lawyer, eh? Of course, they're all parasites. Feasting off human disorder. Doing nothing to make society function smoothly, to iron out the kinks. They create kinks. And make money doing it."

Megan's laughter had a strangled quality. "Uh, yes, well, uh, he hasn't exactly asked me out."

"He will, he will. You're edgy. Is something wrong?"

"No, nothing's wrong." Megan's pleading look was painful to witness.

"You're seeing him again?"

"Maybe. It's not a big deal." Megan rubbed the neck of the wine bottle. "I'd better check the pasta."

She retreated into the tiny kitchen.

Over dinner, they rapidly drank the first bottle and were well into the second as they ate their pasta. Megan rattled on about her upcoming courses at Hunter. As the wine took hold, she behaved less nervously.

Rhythmic noises started overhead.

Nita pointed toward the ceiling with her fork. "Who are the love birds?"

"My neighbors. They're a sweet couple."

The bed upstairs creaked savagely.

Megan emptied the last of the second bottle into their glasses. "Nita, don't you ever want . . ."

"Want what?"

The candlelight played over Megan's awkward smile. "Want, like, you know, a man?"

The thumping overhead speeded up.

Nita took a long drink of wine. "Whenever the term 'man' comes into your head, think instead: 'unneeded distraction.' You'll be a lot better for it."

"I guess," Megan said, and poked at her pasta.

The noise stopped overhead. Nita and Megan ate and drank without saying a word. Megan fetched the veal and uncorked a third bottle.

"Delicious," Nita said, tasting the veal. "Actually, lust is an urge that we can control."

"Love too?" Megan asked, feeling a little tipsy.

Nita, while buzzed, had hardly lost her head. Bergstroms, her father had said, could drink when they had to. "Doesn't exist. An illusion conjured up by weak minds."

At least Megan was too drunk to be nervous. "Nothing like a good man, with a nice smile and a nice bod and —" She took a drink. "Haven't you ever wanted someone?"

Nita reached across the table, took Megan's wineglass from her, and held both the younger woman's hands firmly. "Yes," she said softly, "I have."

The next morning, with a boiling black mass of spring storms gathering, Jimmy Conlon ambushed Nita as she approached the crisis center.

"Looks like rain," he said.

"Who are you?" Nita snapped, still walking.

Jimmy smiled at her, captivated by her dark beauty. "Jimmy Conlon. We spoke yesterday."

"And I have no more to say today than I did then." She had terrific legs and an amazing figure. "Goodbye."

"My sources tell me all the Ladykiller victims had a connection to your crisis center," Jimmy said, keeping up with her. He had out his notepad and pen.

"Do they? How inventive."

"And one of your, uh, psychologically challenged clientele is probably the killer, but you won't let the cops interview anybody."

Nita stopped and faced him. "Who told you this?"

"I can't say."

"You can't?" Nita was taller than Jimmy by half a head. "How very convenient. Didn't people do this in Stalin's time? Unnamed accusers?"

"You're denying it?" Jimmy asked politely.

"I'm not giving you the courtesy of affirmation or denial because you don't deserve either," Nita said.

"It's not a question of what I do or don't deserve," Jimmy said. "I think the people of this city have a right to know what's going on with this case."

"Right to know? Spare me. You wave that around and hope to compromise the therapy of our clients. You obviously know nothing about counseling. All you've done is scare the people of this city needlessly with all this baloney about a serial killer. But I suppose it sells newspapers."

"And you obviously know nothing about newspapers. Newspapers make their money from advertising, not newstand sales."

"I couldn't care the least bit how you grub for your change," Nita said. "You people are the scourge of society. You do no one any good. Someone should bring you under firm control." Nita seemed to be in danger of losing some of her own control now.

"Talk about Stalin," Jimmy said. "That's what he did. And his pal Hitler, too."

"The only heirs to Hitler and Stalin I see around here are Detective Dillon and his scurvy crew," Nita said. "And certainly, you reporters are their propaganda arm."

"Lady," Jimmy said, "the reality train just left the station and you weren't on it."

"Oh, no? You used to write all the articles about this case, didn't you? Suddenly, I notice another name on the latest story. I bet you've been bumped aside. I bet you are in trouble, like Dillon."

Flummoxed, Jimmy's mind blinked off. All he could manage to say was: "What's going on at the crisis center?"

"I have no comment." Nita began to walk away.

"Hey, what's that gun doing in your purse?"

"I beg your pardon?"

"In your bag," Jimmy said. "I plainly saw the butt of a pistol. Why are you packing? I bet it's for protection. I bet it's because you're scared of your own clients."

"Now you're imagining things," Nita said icily. "Have you people no shame?"

Like the song the white chicks used to sing when she was a teenager, Jamie did believe that pretty girls seemed to find out early how to open doors with just a smile. But the puffy-faced suburban police captain wasn't buying.

"Can't let you inspect the body till a few things get straightened out between us and the NYPD," he said.

"I don't understand," Jamie said. They sat in his steam-heated office with its view of the Bergen County courthouse. A picture of his large family was perched on his desk.

"Your narcotics boys busted those humps in an apartment in Fort Lee — on *our* side of the river. They didn't even notify us. Took them right back across the G. W. Bridge, like they were free to do what they pleased."

"I haven't heard a word about it, captain," Jamie said. "All I want is to go over the body."

"So tell me your interest in the case."

Blake had told Jamie to avoid mention of the Ladykiller investigation for fear of leaks, mainly to Mancuso. "Billy Ray Battle is a Manhattan resident who was released pending his assault trial."

"Big deal. Assault happens every minute in New York. I'm supposed to be impressed?"

Rain clicked against the captain's window like a scattering of pebbles. He turned his attention to the sky outside.

"Please let me take a look at him, captain."

"You're not telling me everything, miss."

"It's detective, not miss." She said it softly, bereft of umbrage.

"Sorry."

"Listen," Jamie said. "Maybe I can help you. While there's this problem between our departments, nothing's probably getting done. Is there some piece of information I can get you?"

The captain brightened. "I got a list of fugitives who I believe are in the city."

"Deal. I'll get you a status update. Once the mess is ironed out, we can pick them up for you."

"Step right this way," he said. The rain's beat steadily increased on the glass.

The morgue had the familiar formaldehyde smell, covering other, even less pleasant odors. It was a cocoon of stark white walls and stainless steel tables, far from the rain and the outside living world. No one else was around.

"Not as busy as the one I'm used to," Jamie said.

"I want to keep it like that," the captain said. "No offense to the nation's largest city, of course."

"Of course," Jamie said.

The captain himself pulled Billy Ray's body out of the meat locker. The big man lay naked and gray on the slab, a tag around his big toe. Crude stitches from his groin to his throat gave evidence to the autopsy. His right eye was a stew of dried blood and matter.

Jamie slipped on latex gloves and felt around Billy Ray's ruined eye. "A knife, all right. Direct to the brain. You can tell where it sliced past the bone in the lower part of the eye socket."

"The perp had good aim. Vicious fucker. See the damage to the guy's nuts? Our guess is that the perp squeezed his nuts, then, when he bent over, zapped him in the eye with the blade."

Jamie could tell that the captain was impressed she showed no squeamishness. The first time she saw a corpse, she had puked. This was the umpteenth time. Although the suburban captain was twenty years older than her, Jamie felt sure she had seen many more dead bodies.

"He was found naked?"

"As the day he was born."

"No evidence of sexual activity?"

The captain shook his head. "His anus hadn't been ruptured. No sign of semen in his penis that we could find. When he went out, his bladder opened, so it might have washed away the semen. But I doubt it."

She peered at Billy Ray's neck and arms. "No indication of ropes or any other restraint."

"Not a one."

Jamie turned Billy Ray's death-stiff hands up to the fluorescent light. "Is this writing on his palm?"

"Yeah. It's numbers. He spent the night in the ditch, which means he got a little wet and a lot of the ink washed away. But you can kind of read them."

Jamie copied down the numbers. "Seems to be a phone number. Seven characters, with a dash after the first three. Hard to say if that's a four or a nine. Or if that's a one or a seven."

The captain moved close to Jamie and squinted at Billy Ray's palm. "I'd say it's a seven. No, wait. A one."

"Hmmmm."

"You doing anything tonight?"

Jamie smiled. Maybe the song was right, after all. "Captain, I like you. And I have dated white men. And I even have dated married men. But a married white man?"

"It's definitely not a seven. Seven's my lucky number."

Ace limped into the solemn, textured dark of his old pool hall, where he first had learned how to lose money. It had a half-dozen tables, their felt tops as green as fresh dollar bills. The click and thunk of balls fired his memories, good and bad. The cream of Rahway's layabouts had fled here to escape the rain that had soaked Ace's greasy hair and invaded his collar.

"Where's Big John?" he asked.

Ivan was the first to recognize him. But the greeting wasn't right for a returning celebrity. "Holy shit. Look what the cat dragged in. Ace Fucking Cronen."

Ace shook hands with him. "Where'd Big John get to?"

Super Hooper glanced up from the shot he was about to make. The ash from his cigarette fell to the felt and exploded in a soft heap of gray. "How about that. The big, bad Ladykiller hisself."

"The cops ain't smart enough to hold me," Ace said tiredly.

"You really do them bitches, Ace?" Ivan asked.

"They deserved it," Ace said.

"I got a question," Super Hooper said. The cue ball smacked into the 12 ball, which careened toward the side pocket but bounced off the cushion short of its destination. "Shit. Why didn't you fuck them chicks?"

Ace didn't like Super Hooper's tone of disbelief. "I didn't feel like it."

"Hell, Supe," Ivan said. "Ace here don't need to hold a gun to a chick's head to get her bod. Chicks swarm over our man, Ace. Ain't that right, Ace?"

Ace wasn't too fond of Ivan's tone, either. "Where's Big John?" No one answered.

Ivan sank the eight ball. "You owe me twenty big ones, Supe."

"Lucky fucker," Super Hooper said as he peeled off a bill. "Hey, Ace, you got any dough on you these days?"

"Lots, man. Why?"

"Care for a game?"

"Can't, man. Gotta keep moving. Cops after me."

Ivan laughed. "You're a dangerous dude to be around, Ace."

"Nobody's after you, asshole. I got forty bucks says you can't take me in eight ball," Super Hooper said.

"Well —"

Big John lumbered out of the back. "That *was* your voice I heard. Can't you stay out of this fucking town?" Everybody in the place laughed. "You look like shit."

"Big John, you heard any word on my mother? Last I heard —" Big John used to be a customer of his mother.

"Oh, her," Big John said. "Who keeps track? Didn't she O.D. on booze in Florida somewhere? Who keeps track?"

"Yeah, well, I figured maybe —"

"You got a phone call," Big John said.

"It's the cops," Ivan said with a laugh.

"Guy name of Jackie Why," Big John said. "From New York. Says somebody told him you used to hang here. The phone's in my office. You can talk to him, but you better fucking not steal so much as a paper clip or I'll have your ass."

Ace's tongue played over his lips. "Jackie Why? I ain't here. Tell him I ain't here."

"I already told him you're here, Ace," Big John said. "You saying you don't want to talk to the gentleman?"

Ace hobbled out the door into the hard, cold judgment of the rain. His ankle burned. He didn't see the puddles and his feet soon were drenched.

Jimmy Conlon kept flipping through his notes and checking out Chip's crowded office, which lay behind glass at the edge of the newsroom. Laird was busy on the phone regaling a pal about some mutual acquaintance. At last, the group that had been meeting around Chip's desk got up and left. Jimmy dashed for the office.

"Chip, I got a great tip."

Chip regarded him with the twisted expression that lay between disgust and disbelief. "Does this have to do with the West Side Crisis Center, by any chance?"

"Absolutely. My source with the cops —"

"I've been meaning to talk to you about that," Chip said. "Sit down, please." He closed the door with the grim efficiency of an executioner.

"About what?" Jimmy asked, taking a chair.

Chip took his place behind his desk. His seat was several inches higher than Jimmy's. "We got a very disturbing call from an official at the crisis center concerning your behavior."

"What?"

"This official, Nita Bergstrom, said you threatened to drag the crisis center's name through the mud unless you went out with her. Is that true?"

"Are you kidding?" Jimmy looked wildly about him, jaw agape like a beached fish. "That's bullshit."

"She sounded very rational. A bit upset, perhaps, but I was astounded to hear what she had to say."

"Me, too. You believe her?"

"The matter merits examination," Chip said.

"Christ almighty," Jimmy exclaimed. "You believe this woman you've never met over a member of your own staff?"

"I'm not saying I believe her or not. Simply that you no longer can work this story until a determination has been arrived at. Are we clear on this?"

Jimmy tried to see some compassion in his cast-iron face. "Jesus, you take the prize. What about my tip?"

"Tell Laird. Maybe he'll follow up."

"Tell Laird," Jimmy mimicked. "His social life is a little too busy for him to follow up a blessed thing."

Chip made a dismissing motion with his hand. "I'd love to chat. But I have work to do."

"That sucks," Dave said. "Those bastards."

"I suppose I can't help you," Jimmy said into his beer.

The after-work crush at McSorley's packed in people next to their stools. The din was deafening.

"Maybe you have, anyway. I bet you've shaken up the crisis center some. They might be more open now with at least the prospect of a bad story in the paper about them. They have no means of knowing that the paper won't run it."

"I'm not that confident," Jimmy said. "She's a devilishly clever one, that Bergstrom. And you know what's funny? As good looking as she is, I wouldn't go out with her for a jillion dollars. That would be a date straight out of hell."

"She's like a god around the crisis center," Dave said. "Those people seem to enjoy being manipulated by her. Especially Megan. It's scary, really."

"Date with Megan tonight, right?"

"Yep. Maybe I shouldn't be taking the time to see her now, with everything heating up. But—she's special. Say, I better get going. I need to feed the cat, then clean up. This date is important. I want it to go right." Dave flopped some money on the bar.

Jimmy made him take it back. "This one's on me. Tell Megan to say hi to Nita for me, okay?" After his friend had left, Jimmy remembered that he had wanted to tell Dave about the gun that Nita carried in her bag.

FIFTEEN

Jimmy took a long walk home in the evening rain. People scurried past to their safe, warm places. Jimmy's hat did a fairly good job protecting his head, but the rain had begun to seep through his raincoat. He didn't care. Then a taxi zoomed close to the curb and doused him with gutter water.

"You fucker," Jimmy called out to the cab as it disappeared down the block. He put every ounce of his anger at the day and at his life into the curse.

The rain came down harder, ricocheting off the pavement, turning the world into an aquarium. Jimmy got a pizza on the corner beside his building and hurried upstairs before the rain could eat away the cardboard box. He peeled off his clothes, got into some dry togs, then opened the box. It wasn't what he had ordered — peppers, not pepperoni — yet it would have to do. He sat down to his lonely meal, and he discovered he wasn't hungry. As the cheese congealed on the pizza, he pondered what to do with his wrecked career. He loved journalism. He was good at it. No one, though, would let him practice it right.

The phone trilled.

"Yes."

"I have some news for you," a woman's voice said. Muffled. Almost recognizable.

"Like what?"

"About the Ladykiller," she said.

"What is it?" Jimmy, as a newspaper reporter, talked to call-in nuts a lot. They seldom phoned his home.

"I can tell you who he is."

"Give me a clue." Jimmy fingered the cold pizza.

"He doesn't have anything to do with the West Side Crisis Center."

"How do you know I think that?"

She paused. "I have sources in the police department."

"I'd love to talk to you, lady. But I'm tired. So unless you get real specific, real fast —"

"Meet me outside your building. I can show you his picture. I have it with me. Him and his .45."

The woman sounded authoritative, not crazy. Still . . . "It's raining outside, lady. Can't you mail it to me?"

"The killer has targeted another victim. He's going to strike tonight. I know the killer."

Now Jimmy paused. "You know him?"

There was a stifled laugh. "I've known him all my life."

"Why does he do it?" Jimmy asked.

"To help—" She stopped herself. "Meet me outside your building. Walk toward Lexington Avenue." She hung up.

Jimmy didn't even consider not going. He grabbed his notepad and a yellow rain slicker, which would do a better job than his soaked raincoat. He scratched a few notes in the pad as he went down the stairs.

The rain on the street was even more intense, drumming the sidewalk in cold, wild abandon. The living had fled indoors. Jimmy hunched over and trudged toward Lexington, hard drops peppering his face.

Midway down the block, a figure in a poncho and a low-pulled hat stepped out in front of him, materializing out of a doorway in the long brick wall of a school building. Across the street loomed the dark shape of a church. Jimmy, the native New Yorker, was suddenly aware that no apartment windows overlooked them.

"Thanks for coming." It was a woman, dressed in jeans. Jimmy recognized the voice.

He squinted at her in the rain and dark. "Ms. Bergstrom?"

"I had to meet you," she shouted over the wind. "Did you tell any-one about my .45?"

"No. Why? Do you carry it because you know who the killer is? Do you feel you're in danger?" Jimmy already had his notebook out and was about five questions into the interview in his head. Jimmy was a pro even in bad weather.

Her leather-gloved hands, folded into her poncho, emerged gripping the gun. And she pointed it at Jimmy in the rain.

At first, Jimmy didn't understand. "What's that? What are you doing?"

"Kneel down," she commanded. "Now."

The fear surged up Jimmy's spine. But he had been in tight spots before. "Fuck you, lady." He turned around and headed back to his apartment.

"Stop," she cried.

Jimmy broke to the right and dodged between two parked cars into the street. Nita fired and missed. She raced after him. As Jimmy sprinted across the empty asphalt, she fired again and grazed his shoul-der. He yelped and almost tripped. That earned her several yards. Jimmy skipped between the parked cars on the street's far side. Nita's third shot punched through his right bicep. He spun around and fell to the wet sidewalk.

Nita, watching him, tripped on the curb and herself fell hard to the pavement. Jimmy, jangled by pain and shock, scrambled to his feet.

Disoriented, he saw the church and fell again onto its hard steps. He struggled to climb up the long steps to sanctuary on his hands and knees. His pain-clouded mind had the idea that if he could get to the top of the church steps, he would live.

Nita, drenched and panting painfully, came after him. Her gun bobbed as she aimed at his heaving back in its yellow slicker. This wasn't going to be a Ladykiller slaying. No neat shot through the right side of the brain. Just an ordinary street murder for Jimmy Conlon.

As she targeted between his shoulder blades, Jimmy suddenly turned over on the stairs. "You bitch," he sobbed.

She readjusted her aim at his chest. Then he launched himself off the stairs and charged her, howling. She pulled the trigger and his momentum slowed for an instant as the bullet tore through him. His body hit her with considerable force. They fell in a tangle on the sidewalk, him on top of her.

Nita's last shot had hit him in the neck, piercing an artery, and jets of hot blood splashed over her face, into her eyes and mouth. She gagged, pushing frantically at his weight. He was twitching now, writhing spasmotically.

She finally climbed out from under him. She retched violently, yet nothing came up. He continued to jerk beside her, dying.

The .45 lay a foot from her. She grabbed it and put the barrel against his left ear. His brains splattered out the other side of his head, and the hard rainfall sluiced them toward the gutter. Nita had the presence of mind to feel his pockets for a wallet. Thankfully, she found one. Robbery.

Weaving down the sidewalk, numb with shock, she let the rain wash her bare, blood-sticky head. Then her mind cleared and she remembered something. Something important.

She forced herself to retrace her steps. She went back to the body in front of the church.

Her hat lay crumpled on the steps. She picked up what would have been a superb piece of police evidence and jammed it on her head, hoping it would disguise the blood in her hair. At the corner she reached down to the dirty water rushing into a storm drain and splashed a handful on her face. Though shivering, she walked the endless blocks to home. It was taking a chance to go into her building, yet she met no one on the stairs.

Once inside, Nita bolted for the bathroom. Blood was all over her jacket, gloves, and skin. The rain had washed away some of it. But it still streaked her face and clung greasily to her twisted hair. Blood had stained her teeth a garish red. She looked like a warrior, direct from hell.

She had never been in such physical danger before. Even with Billy Ray, she had felt sure her wits were a match for him. No one had ever attacked her with the crazy momentum of Jimmy Conlon's desperate leap at her on the church steps. It was a new sensation and she had hated it. Now, her elation returned. She had won. Covered with his blood, Nita laughed hysterically for several minutes before she threw up.

Dave and Megan sat down to dinner as the rain thrummed against the restaurant window. "I haven't told Nita I'm with you tonight," she said. As if to reward herself for candor, she took a long drink of wine.

"Good," he said. Then, with a sly smile, "Seems Nita doesn't exactly like me."

Megan found herself smiling back. "No, she doesn't."

They shared a laugh, the kind where they locked wide, hungry eyes. The talk flowed more easily from there. About their childhoods and parents and the types of people they liked and disliked. In fascination, they quizzed each other about their interests, what they valued. The answers delighted them, made them laugh for no reason. Their knees bumped beneath the table. Their hands drifted together.

Once more, as the meal ended, their mutual destination was unspoken. He excused himself for a moment to call in. He had memorized Megan's address and phone number, gave them as his next location — the gospel according to Mancuso. Defying the relentless rain, fortune provided a taxi for them in front of the restaurant. In the cab, they kissed in heat, their tongues exploring each other's mouths.

Inside the welcoming warmth of Megan's apartment, they didn't bother with lights or talk. They tugged off each other's clothes. Dave picked up Megan and carried her to the bed. She brushed the stuffed animals onto the floor and drew him needfully into her arms.

"Slow, slow, slow," she gasped.

"Yes, yes."

He entered her with agonizing, exquisite slowness. With each hard, hot inch, she cried out. Her thighs squeezed his hips. At last, Megan eagerly locked her legs around him.

The pounding on her front door almost matched their rhythm. It took Megan a minute to realize it was not the pounding of her heart. Then she heard the shouting.

"Dave? You in there? Dave? Miss Morrison? This is the police."

"Jamie?" Dave panted.

Megan moaned as he withdrew from her.

"Dave," Jamie called from the other side of the door. "Bad news, Dave. Real bad."

Jamie didn't want to tell him. The car sped to the scene, siren shrieking as the watery colors of the rain-swept night reeled past. She kept her concentration on the driving. Images of Dave kissing Megan good night at her door — Megan with her hair every which way and her face puffy from interrupted lovemaking — replayed in Jamie's mind. She thought of the anguish that awaited Dave ahead.

"It's not my mother, right?" Dave said.

"No."

"You don't want to tell me, do you?"

"No, I don't."

"Tell me."

"This isn't a Ladykiller case, Dave," she said. "I just happened to be around when the squeal came in."

"Who is is it, Jamie?" He asked with the mournful quality of one who already knew.

She told him. Not daring to look at him, she told him.

Dave made a small, gasping sound. And said no more.

The siren blared its wolf song. The wipers slapped aside the ceaseless wash of water that teared across the windshield. And Dave said nothing.

"I was in New Jersey today," Jamie said to fill in the painful silence. She related what she had discovered. "The numbers on Billy Ray's palm appear to be the phone number of the hotline at the West Side Crisis Center."

Dave still said nothing.

At the scene, Jimmy's block, radio cars with their flashing red strobes clogged the street. A couple of news vans had arrived already. Even in the hard rain, a crowd was gathered outside the yellow tape.

Forgetting to put on his hat or button up his raincoat, Dave left the car and walked like a zombie through the rubberneckers.

He didn't show his badge as he ducked under the tape. A young cop bellowed at him and grabbed his shoulders to shove him back.

"It's Detective Dillon, you asshole," an older cop shouted, and the embarassed young officer quickly unhanded Dave.

Smithers, who Dave first met at the Academy, was in charge of the uniforms at the scene. He intercepted Dave. "You a friend of this guy, right?"

Dave nodded. The rain did a good job covering up his tears.

"Word got out that a reporter was waxed," Smithers said, the rain bouncing off the plastic sheathing that covered the patent leather bill of his hat. "News teams are here, with more coming."

Dave was transfixed by the canvas-covered form that lay beside the church steps. Hands and feet protruded from the canvas. A crowd of detectives and uniforms clustered over it like indecisive buzzards, their movements slow and deliberate in the downpour. A couple of technicians were trying to rig an awning over the body, but the wind was defeating them.

"Mancuso will be here any minute," Smithers said. "He's pissed to be called out. But a reporter —"

Dave edged through the group around Jimmy's body. A couple of people called his name in the wind. He ignored them. He pulled aside the canvas over Jimmy's head. The rain quickly ate at the chalk framing his ruined, blown-out skull.

"Robbery," a detective said into Dave's ear. "Signs of a struggle. Shot four times. Neck, shoulder, arm, and head. Wallet gone. Pocket inside out."

Dave explored beneath Jimmy's yellow, dirt-and-blood-grimed slicker. He felt for Jimmy's back pockets and fished out his friend's notepad. Sheltering it inside his raincoat so the ink wouldn't run, Dave examined the pages with a uniform's borrowed flashlight.

One entry, with that night's date and the time, two hours before: "Sez knws LK. Has pic."

"Body was lying here awhile," Smithers said. "Nobody called it in. Bad rain, right?"

"Must've thought he was homeless. Drunk or some shit," a uniform added disgustedly. "People."

Jamie trotted up. She said into Dave's ear, "Mancuso's here. Let's get out."

Dave surrendered the notepad to one of the detectives. He looked at her dumbly.

"You're getting wet, Dave," Jamie pleaded. "I'll take you back to Megan's. There's nothing more you can do."

The Mancuso entourage barged onto the scene. The man himself was dressed in a tuxedo under his raincoat. One of his flunkies held a giant umbrella over his head like a dark halo. The umbrella needed two hands to steady it in the gale.

Mancuso's bray carried over the weather. "Do I have to give a statement to those fucking jackals?"

"Sir, it would be best," his top aide said.

Mancuso gazed with contempt at the television lights on the nether side of the tape. "What's worse, the city clerk's testimonial dinner or this gang bang? At least the dinner's inside. I know this reporter, don't I?"

"Yes, sir," the aide said. "Jimmy Conlon. He's the one who broke the story —"

"I remember, I remember." Mancuso waved at him to shut up. "What's the big deal here?"

"He *is* a reporter of some importance, sir," the aide said.

"To who?" Mancuso sneered nastily. He scanned the group around the body. "Dillon? That you? Christ."

"Sir, let's get you briefed before you talk to the media," the aide suggested.

"Let's just make it a photo op." Mancuso said, staring at Dave as he talked to his aide. "I was here to show my concern and all that crap. I mean, really. So we've got one less pushy Jew reporter. So what?"

"You bastard." Dave lunged at Mancuso. Jamie and Smithers grabbed him and pulled him back.

Mancuso jerked away and momentarily lost his footing. The

umbrella caught the wind and the rain splashed his elegant shirt. He stabbed his index finger at Dave. "That son of a bitch is crazy. I'll pull his badge, by God."

"Come on, Dave," Jamie said. "Let's get out of here."

Dave twisted free from Jamie and Smithers. He ran to the intense TV lights that shone like supernovas beyond the tape. Dave palmed his badge and held it aloft for the reporters and cameras.

"I'm Detective Dave Dillon. I'm on the Ladykiller task force. Jimmy Conlon was my best friend. He was going to meet somebody who said they'd tell him the identity of the killer. That's why he died tonight. It's related to the Ladykiller series. He was shot four times with a .45. Not the way the Ladykiller victims always are. But it's related." He paused to stop himself from sobbing. "Believe me."

The reporters called questions, but Dave shook his head and threaded through the throng. He broke into a run.

He ran through the freezing, silver curtains of rain for blocks. Until he got home. The cat tumbled out to say hello, then after one good gander, ducked under the couch.

Dave phoned Megan, standing there in his sopping clothes, a puddle forming at his feet. He was still out of breath.

"I was worried sick," she said. "Why don't I come over? Let me be with you, Dave."

The idea of her arms around him beckoned like smooth, rich sunshine. "I want that more than anything," he said. "But I've got to figure it out. I've got to get this killer. There's a pattern. Somehow. If I can just —"

"Shhhh. I know."

And all over the city as the clock edged toward twelve, the vast cloud of rain and wind cascaded its anger, rattling windows, chilling hearts. The evening news beamed the dramatic footage of Dave Dillon to every dry place in town. The living took shelter that night and held each other close.

Keeping his own vigil through the night, as it howled its wet and malignant majesty outside, Dave Dillon sat on the floor at the foot of his bed, sat before the wall and the bloody pictures of the dead.

As the gray morning rain whipped at his window, Dave understood what he had to do. He slowly disengaged from the shocked, blood-blasted faces of the victims' photos and brewed some coffee.

The cat, who had left him alone during his long vigil, padded into the kitchen and rubbed Dave's legs. Dave bent down with the slow and deliberate care of the deeply weary and stroked the cat. After he fixed his pet's breakfast, he took his coffee to the window and let his bleary eyes dwell on the storm-swept street. Early risers scurried forth, bent under the rocking tempo of the continuing wind and rain.

The coffee, plus a shave and shower, brought him fresh energy. He briefly considered calling Jimmy's mother, but what would he say to her? That he was responsible for Jimmy's death? That if he hadn't enlisted his friend's help, Jimmy would still be alive?

As he was leaving, the phone rang. Although he wasn't ready to talk to anyone yet, he somehow knew that he should answer. Megan's voice had a soft, cottony, caring quality.

"How are you?"

"I'm okay. Really."

"I couldn't sleep," she said. "I worried about you all night. I wanted to call, but hoped you were sleeping, so —"

"You're wonderful," Dave said. "The next few days won't be easy. If I know you're there for me — Well —"

"I'll be there for you," Megan said firmly. "I love you, Dave." She was surprised to hear herself say it. She held her breath.

"I love you, too, Megan."

The first person Dave encountered at work was Blake. The skin of the lieutenant's face was tight and his mouth was a grim crease. "Come into my office."

Dave nodded and followed him. Jamie stood at the coffee urn, talking quietly with Safir and Wise. She first sensed Dave's passing presence, and stared at him, her open mouth a small oval. Safir and Wise watched Dave walk past in Blake's wake with a morbid raptness. Unblinking, Dave met their gaze.

Blake closed the office door behind them. He didn't bid Dave to sit and didn't sit himself. "Dave, I'm sorry as hell about Jimmy but —"

"Hear what I have to say," Dave said.

"Jesus Christ, Dave, Mancuso called me last night and twice already this morning, demanding — and I mean, demanding —"

"Hear what I have to say."

Blake shook his head. "After all I've done for you, how could you go to the media like that? How could you try to assault Mancuso like you did? My sweet Lord, how could you, Dave?"

"Hear me out," Dave shouted.

Blake stopped. "What? What can you possibly say?"

"Listen," Dave said, "I still can't tell you who the Ladykiller is. And I don't give a damn about Mancuso's feelings or what I told the media. It's irrelevant."

Blake emitted an exasperated gasp. "Irrelevant? He's got you off the task force. And pending an investigation, I have to take your badge."

"Today is Wednesday," Dave said. "Give me until Friday. What difference does it make? The task force is going away, and I am too. No matter what. But I can see now how to catch this fucker."

Blake shook his head and gave a small chuckle of disbelief. "You tell me how, Dave. You tell me how, after all the time we've put in, after all the false starts, how we can collar this bastard by Friday." This taunting tone was new to Blake. "You tell me, Dave. Come on. Tell me."

"The key is the West Side Crisis Center."

"You keep on harping about that," Blake said. "And what have we got to show for it? We got shit, my friend."

"Listen," Dave said, "Ace linked each of the victims with the crisis center. We were able to corroborate that with others."

"Oh, please. Where has that gotten us?"

"Listen," Dave said, "Reuben Silver and Jimmy Conlon also died because of their association with the crisis center. And I think Billy Ray Battle did, as well. He and Ace were friends. I think Billy Ray stumbled onto something."

"You think, do you? Your buddy Conlon was a robbery victim. His wallet was gone. He wasn't shot in the right eye."

"That doesn't matter," Dave said. "His notebook suggests he was lured outside to his death. He must have known something. Must have had enough for the killer to move on him."

"Dave, you listen to me for a moment," Blake said. "Your theories and suspicions don't get us anywhere. There's not a chance we can win a court fight to interview the loonies at the crisis center. Not with Mancuso on our ass. And not by Friday."

"Listen," Dave said, "The phone is the way in."

"The phone?"

"The West Side Crisis Center hotline. A lot of their clients use it when they get too weirded out. Reuben Silver was on the hotline the night he was killed. I bet the killer called him and made him go outside, where he got shot. Billy Ray Battle had the hotline number written on his palm."

Blake sat down heavily on the edge of his desk. "What do you want, Dave?"

"Tap their phones," Dave said. "It's our last chance. But why not? What do we have to lose? We can get a court order, without the crisis center learning about it. They can't stop us in court if they don't know."

"We're so deep on Mancuso's bad side that he wouldn't piss on us if our guts were on fire," Blake said skeptically. "We need to go through him for any court order."

Jamie knocked on Blake's door and poked her head in. She tried not to look at Dave. "Chief Mancuso's here."

Dave looked at Blake, waiting to be asked for his badge again. "Stay out of sight," he told Dave.

Dave disappeared down a hallway seconds before Mancuso and his procession stomped into Blake's office.

Jamie found him and took his hands. "Oh, Dave," she said.

They stood mutely in the hallway, holding hands. The yelling from Blake's office carried down the corridor with the force of a spring squall. Safir and Wise wandered by. They both patted Dave slowly on the back.

At last, Blake appeared at the head of the hallway with an odd grin. "Let's get that court order."

"What happened?" a bewildered Jamie blurted.

"We're going ahead with the wiretap on the crisis center," Blake said. "I told Mancuso I'd bring him up on charges. He regularly made ethnically insensitive remarks. Not smart in a multicultural urban environment. I bought us till Friday."

"What happens then?" Wise asked. Blake's grin faded.

"What happens, Loo?" asked Saffir.

"If we don't deliver by Friday, Mancuso's gonna hang us," Blake said. "No, before, he was gonna hang us. Now, he's gonna hang us, draw us, and quarter us. So this had better work."

"Big Dick Mancuso," Wise said.

"Before he dicks us," Saffir said darkly.

"We better be successful, Dave," Blake said quietly, back to his old self.

"We will be," Dave said.

Nita, usually fastidious, caused a stir when she showed up for work that morning. Her hair was barely brushed. She had on a wrinkled blouse with a tear at the shoulder seam. Her eyes were a roadmap of red capillaries with dark bags under them.

"Oh, Nita, dear," Rose said. "What's the matter?"

Nita didn't answer. She sat at her desk and pretended to sort through her in-box.

"Can I get you some coffee?" Tim suggested.

Nita shook her head without glancing up.

Control. She was losing control. The scene with Conlon had been chaos. She almost had lost everything. What if he had escaped? Now Dillon was trying to make him into a martyr on television. And Ace remained on the loose. There were too many unpredictable factors. Most frightening was her reaction to the melee with Condon. Her head had been in the toilet the entire night. When not throwing up, she lay on the bathroom floor and shook. In the past, the removals had been clean and efficient. That had to be restored. Control.

Tim met Megan at the top of the stairs and whispered to her. Megan gingerly approached Nita's desk.

"Good morning, Nita," she said. "How about I feed your fish for you?" She had an odd wistfulness about her.

Nita shrugged.

After Megan sprinkled the fish food into the tank, she came up to Nita's desk again. "May I have a word with you?"

"Not now," Nita said shortly. "I'm tied up."

"It's important," Megan said.

Mouth twisted in a pained expression, Nita looked up at her.

"It's about Dave."

"Dave? Detective Dave?"

Megan leaned over the desk and lowered her voice so the others wouldn't overhear. "I can't help myself. I love him. He's what I want. He's smart and strong. He's good and caring. He loves me."

Nita sneered. "He's an idiot. Get together with him and you throw your life away."

"I don't agree," Megan said, striving to stay calm despite an intrusive quaver. "You don't know him. You have some distorted, unreal view of him."

"Unreal?" Nita thundered. She leapt to her feet. "How dare you say that to me?"

Everyone in the large room watched Nita as she stalked around her desk and, with a stiff finger, jabbed Megan on the breastbone.

"How dare you challenge me," Nita cried. She jabbed Megan once more, forcing her to retreat a step backward. "I have made you what you are. I've given you a life. I've given you a purpose. Of all the people I could have chosen, I chose *you*. And you want to defy me? You want to fritter your gift away because you want this Keystone Kop in your bed?" She jabbed Megan again.

"Stop," Megan whispered. "You're hurting me." She moved back another step.

"Do you have any inkling of the cause you serve?" Nita roared. "You're a traitor. That's what you are. A traitor."

Another jab bounced off Megan's chest. "Nita, please," she sobbed. "Don't."

Nita turned to the fish tank. With both hands, she pulled it off the table. It smashed to the floor in a vast explosion of glass. Water sluiced across the tiles. Fish flopped about, dying. Nita, arms akimbo, stood over the ruin, panting. Then she whirled on Megan and pointed at her. "You're a disgrace. You selfish child. I hope you rot in mediocrity."

Hands to face, crying wildly, Megan ran from the room and down the stairs.

A terrible silence followed. The only sounds were the pock-pock-pocking of rain on the windowpanes, and the tiny slapping of the fish in their last spasms.

Dr. Solomon wandered in, filled with dithering anxiety. "Oh, my. Nita? Oh, my. Are you all right? Would you like to go home?"

"Home?" Nita yelled. She burst out into a short staccato riff of hysterical laughter. "This is my home. I have work to do here. I'm on the hotline for the next two nights. And I'm going to do my job. So help me."

Ace sat alone on a rock inside the railroad culvert, where he used to hang as a kid, and listened to the rain batter the world. A cold wind began to howl through the tunnel.

He remembered a whore who hung at the pool hall. Working girls weren't as plentiful in Rahway as on the Deuce, but if you looked long enough you could find them. He ventured back to the pool hall and managed to find the number written on the wall next to the pay phone.

"Fifty bucks," the girl at the other end of the phone said. "Twenty-five for a blow job. I should charge more, but you sound like a nice kid." She laughed mirthlessly.

Ace fingered his dwindling billfold. "Okay."

He went to the girl's tiny room above the hairdresser's, across the street from the pool hall. She was a little chubby and had broken teeth. Yet the mole on her cheek reminded him of Madonna.

He told her so as he watched her undress.

She lay back, naked, on the stained mattress. "Yeah, lover, I'm a real Material Girl. Say, you could use a shower."

"I don't want a shower," he said, removing his shirt.

"Uh-huh. Well, then, I get hardship pay. That'll be seventy for the trip, lover."

"Okay," Ace said glumly. He slid out of his pants and wondered if he could afford dinner.

She gestured at his crotch. "What's the matter, hon? Don't like what you see?" She jiggled her breasts and smiled.

He sat on the edge of the bed, not touching her. "I got a lot on my mind. Sorry."

"Shit. I get paid anyway, you know. You pay up whether or not you get interested, okay?"

"I got nobody to talk to," Ace whined.

"Yeah, yeah, yeah." She pulled a stick of gum out of her bag but didn't offer him any.

"Only one person in the world I can talk to. I love her. She wants to kill me, though."

"I know how she feels," the whore said matter-of-factly.

Ace watched a roach climbing the filthy wall. "I can't live without her. She's a goddess. What the fuck can I do?" A tear started down his face.

"Oh, Jesus. So she's a goddess? She any good in bed?"

"She's crazy," Ace said. "I thought I was out there on the edge. She scares the shit out of me."

The door splintered open and crashed against the wall. Jackie Why stood in the threshold. Water dripped from the brim of his white Borsolino. The ember at the end of his cigarette glowed furnace red.

"What, what, what?" Ace spluttered.

The whore screamed and covered her breasts.

"Hey, shit-for-brains," Jackie Why said. "You owe me four bills. It's collection time."

Ace and the whore scrambled into their clothes as Jackie Why laughed at them. She eased past Jackie Why and ran down the stairs.

"You come all the way from the city to get a lousy four hundred?" Ace said, his mind whirring to come up with a peace plan. "That's chump change for you, Jackie."

"I had nothing better to do," Jackie Why said. "Give me the money, and maybe I won't kill your sorry ass."

"I don't got it," Ace said. "I mean, I got maybe seventy-five. But I ain't got no four hundred."

Jackie Why took a huge drag on his cigarette. "You been spending your money — which is *my* money — in the wrong places, my man. How much did it cost you to fuck that little butterball?"

"Nothing," Ace said. "I didn't fuck her yet. Hey, I can pay you back. Honest. I need a little time."

"You don't got no more time," Jackie Why said. He unbuttoned his leather jacket. He wore his gun in a holster on his left hip. The butt pointed frontward.

Ace started to hyperventilate. "Please, Jackie. Please give me a chance."

Jackie Why pulled the cigarette from his lips and, grinning widely, jammed it against Ace's forehead.

Ace hollered as his flesh sizzled.

Then Big John suddenly appeared behind Jackie. He grabbed his shoulder and turned him around. Ace scuttled backward behind the bed. He thought he saw Big John reach for Jackie's gun. He ducked his head and could only hear the scuffle until the gun went off.

Torn between hiding his face and desperately wanting to know the outcome, Ace burrowed down for another full minute of silence and then gingerly peered over the edge of the bed. He saw Big John standing over Jackie. Ace couldn't tell if Jackie was alive or dead, but as he watched, Big John shoved the gun up against the pimp's chin and pulled the trigger. The pimp's Borsolino blew off his head in a fountain of blood and brains.

Ace, stunned, watched in silence. Eventually, Big John looked at him. Numbly, Ace clambered to his feet and staggered toward the door, skirting Jackie Why's sprawled body in awe and wonder. A crimson lake was growing around the pimp's mangled skull.

Big John tossed the gun at him and Ace caught it awkwardly. "You stupid little turd. Christ almighty."

"I'm sorry," Ace babbled inanely. "I didn't mean to."

"You're dead fucking meat, is what you are," Big John said. "Now get the fuck out of here. I'll clean this here up." He rummaged in his pocket and shoved a fistful of bills at Ace. "Go on. Get back to the city. Where you belong."

A light seemed to go on again in Ace's eyes. "Where I belong," he tittered excitedly, thinking of Nita.

⇛ SIXTEEN ⇚

Dave was sitting in his unmarked car in the rain, staring at the West Side Crisis Center, when Megan charged out of the door.

As she ran past, her face wild with rain and tears, Dave sprang from the car and grabbed her. He crushed her to him.

She fought his arms for a minute until she realized it was him. Then she sobbed against his shoulder.

"We're getting wet," he said as he held her. "Let's get in the car."

He led her, like a child, into the car. Inside, with the storm pounding on the roof, she cried harder.

"Nita?" Dave asked gently.

Megan nodded, just once.

"What happened?"

Megan shook her head, took out a Kleenex, and blew her nose.

"Was it about me, by any chance?"

"Yes," Megan said, hiccupping against her sobs.

"Did she ask you to choose between us?"

"Can we do something? Drive around?"

"Sure." Dave fired up the engine, called in on the radio that he was changing locations, and eased through the cascading downpour. "Anywhere in particular?"

"No," Megan almost whispered.

By its own instinct, the car found itself rolling over the bridge into Queens. The Dillon house, identical to all those to either side, had a damp bleakness.

"Come on in," Dave said. "There's someone I want you to meet." He smiled encouragement.

"Oh, God. I look terrible," Megan said. "My make-up —"

"You look beautiful," Dave said. "You're the most beautiful woman in the world today. Or any other day."

He took her hand, and led her into the house.

His mother sat beneath a shawl, a trashy paperback on her lap. She didn't smile or move.

"This is Megan Morrison," Dave said. "I told you about her. I decided that, well, you two should meet."

Megan summoned up a smile and shook the old lady's reluctant and brittle hand. "I'm so pleased to meet you, Mrs. Dillon. Dave has told me a lot about his childhood and this house and you and everything, that, I . . . uh . . . am delighted to be here." Aware she was babbling, Megan subsided nervously.

"Good to have you," his mother said shortly with a saccharine smile. Then to Dave, "I'm getting tired. Could you help me into the bedroom before you make your friend some tea?"

As he eased his mother to her feet, the old woman said, "The Conlon wake is tomorrow night. So quick."

"I know," Dave agreed. "I got them to release Jimmy's body early from the medical examiner's. Usually, in a homicide — Well." He didn't want to talk about that.

Dave shrugged at Megan apologetically and escorted his mother slowly along a creaking passage to the bedroom.

In the bedroom, his mother regained her strength suddenly. She held his arm and shook her head. "Get rid of that one. She's no good. I know a bad girl when I see one."

"Ma, that's silly. Megan's a sweet girl." Dave was caught totally off balance.

"Your father went wrong because of a bad woman. I can sniff them."

"Ma, I'm not going to discuss this with you," Dave said, beginning to be angry. "I'll take you to the wake tomorrow. Goodbye."

"I can sniff them," she said with a hiss. He practically had to pry her hand off his arm.

Running out to the car, Megan said mournfully, "Your mother hates me."

"She's just hard to warm up to. It takes a while. She'll be okay."

As the row houses slid past the car windows, Megan said, "Nita went off the deep end when I told her about us. She smashed her fish tank. She loved those fish."

They rode in silence into Manhattan. Megan asked to be dropped off at the crisis center. They made plans to meet that night.

She kissed him briefly but with the promise of passion, and he watched her hurry into the building. The rain seemed to be letting up.

Before Dave could pull away, he noticed Nita go past, wearing no raincoat, carrying no umbrella, soaked. She had been someplace else and was headed for the crisis center, as well.

On an impulse, Dave leaned out the window and called her name. At the sight of him, Nita's lip curled. "The great lover himself," she said. "Enjoying your latest conquest, Dillon?"

"You don't need to talk like that to me."

"Why not?" Nita taunted. "Is there a law against it? Are you going to arrest me? Take me back to the precinct and book me, so I can listen to you brag to your buddies what a great lover you are."

"What do you know about love?"

"That it's a foolish illusion." The rain made Nita's hair hang in ropes about her face. She laughed without mirth and a little too long. "You're trying to make me lose control, aren't you, Detective Dillon? Aren't you?"

"Control of what? Of Megan?"

"You're not going to do it, Detective Dillon. Oh, no. I swear that to you."

"Lady," Dave snapped, "the only things you control are your fish. Or should that be past tense?"

Nita opened her mouth to reply but didn't. She was clearly stunned by Dave's remark. She turned and walked into the building.

•   •   •

Ace cruised along the Deuce in Jackie Why's Mercedes. Aside from the bills that Big John had given him, Ace carried Jackie Why's fat billfold in his pocket and Jackie Why's gun in Jackie Why's holster on his hip, hidden by Jackie Why's own leather jacket. There were only a few flecks of blood on the jacket. The gun rode on the left hip, butt forward, just as Jackie Why himself had worn it.

The rain had subsided to a spattering. Ace had the windshield wipers on intermittent. They swiped the glass clean at their own occasional pace, like a sudden and unexpected twist of good luck.

Spotting Falstaff, who had come out to panhandle now that the rain was ending, Ace slid the Mercedes up to the curb. "Hey, my man," he called to the wino, "you want a ride?"

Falstaff's beard bristled in surprise. "Odds bodkins. Is that you, Ace?"

"I'm coming up in the world. And I'm back in town on serious, big-time business."

"Per chance, is that Jackie Why's car you're driving?"

"Damn straight," Ace said with a bright grin. "I killed him. I shot his ass. He came out to New Jersey, which is my turf. And the fucker died for it. Well, guess what? The Deuce is my turf now. Hell, the whole fucking city is my turf." He cackled in glee.

"Stone the crows," Falstaff said in genuine amazement. Then he seemed to get an idea. "That being the case, would you be kind enough to part with some change?"

"Change?" Ace rummaged in his pocket and produced Jackie Why's bulging wallet. He peeled off two twenties. "Here you go. Time to get gooned out of your mind."

Falstaff accepted the money in lip-smacking appreciation. "Bless you, good sir. My first drink, I'll raise the bottle to you. Then, I'll toast the late, great Jackie Why."

Ace's smile vanished and his face slid into a dangerous frown. "You don't believe I popped him, do you?"

"Ace, drunkards are God's innocents. We believe all. If you say you dispatched Jackie Why to his reward, it is as good as true."

Ace pulled out the gun and pointed it at Falstaff. "I popped him with this fucking piece, you sack of shit."

Falstaff held up his hands, the bills clasped between thumb and index finger. "I believe, I believe. Sirrah."

Lowering the weapon, Ace said, "Good. Lots of people don't believe me. Before the day's out, they sure as shit are going to. Hear me?"

"Perfectly, perfectly. Yes indeed."

Ace nodded and drove on. He parked the Mercedes in front of the Foxy Lady. Tony Topnut, standing at the front door in a Hawaiian shirt that pictured hula girls giving fellatio to elongated pineapples, grabbed Ace by the shoulder.

Ace jerked away from him and drew the skirt of his jacket back to reveal the holstered gun. "Hands off, you fat turdball."

Tony ignored the gun and shook his prey until his teeth rattled. "Where's my fucking two hundred, you fuckhead?"

"Keep it in your pants." Ace pulled away and slid out Jackie Why's billfold. He counted out the money. "I got money and I want a drink."

"Fuck," Tony Topnut said, pocketing the bills. "Go on in."

Ace swaggered in, barely limping now.

At the bar, he laid out some bills. "Scotch. And none of that watered-down piss you serve."

Finesse sidled up. "Well, if it ain't Mr. Dude. Where'd you get that bodacious jacket?"

"Popped Jackie Why for it." The bartender put Ace's drink in front of him. Ace took a slug.

"Mmmm-mmmm-mmmm. You are one crazy motherfucker."

"Give this black bastard what he wants."

Finesse cocked an eyebrow and ordered a Manhattan. "And after that, my friend here's gonna buy me the Bronx and Staten Island, too."

"Friend, shit. You don't like me."

"Nobody likes you," Finesse said. "So, you living large now. Considering that the police want you for questioning and that Jackie Why wants you for four hundred semolians, that's a good idea. Where'd you get the money again?"

Ace bared his teeth and snarled, "I fucking told you. Don't you listen, you black bastard?"

Finesse, unperturbed by the outburst, accepted the Manhattan from the bartender and took a sip. "My, my, my. You are the racial-sensitivity poster boy today. What brings you back to town? NAACP meeting?"

Angry, Ace dismounted his barstool. "I'm going to straighten it out with my woman. The only person who ever cared about me."

Finesse savored another sip of Manhattan. "A woman? Let me guess. She's deaf and blind. And she lost her sense of smell."

Ace smacked the glass out of Finesse's hand and screamed, "Damn you."

He yanked out the gun. "Talk about her like you done, and I'll kill you."

Finesse edged away, bumping into the stools. "I didn't mean nothing. Hey, brother, be cool."

Tony Topnut flung the door of the bar open and Ace saw the wrecker hoisting the Mercedes outside the bar's front door.

Ace ran toward the door. "Put that down," he yelled, waving the gun.

Tony flung his bulk forward and managed to bearhug Ace from behind, locking his scrawny arms to his sides, the gun pointed at the floor. "Give it up, you little scumbag," he shouted in Ace's ear.

Ace, squealing in pain, accidentally pulled the trigger. The bullet ripped through Tony Topnut's shin. The bar owner howled, dropped Ace, and fell to the floor. He held his bloody leg, wailing. His bladder let go and his urine formed a puddle that spread faster than the blood that oozed from his shin.

"Holy shit," Ace yelped and backed away, knocking over two chairs before he turned and ran out the back door.

The eternal day finally over, Nita headed back to her apartment. She had to get out of there, give herself some respite before the hotline shift began. Tim was on with her tonight, which was annoying. In fact, everyone in the center was annoying. Dr. Solomon had approached her and asked if she wanted to chat. Her vehement "no" had sent him back to his office refuge, not to be seen the rest of the day.

No one else dared to talk to her. Megan stayed away and kept her back to Nita. Just as well. Megan's simpering concern was more than Nita could stand. Fortunately, someone had cleaned up the mess from the shattered fish tank.

Nita paced along the drying sidewalk, her attention focused immediately in front of her. The cracks and stains and oily puddles of the concrete stood out like the world's imperfections. She had to get a grip. Control. Where had it fled? She wanted to smash anything in her way. Simply destroy it. The hell with cool planning. She was making too many mistakes. She had to get back her control.

She needed a plan. To deal with Ace. With Megan. With Dillon. She wished she could smash Dillon. How dare he presume to judge her? She visualized his empty cop head lying in a spreading pool of blood. Like Jimmy Conlon's. Yet a plan wouldn't come to her. The sidewalk unrolled its ugliness beneath her feet.

Almost home, she heard footsteps behind her. Gripping the .45 inside her bag, once more she whirled around.

There was nothing there.

At home, she ripped off her clothes, left them carelessly in a heap on the floor, and turned on the shower as hot as it would go. The scalding, thudding water punished her skin. At last, when she could take it no longer, she shut off the shower. She was panting.

Slowly, Nita patted her reddened body dry with a towel. The shower restored her to life. Pain cleansed. She blow-dried her hair and slipped into fresh clothes—a light sweater and leggings.

She had the feeling something would happen tonight. The air, breathless from the rain, had that expectant quality. Well, let them throw the worst at her. She was ready. She checked the action on her .45 to assure herself that it fed rounds smartly into the chamber. Control. She was getting it back.

Then she noticed the fish tank. What was wrong with the fish? She squinted toward the bright stillness, remembering that she hadn't fed the fish for — How long? In dread, she tiptoed past her desk with its silent computer, to the tank.

Only the large blue fish was alive. A few scales and fins from the others were floating in the murky water. The blue fish, eyes wide as it stared at Nita, had the guilty look of the reluctant cannibal.

Nita looked at the acquarium. Somewhere deep inside her a bubble of pure rage swelled. She began to scream at the blue fish, her voice rising to a shriek of frustration and fury. She screamed and screamed.

The spring air was blessed with a blossom smell. The rain had washed the city nearly clean. Puddles sat like mirrors, reflecting the last pinks and reds of the sky. Dave walked around them and told himself that miracles were waiting to happen on such a fine night.

Standing in the small foyer, he buzzed and waited until Megan came down the stairs. She looked smart: blue silk blouse, white linen jacket, black short skirt, expensive pumps. Her welcoming smile had an incandescent warmth.

They kissed for a full minute. When she touched the holstered revolver under his armpit, she broke the embrace. "Dave, about your friend Jimmy. I'm so sorry."

His eyes filled and he held her again, close, until the feel of her body drove away his grief. He kissed her hard, his mouth demanding.

"Detective Dillon," she gasped, pulling away for air. "I'd like to take you right back upstairs."

"Let's go," Dave said hoarsely, pulling her back to him.

The street door opened and a couple entered, embarrassed to have interrupted.

Dave and Megan released each other. "Oh, hi," Megan said awkwardly. They nodded and smiled.

"Maybe we should go to dinner," Megan said, taking his arm. "I do have us a reservation at a great place nearby. And then —" She giggled throatily.

Dave stroked her face and joined in her smile. "Whatever you say."

"I'll remember that," Megan laughed.

They walked to the restaurant in the buoyant air. Megan held Dave's arm with both hands, pressing her body against his. They passed the doughnut shop and the men inside waved.

"Isn't one of those guys a congressman?" Dave said.

"I don't know. I'm only looking at one guy tonight," Megan said archly and he leaned down and kissed her cheek.

"Listen, let's not talk about serious stuff: Jimmy, Nita, the case. Let's just talk about us tonight, okay?"

"That sounds wonderful," Megan agreed with a smile. "Carlo is giving us an alcove in the back. Practically no one can see us there. It'll be lovely."

"Nobody can see us?" Dave caressed her forearm. "Sounds kind of dangerous to me."

"I am dangerous, my love."

Nita walked briskly toward the crisis center. Tim would already be there for the hotline shift. She was late. She was never late. But an hour had simply slipped away. More. She remembered hearing the screaming as if it had come from someone else. And catching the blue fish, flinging it hard against the wall, then stomping it into a pulp. She remembered the neighbors pounding on the door and asking if she was all right. She remembered yelling at them through the door to go away and leave her alone. She remembered sinking to the floor, sitting on the hard surface, her head in her hands.

Control? Where had it fled?

Two blocks from the crisis center, the footsteps started again. Right behind her. Keeping pace. When she spun around, she actually had the gun half out. A shadow seemed to slip into a dark doorway.

"Ace, is that you?" she growled. She approached the doorway, gun pointed ahead of her, combat ready. There was no one there. Of course. She stuffed the .45 back into her bag and resumed walking, resisting the impulse to check over her shoulder.

At work, Tim buzzed maternally around her. "How are you? You look awful. Do you want to go home?"

"No, I do not." Nita's voice was a bark. "Leave me alone."

Tim backed off. "Sorry for breathing, I'm sure," he said petulently.

Sweeney was not in his customary position. Still hurt, Tim said he'd finally been reassigned. He had asked Tim to tell her goodbye. "Why, I don't know, Miss Grumpy."

Nita ignored him and sat at her desk. The paperwork in her in-box had piled high, yet she didn't feel like touching it. She stared at the mound and did nothing.

"Want me to help you deal with this," Tim offered tentatively, gesturing at her in-box. "It's really overflowing."

Nita picked up the in-box stack and dumped it in her wastepaper basket.

"Well," Tim said. "Somebody has the rag on tonight." He returned to his desk.

The phone rang. Nita reached for it.

Ace sat on the overpass wall beside Grand Central, legs dangling over the rushing cars below. He had been laughing for some time.

He glanced up at the huge clock on the building stories above. He adjusted the gun, which was sticking unpleasantly into his side, patting it fondly. He frowned suddenly and checked his jeans pocket. He dug until he found a quarter, put it back, and resumed laughing.

Secure in their alcove in the back of the neighborhood restaurant, Dave and Megan drank their wine and looked at each other dreamily in the glow of the table's single candle. Everything they said to each other provoked delighted laughter.

"You could move into my place —" he said.

"That photo collection will have to go, of course."

They laughed, never taking their gaze from each other.

"No need for them if I'm off the force," he said.

She stopped laughing and gripped his hand. "If that happens, what will you do?"

Dave shifted his attention to his wineglass. "I'll figure it out. See, I've always been a cop. Police work is in my family. There has to be something beyond that, though."

Megan squeezed his hand. "You'll be okay, darling. I believe in you."

Dave met her eyes again and leaned over to kiss her. "Thank you. And you, what will you do?"

Now it was Megan's turn to turn her attention to the wine in her glass. "Finish my degree. Get on with my profession."

"Maybe we should start over someplace else. Get out of town." He laughed to show he was kidding, but for the first time his laughter sounded forced.

Luckily, Carlo chose that moment to bring the veal.

Dave and Megan were eating lustily in perfect harmony, the wine heating their blood and their teasing taking on overtones of foreplay, when Dave's beeper went off.

Dave listened intently to the recorded conversation. "So, she never says exactly where she's going to meet him?"

Jamie was close to him, leaning against the console in the cramped surveillance van, her polished ebony cheekbones gleaming in the dim lighting. "Just that it's somewhere they met before. I presume it's nearby."

"And she hasn't made a move?"

Safir, his eyes glued to binoculars in the front seat of the van, shook his head. "Nobody's left the crisis center since the shift changed and she and Tim got there."

"Nobody at all," echoed Wise, waiting his turn in the driver's seat.

"Play that last part back again, would you," Dave asked.

Jamie hit a button and Nita's voice filled the van.

"I know you're upset. If you've killed a man, I know you feel hurt and depressed but I don't want you to do anything —"

The side door of the van slammed open, startling all of them. Wise had his gun out of his holster first, pointing it two-handed over the back of the front seat. Dave was on his feet in a split second, moving in front of the gun, reaching out.

Megan stood in the open doorway, half scared, half puzzled,

taking in the scene before her. Nita's voice continued to talk sooth-ingly, intercut with Ace's jittery staccato, alternately cajoling, threat-ening, begging.

Dave grabbed Megan's arm and pulled her inside. "You were supposed to wait in the car." Jamie slammed the rolling door shut behind her. With a curse, Wise holstered his gun.

Nita's voice purred, "Ace, you know I can't say I'll meet you out-side the crisis center, especially at night, but perhaps you should go back to the place where we last saw each other —"

"I can't believe this," Megan shouted, as the reality of the situa-tion sunk in. Belatedly, Jamie hit a button and Nita's voice was cut off.

"You're spying on us." She angrily shook off Dave's hand.

"Listen, Megan —"

"Listen, nothing."

Safir cut them both off. "She's leaving the building. Let's roll."

Dave shouted, "Stay back. We don't want her seeing us, but don't lose her."

Megan was furious. "You're using her as bait! I don't believe it."

"Keep her here," Dave said to Jamie as he took out his weapon, checking the clip.

"Dave!" Jamie protested.

"Don't bother," Megan snapped indignantly. "I'm leaving."

Dave was frantic, trying to switch gears from cop to caring in sixty seconds. "Please, Megan," he begged, "I'll explain later. I promise."

"How could you? You're letting her meet some lunatic out there. You could get her killed."

Dave and Jamie both lunged for her but Megan ducked out of the van's side door before either of them could grab her.

"Stay here," Dave commanded Jamie, jumping out the door be-hind Megan.

"Dave —" Jamie protested.

Safir and Wise got out and slammed the side doors, too. They glanced at Dave.

"She's already at the corner," whispered Saffir.

"Let's not lose her," whispered Wise.

Jamie leaned out the open side door. "What about Megan, Dave?"

"Forget her. We go after the other one."

The three men raced off into the night.

The street was swept clean of humanity. Events were clicking into place like the sound of Nita's shoes on the nighttime pavement. Nita felt that old tingle of anticipation, heightened by the thrill of being back in command again.

She hurried along the dim street, the occasional tree making strange shadows and stranger murmuring sounds in a light breeze off the river. When she heard the footsteps behind her, she almost broke stride but did not. She did not look back.

Megan cursed under her breath. She wasn't sure which way Nita had gone. She hurried as fast as she could past the crisis center and west, toward the river, toward the darkness. She couldn't be sure, but she thought a man ran silently past on the other side of the dim street. She cursed the pumps she was wearing that slowed her. She cursed herself.

The playground loomed ahead in the darkness. Nita hesitated before entering. No sign of Ace. The playground, a phantasmagoria of bars and slides and swings, cast strange angular shadows. Nothing breathed there, other than the air, faintly stirring off the river.

Nita crossed the dim, desolate lot. When Ace popped up, part of the long shadows of the jungle gym, she stopped. He approached her cautiously. In the half-light, his sickly pallor seemed ghostly.

At the corner, at a nod from Dave, Safir turned south, Wise north, and Dave ran straight on alone.

Sobbing with frustration and fear, Megan paused to take off her pumps. When she glanced up, she was sure she saw Dave, illuminated in the light from a passing car, at the intersection at the end of the block. He was running easily and he had his gun out.

"Noooooo," she cried, flinging the shoes away and sprinting after him.

Ace pulled back the leather jacket to show Nita his holstered gun. "I killed someone. I did. I did it for you."

Nita pulled the .45 out of her bag. "Thanks."

"Nita," Ace croaked. "I did it for you."

She took perfect aim at his head.

"Please." Ace began to sob.

"Freeze. Police."

Nita swiveled to face the shouted command. There was a man behind her. There was a running man, coming into the playground. He had a gun out. Dave Dillon.

"Nobody move," the detective bellowed. As if he owned the city. As if he weren't just another parasite.

Nita pulled the trigger.

Megan's heart was beating wildly and she was running as fast as she could, her skirt hiked up her thighs, her long legs pumping.

When she heard the shot, she nearly stumbled and she screamed Nita's name. The second shot seemed to propel her forward as she raced into the darkened playground, her head light with fear.

There were more shots but Megan ignored them. A child's swing was moving, and in the light reflected off its metal surface she glimpsed a figure on the ground.

Screaming, oblivious to everything else, she raced to the fallen figure.

At first, kneeling, panting, beside Nita, Megan thought she might have just fallen. She was lying on her back, her head to one side. Megan slowly, tentatively, reached for her friend. She touched Nita's perfect face, traced the line of her exquisite cheek with her hand. She spoke Nita's name softly, like a caress.

Somewhere behind her, there were shots being fired and gruff men's voices. Someone was shouting her name, telling her to stay down. None of it registered.

Nita's eyes were open and Megan thought she was about to speak to her. Megan leaned closer. She thought that Nita was crying. Nita's right eye, the side of her face that was down in the shadows, seemed to have shed a tear, a solitary red tear. Megan gently put her fingertips to the point of Nita's chin and turned her face toward her.

Then she saw the blasted eye, the skull shattered and dripping, the horror of a beloved face exploded in violent death. Megan's stomach churned, the blood drained from her head.

Her first shriek was thin and strangely high-pitched, as if from a small wild animal. But soon her throat cleared and her tortured screams, full-bodied and awful, shook the night.

⇛ *SEVENTEEN* ⇚

From then on, time fast-forwarded for Dave through curtains of static. He moved through it as if in a trance.

Lt. Blake materializing at the playground to personally take his statement. Surrendering his service revolver to Blake, so the crime-scene people could inspect it and log it. Safir and Wise coming back, reporting that they had once again lost Ace, whose talent for disappearing in this city was becoming a legend.

Making a longer, videotaped statement at the precinct. Drinking cup after cup of coffee, Jamie always at his side. Blake recommending that he take a leave. Take a few days.

Asking Jamie and Blake about Megan. Getting no good answer. She was hospitalized, sedated. No one would let him know where.

Going home as dawn neared and ripping down the photos of the Ladykiller victims. Trying to sleep. Awakening from nightmares with the cat licking his face.

When he went in to work, over protests from Blake, Dave learned that Nita had kept a record of all her clients on a computer disk at her apartment. Safir and Wise had turned that up in their search.

Ace was still missing.

Dave asked about Megan but he knew he was being stonewalled.

Blake went with him downtown to One Police Plaza where he had to endure Mancuso's back-slapping and fake smile. Dave accepted his clammy handshake for the cameras. He was numb. He could think only of Megan.

Standing next to Mancuso at the press conference with no other Ladykiller task force members present, not even Blake, Dave listened to how Mancuso had all but cracked the case. He was lauded by Mancuso for blowing away the dread menace. He listened to Mancuso say that the city's streets were safe again.

Jamie drove him to Jimmy Conlon's wake. He hugged Jimmy's mother, who thanked him for killing the demon who took her son. He overheard Jimmy's fellow journalists complaining bitterly that Chip, Laird, and the other office politicos couldn't attend the wake because they were dining with the publisher. The newspaper had sent a big wreath.

Jamie was at his side always.

Dave watched his mother whisper to Mrs. Corrigan, as they sat in the corner of the room, about the black girl who was after her Dave. He didn't need to hear the words to know exactly what they were saying.

Jamie knew, too, but she didn't care. She knew that Dave was like an invalid, still in shock, and badly in need of care. She tried not to think about the future, but a tiny voice kept whispering that patients always fell in love with their nurses eventually. She could wait.

Dave heard not a word of congratulations from his mother to her boy, the hero cop.

Standing beside Jimmy's closed coffin, passing his hand over its fine wood, Dave said farewell.

Dave called the crisis center and got the runaround about contacting Megan. He left repeated messages on her answering machine, hearing her cheerful, sexy recorded voice, until the machine was turned off or stopped functioning. Then the phone just rang and rang.

At home, Dave tried to sleep, awakening once more to the rasp of the cat's tongue.

He bought all the newspapers.

The most telling headline: LADYKILLER WAS A LADY. The subhead read: COP BLOWS AWAY KILLER SOCIAL WORKER. The tabloid had a large picture of Nita on its front page. She looked beautiful.

After a wasted day at work, pushing papers around like a zombie, Dave gently turned aside Jamie's suggestion that they have dinner.

"Not hungry," Dave said. "Sorry."

"Then you gotta be thirsty," Jamie purred.

Wise butted in: "Yeah, let's party. You know the rules."

Safir added, "You got to, Dave. You crack the case, you buy."

Dave let himself be taken to McSorley's. A couple dozen cops with beers in their big hands came up to touch their glasses to his, clap him on the shoulder, punch his arm. Jamie, a fixture on the stool next to him, kept finding excuses to touch him.

Blake on the other side, asked: "So, Dave, you gonna take some time off?"

"Yes, sir. Maybe a little while. I've got some, uh, personal matters I'd like to handle."

"Fine," Blake said. "Just tell me how much time you need."

Dave stood up. The others looked at him, a little drunkenly, expectantly, as if he were going to make a speech. "I'd like to start now, if that's all right." He threw some money on the bar and headed out.

"Dave?" Jamie called after him.

Blake put his arm around her. "Don't," he said.

Encouraged by the recent rainfall, pink blossoms had burst forth on even the scrawniest tree that poked out of the Manhattan bedrock. To Dave, however, they barely existed. He headed toward the West Side Crisis Center, dead to the flowery morning that proclaimed itself around him.

When he entered the customary bedlam of the crisis center, the clients stopped their bawling, crying, and drooling at once. Silently, they watched him pass, headed for the stairs. The heat of their staring prickled his skin.

Only one of them approached him, the fellow from outer space. "She was a goddess," he said to Dave, and he about-faced indignantly, marching back into his madness.

"A goddess," someone in the crowd cried.

"Goddess," another client echoed, more loudly.

By the time Dave got to the stairs, the entire group was shouting, "Goddess."

At the top of the stairs, the social workers at their desks also stared at Dave. No sign of Megan.

The young gay guy, Tim, stood up as Dave passed. "Nita Bergstrom was no murderer," he said, his voice shaking.

Dave didn't even slow down.

Dave met Dr. Solomon in the corridor outside his office.

"Oh, dear," Dr. Solomon said, dismayed to encounter Dave.

"I want to see Megan," Dave said.

"She isn't here, I'm afraid."

"How is she?"

"She's fine, physically," Dr. Solomon said. "I put her in the hospital for some rest. I regret to say I'm not going to tell you which one. They're sending her home tomorrow. I asked her to stay with Mrs. Solomon and me for a while, but she refused."

"Is she — calmed down?"

"She's on Valium. You've got to realize that she's had a horrible shock. Nita was her best friend and mentor."

Dave nodded. "I know."

"And I gather that you meant something to her too." Dr. Solomon's demeanor was kindly.

"I was hoping that I meant a lot to her. I'm in love with her," Dave said.

"Well," Dr. Solomon said, "when your boyfriend kills your best friend, that's a pretty major trauma, wouldn't you say? Her whole world is shattered. She needs time to pick up the pieces."

"Yeah. Thanks, doc."

"We all need some time," Dr. Solomon said.

"Time," Dave said hollowly.

"Yes. I'd have staked my professional reputation on Nita. Hard to conceive of her as a killer. What a remarkable woman." Dr. Solomon walked sadly away.

Dave leaned his forehead miserably against the corridor wall. "Time?" he said plaintively to himself.

• • •

The next day, Megan left Mount Sinai Hospital and caught a cab down Fifth Avenue. The blossoms of Central Park were explosions of joyous pinks and whites, and as they bobbed past the cab window in bright-spirited array, she tried to interest herself in their beauty.

She spotted the tabloid on the floor. Yesterday's. With Nita's picture on the front page. She picked the paper up and held it in her lap, examining it while the cab slid down spring-blessed Fifth Avenue. With her fingertip she traced the contours of Nita's dear, familiar, exquisitely beautiful face. She stared at it for a long time.

Then Megan slowly crumpled the front page in her fist.

Finesse and Falstaff were assuming the position against a fence that sported a massive poster for the Big Apple Circus. Palms open against the poster's clown faces and animal acts, feet spread over the filthy sidewalk.

"Why do I gotta do this?" Finesse complained. "This is shit."

"I wouldn't anger the gendarmes," Falstaff advised.

Blitzer, the young cop, stood behind them, within whacking distance with his nightstick. "Where is he?"

"I ain't seen him since he went batshit in the Foxy Lady," Finesse said.

"Our good man, Ace, has developed into quite the will-o-the-wisp," Falstaff said. "He doesn't vouchsafe his whereabouts to the likes of us, I assure you."

"We'll be coming down hard on you till we find this asshole," young Blitzer said. "A word to the wise."

Martino came running up. "I think we got him," she said.

The two uniformed cops ran along the Deuce to a shanty of cardboard boxes. Something was inside, moving.

Martino radioed for backup. She and Blitzer both drew their sidearms. "Come on out, Ace," she commanded. "We know you're in there."

But the face that appeared was that of Stinky, the old bag lady. "Can't I get no rest?" she growled.

As the two cops slumped away, Blitzer asked his partner, "Why do they care so much about bagging Ace? He killed one useless hump and wounded another. We ought to give him a medal."

"Lt. Blake feels he'll go after Dillon."

"Dillon?"

"Ace was obsessed with Nita Bergstrom," Martino said. "And who put a bullet through his beloved's head?"

"Shit."

The phone was ringing in Megan's empty apartment. Then came the jangle of keys in the lock She came in carrying several packages.

She kicked the door shut behind her. The phone rang again. Megan glanced at the phone as she put down the packages. The answering machine clicked on. She had erased all the messages without listening to them. The tape was rewound.

Dave's voice, warm and rich, filled the apartment. "Megan, I know you don't want to talk to me just yet. But I want you to know I'll be here. When you're ready." The voice faltered toward the end. After a moment, he hung up.

Megan ignored the phone. She carefully opened the small package and held her new prize up to the light. The plastic bag was filled with water and it revolved slowly as she held it aloft.

Inside the plastic bag of water swam a beautiful, bright blue fish.

The crisis center staff was assembled but the meeting was not yet in full drone. They were awaiting the arrival of Dr. Solomon before it officially began. No one had seen him, and the question was whether he had remembered. People tried to talk about any other topic than the one foremost in their minds.

Then Tim chimed in, bad taste as usual getting the better of even his own sentiments.

"Did you hear the one about the social worker who wanted to change the world?" he asked archly. "She really took a shot at it."

There were scattered gasps and nervous giggles. Tim didn't notice Megan when she came in behind him.

"Did you hear the one about the social worker who wanted to challenge her clients?" he pressed on. "She blew their minds."

The silence this time was ominous. Tim turned around and saw Megan in the doorway, standing there without expression. Tim grimaced apologetically.

"Everybody knows how I felt about Nita," Tim said. "Well — life goes on, doesn't it?"

Dr. Solomon entered the room in his customary fog. He conducted the entire meeting without noticing Megan. It was only at the end of the session, when Rose made a fuss over Megan, that he saw her. He asked Megan into his office, where she stood stiffly before his desk. He sat looking worriedly at her.

"Don't you think it's a little soon?" Dr. Solomon asked.

"I need to get back to work, Dr. Solomon," Megan said. "I need the routine. I need to feel useful. I need to *do* something."

"Well —"

"And I'm on the schedule to work the hotline tonight anyway, with Rose. She gets scared at night, and I can soothe her," Megan said.

"Oh," Dr. Solomon said, "I couldn't possibly —"

"This will be the best thing for me, sir," Megan said, and she moved to leave. "Thanks, Dr. Solomon."

She smiled and walked out briskly. Dr. Solomon sat behind his desk, pondering.

That night, the wind invaded the streets from the west, jostling the blossoms, threatening to strip them from the tree branches. Megan poured herself a cup of coffee while Rose nattered on.

"So tell me how you really are, dear," Rose said.

"I'll be fine, Rose," Megan said. "But I don't want to talk for a while. Is that okay?"

"I understand completely," Rose said. "I won't say a word." And of course, as soon as she perched on her desk chair, she started her running commentary. "We're going to be in for another big rain-storm. I heard on the radio —"

Megan blocked it out. She sat behind Nita's desk and went through Nita's drawers. They all were empty.

"The police did that: emptied the drawers and took all Nita's belongings away," Rose said. "They came in here, with that black girl detective. The one that's so pretty —"

The desk, with its vacant drawers pulled out, transfixed Megan.

Rose wasn't sure whether Megan would cry, so she chattered still louder. The phone rang, startling them both.

Megan gestured at Rose that she would answer. She picked up Nita's receiver. "Crisis center," Megan said into it. "Can I help you?"

"Do you know who this is?" the voice at the other end muttered. A sizzle of lighting made the crisis center windows glow.

"It's Ace, isn't it?" Megan said. The following thunder erupted loudly. Another phone rang and Rose answered briskly.

"You saw her dead, didn't you? You saw what they did to her, didn't you?"

"I saw," Megan said. She felt her throat dry up.

"You know she didn't do it, don't you?" Ace said.

"She didn't do it?" Megan said breathlessly.

"I'm the one," Ace said, anguished. "I'm the Ladykiller. I did them all. Every one."

Megan could hear her heart pounding. She was gripping the phone so tightly her knuckles were white.

Ace continued, "She was innocent. And I can prove it."

The lightning lit up the windows again. The thunder came more quickly this time. The storm was closing in.

"Tell me."

"I can do better than that," Ace said. "I can show you."

Megan gasped, her hand to her throat. "Where?"

The night air held the electricity of the approaching storm. Eerie shadows jumped and writhed in the rising wind, which coursed down the street from the west like a great wickedness.

Megan, who had left ignoring Rose's petulant queries, came out of the crisis center onto the street and locked the iron door behind her.

She turned and started at the appearance of a man who seemed to thrust up out of the nightmare-deep shadows.

It was Dave.

"You," she said.

Dave grabbed her by the shoulders. "I've got to talk to you," he said. "You've got to listen."

Megan, first rigid in his grasp, began to struggle, trying to get away. "Let go of me."

"Megan, please. You've got to listen."

A sudden fusillade of rain pelted them. It was hard and stung.

"You killed her," Megan cried. She lashed out with all her strength and anger, punishing him. The wind and the rain fueled her fury. She pounded at his head. He covered himself to deflect her fists.

Then, over Dave's shoulder, a new figure rose, as if from the earth. Ace gripped the gun in one hand. Confusion, fear, and hatred shone in him as the storm blew about his greasy hair.

Megan froze. Dave whirled around.

Ace wavered. The gun dipped. Dave grabbed the arm with the gun and twisted it. Ace slammed to his knees on the rain-swept sidewalk. He sobbed in pain, frustration, and failure.

After a moment, Dave released Ace and picked up the gun where it had fallen on the pavement. Dave looked at Megan, who leaned against the building wall, limp and emotionally spent.

Dave turned to Ace. "You're under arrest," he said mechanically.

Yet before Dave could bring out his cuffs or read him his rights, Ace bolted.

Dave lunged to give chase, but Megan called out, "Let him go."

Dave stopped instantly.

"I've got to take him in," Dave said without conviction.

"No. He's not going to hurt anybody," she said tiredly. "He doesn't have it in him."

After pocketing Ace's weapon, Dave reached out to her. Megan took his hand and let him lead her in the rain down the block.

Exhausted and wet, they got into the car.

In Dave's apartment, the pictures were off the wall and the cat was in hiding. The storm howled outside, rattling the windows, a beast let loose on the earth. Megan's clothes hung over the bathroom shower curtain bar to dry. She sat in a chair, wearing Dave's terry cloth robe, and dried her hair with a towel, her purse at her feet.

Dave sat on the floor before her, barefoot and shirtless, talking earnestly.

"It all fits," Dave said. "Nita's thesis adviser at Columbia said her work had gone off the deep end. She couldn't focus on one narrow topic. She had to take on all urban ills. And when she found out that, in the real world, she couldn't cure them, it drove her mad."

Megan continued to dry her hair, not looking at him.

Dave got up on his knees and took her hands. "She set them up, Megan. The ones she considered incurable. The social misfits. She shot them. In cold blood. She arranged to meet them in lonely places. And she murdered them."

"Did you have to kill her?"

Dave peered at her. "She was going to kill me, Megan. I had no choice."

Megan returned his gaze evenly.

"For God's sake, Megan. She was a murderer."

"And what are you?"

Dave smacked the floor with his fist. He gave her an anguished look. Their eyes locked.

"Don't do this," he pleaded. "I love you."

For a seemingly endless time, Megan stared into Dave's eyes, as if searching for something. Her expression very gradually softened.

Dave took her hands once more. Megan smiled wanly at him. She sighed and leaned back in the chair.

Dave grinned with relief. He got up and made for the kitchen. "I'll get us some wine."

His phone rang. He didn't even pause as he busied himself with the corkscrew. "The machine will get it," he called. He hummed as he rummaged in a cupboard for the stemware he seldom used.

The answering machine clicked on. Jamie's voice, low, musical, and troubled, filled the air. "Dave, something strange. It all checks out except for one killing, the murder of Kimberly Worth. Nita was at Dr. Solomon's house for a dinner party with some heavyweight grant people and nobody went home till late, after the body was found. We'll keep plugging, but I thought you'd want to know."

"Christ," Dave said in the kitchen.

The dial tone sounded briefly before the machine clicked off.

"I'm sure they're wrong," Dave called after a pause, pouring red wine into elegant glasses. "They'll figure it out."

Dave came out of the kitchen holding the glasses aloft, his expression tenderly triumphant. "Anyway, we have our future to think about."

Megan's own triumph was written on her face. The .45 felt natural in her two-handed grasp.

She aimed carefully and squeezed the trigger.

Dave took the bullet through his right eye. Perfectly.

If Dave could be said to have had a last thought or could have put the fleeting, half-formed image into words, it would have been the glimpse of another woman, also beloved, pulling a trigger. A woman who had killed and left him to take the blame.

The thunder seemed to echo the report of the weapon.

On the way out, Megan carefully took with her every item of her clothes and the robe and the towel. She didn't worry about fingerprints. She had been his girlfriend, after all.

Control.

The next morning, when the rain ended, the sound of the cat's incessant yowls caused the super to enter Dave's apartment. He threw up all over the floor in front of the chair where Megan had sat.

By the time Jamie arrived, the crime-scene people were hard at work. Dusting for prints, making measurements, taking photos, writing in notebooks. Safir and Wise stood off to the side, muttering to each other.

Dave's body was surrounded by a neat chalk outline.

Jamie stood over him, her face vibrating with grief.

Lt. Blake came over to her, and she pulled herself together.

"Well, Loo," Jamie said softly, "Dave was right in one respect."

"What's that, Jamie?"

"There's a plan here. By a very smart, cool killer. And he's rubbing our noses in it."

Safir and Wise joined them. The four watched silently as Dave's body was covered with a sheet.

"So we start over?" Wise asked.

"We start over," Blake said.

And off in the night, a phone rang in a high-ceilinged, almost empty building, guarded by an iron door. The ghostly ringing sounded tiny in the large room — a drab place except for the new fish tank.

As always, Megan picked up the phone. "Crisis center. Can I help you?"